T0354473

RIGHT NOW IS WORTH IT

THOMAS CORRIGAN

RIGHT NOW IS WORTH IT

iUniverse books may be ordered through booksellers or by contacting:

iUniverse
1663 Liberty Drive
Bloomington, IN 47403
www.iuniverse.com
1-800-Authors (1-800-288-4677)

ISBN: 978-1-5320-7355-7 (sc)
ISBN: 978-1-5320-7357-1 (hc)
ISBN: 978-1-5320-7356-4 (e)

Library of Congress Control Number: 2019942681

Print information available on the last page.

iUniverse rev. date: 09/27/2019

PROLOGUE

It was no surprise the highway was silent, save for the occasional chirp of a bird from a nearby tree. It was nearly ten thirty at night. The fields on either side of the cement stretched for miles, and cows lay down with one another, nestled together in small groupings.

A few homeless men had started a fire under one of the trees in the highway divider when it began to drizzle. They hastily covered the fire with blankets to shroud it from the rain, which grew to a shower. The rain slowly and insidiously made its way through the branches of the trees to where the homeless encampment lay. All three men surrounded the fire and protected it from the rain.

Eventually the rain stopped, and the fire was still burning. One of the men, who bore a heavily thick beard, sighed, took his blanket, and threw it onto a child lying asleep under a tarp. Pieces of asphalt tried to roll along the ground with each breeze that came through but remained still. The breezes stopped, and everything was hushed.

A police siren blared in the distance. Ears on cows perked up, and they turned their heads to the sound. A red Camaro raced down the highway, and with the muffler off, it sounded like the Indy 500 rather than a single car. The Camaro flew over a hump in the highway, and the wheels jerked and spun over the pieces of asphalt below. Rubber hit the pavement again, and the driver slammed her foot on the gas. The speedometer flew past eighty miles an hour to ninety to one hundred and began to jerk and fly around its limit.

Christina knew she had one option as the police cruiser gained on her: drive. She couldn't turn back, not now. But the siren blared just fifty yards behind her, and she feared she might be at the end of her ride.

"Stop the car! Put your foot on the brake, and stop the car!" yelled a policeman through the megaphone attached to the exterior of the cruiser.

Christina looked in the rearview mirror and saw the front bumper of the cruiser coming ever so close to the back of her car. She shook her head and adjusted her grip on the wheel. Christina looked down at her left leg. A shard of glass protruded from the knee. She knew she couldn't go back to the house yet. Christina wiped the wet perimeters of her eyes and took the Camaro into the highest gear.

"Stop the damn car!" shouted the policeman.

Christina's knee stung like a thousand wasp stings, and she took her hand off the wheel to apply pressure. She adjusted the way her pants fit around the glass and drove over a hill on the highway. An upcoming curve, which had been hidden behind the hill, surprised her. She jerked the wheel to the left, but the wheels didn't agree. Christina knew she wasn't going back to the house ever.

The Camaro hit the highway divider. Christina pulled hard on the steering wheel to maintain control. It was too late. The Camaro's front bumper fell off and got caught in the front tire. The car flipped repeatedly as bits and pieces of steel and glass flew off it. Christina heard the siren turn off. The red Camaro flipped for the fourth time, and Christina shot through the windshield. She rolled to a stop on her stomach, her face bleeding from every orifice. The car came to a rest on its back.

Christina saw the policeman walk toward her. Her eyes strained to stay open.

"All units, we have an 11-83 on Highway 280. I need an ambulance on the ninth mile marker ASAP. I repeat—there is an 11-83. Ambulance needed on the ninth mile marker ASAP," the policeman said into his microphone. He walked up to Christina, and she closed her eyes.

A siren echoed in the distance, and an engine running eventually sputtered out into nothingness.

EMMA

Five Weeks Later

"Emma?" Ted, her stepfather, asked outside of a closed bedroom door.

"Yeah?" she responded, still lying in bed with the sheets pulled up to her nose.

Ted knocked on the door. "You awake yet?"

"Take a friggin' guess, Ted," Emma responded exasperatedly.

"Hey," he said, opening the door.

Emma could smell the cigarette smoke on his breath and the beer from the stains on his cutoff. She watched him push his hair back out of his face and scratch the mole on his neck.

He snorted snot up his nose. "If this is gonna work long term with you and your mom, we need some respect in this goddamn house, so no more of this Ted bullshit, got it?"

"Fine, Ted. Just please get out of my room now, Ted." Emma got up to close the door.

"Smart-ass." Ted walked away from the door. "Make your own damn breakfast. I'm going down to Johnny's to play pool."

"Fine, whatever!" Emma shouted through the door and then said under her breath, "Lazy prick."

Emma wiped her face and sat up in bed. It was too early to have to deal with her stepfather, but it was always too early. She leaned over to her nightstand and grabbed her phone. The blue light illuminated her face, and her eyes watered, straining to adjust.

She clicked in the password and went into Instagram. Although she wasn't close enough with anyone in school to rant to, she felt comfortable posting her disgust with Ted to hundreds of people she'd met and talked to either once or never at all.

She posted a picture of a wilting flower that she had downloaded from the web. The artsy caption, which Emma only typed for the most amount of attention, read, "U know it's gon be a long day when ur own parent act like they don't want u."

Compassionate comments and likes flowed in. Emma knew they weren't sincere, but it relieved some of her anger toward Ted. She turned her phone off and jumped in the shower. She got out and changed into some black jeans with a shirt and a Panic! at the Disco hoodie. Emma grabbed her schoolbag and left her apartment complex, the Deepcrest. Most people living there were happy they had finally been able to afford a place to stay, but Emma was ashamed of the run-down housing.

When she had made it out of her neighborhood without anyone from school seeing her, she gave a sigh of relief. The warm postsummer air blew through the trees and made the morning dew fall all around Emma. She strolled past the white Victorian-era mansions; she watched parents strap their children into booster seats in their Cadillacs and Porsches. Emma was jealous that the rich resided just three streets over from her shitty apartment. She felt more comfortable walking near a place Ted couldn't afford than she did in her own home.

The sound of a car revving caught Emma's attention. She turned around, and a midnight-blue Porsche full of high school baseball players drove past her. Emma shook her head and kept walking. She looked at the car from the corner of her eye. *Stupid jocks*. The Porsche paused in the middle of the street and drove back toward Emma.

"Whoo, shawty!" one of them yelled. "Give me a quick shake, cutie!"

The rest of the guys laughed, their eyes fixated on Emma. She grimaced and flipped them off.

"Oh shit! She feisty, boys," Dillon said. He revved the engine and drove off to the school.

Emma looked down at the ground. An orange had fallen off a tree. She kept kicking it and dribbled the orange the whole way to her classroom, at which point she picked it up and aimed for a recycling bin to throw it in. She threw it and completely missed.

A few girls around her snickered. Emma rolled her eyes and walked into her world history classroom. She brushed her hair aside and looked around the room for a place to sit down. Every seat was taken except for the one right next to a boy who was chewing gum and sticking it under his desk and then chewing it again. Emma looked for another seat, but the bell rang, and she had to sit down next to him.

The teacher walked across the classroom, straightened her hair out, and closed the door to the classroom. Mrs. Morton's Coke-bottle glasses rested on her nose, and she smacked her lips before popping open a can of tonic water. Emma watched her nearly chug the whole can and tried to ignore the sound of her unsettling guzzling.

"All right, sophees," she said. "Second semester, which means only five months until summer and two months until winter break."

"So only two months until I get a nice, long taste of Sophia," whispered one of the baseball players to his friend.

He took his cap and shook it out. The sweat from the baseball team's early-morning workouts drenched the desk of the kid behind him. He leaned back and stretched his skinny, toned arms out to reach his friend. They fist-bumped each other and laughed it off.

"Jackson!" the teacher shouted across the room. "Anything you'd like to share with the rest of us?"

"Sure, although I'm not sure how you would feel about my

objectification of a certain nice piece of ass," Jackson said and winked at Sophia.

Sophia turned red, and she put one hand on her eyebrows, shading her eyes from the rest of the class.

"Jackson, that is enough," the teacher shouted.

"My bad, Mrs. Morton." Jackson grinned.

"Thank you, Jackson." Mrs. Morton went on, "I was hoping to hear about all of your holiday vacations. Maybe we can start with—let me see …"

Emma averted her eyes away from her teacher. What was it with teachers being completely wimpy these days? She wished schools went back to the old days where Jackson would have been hit for that stuff he said and that would've been that. Emma was reminded of her stepfather's vernacular every time Jackson spoke about a girl.

Mrs. Morton scanned the room for a volunteer to share what they'd done over the holidays. Emma stared out the window and tilted her head away from the rest of her class in an effort not to be picked first. She brushed her hair back over the right side of her face to hide it and seem unimportant to Mrs. Morton. Unfortunately, it only brought more attention to her.

"How about … Emma?" Mrs. Morton asked with a fake smile.

Of course. Force the girl who clearly doesn't want to talk about her sister dying to tell everyone about her life.

"Would you like to share what you did on your break with us, Emma?"

"Um, well, I went up to the city and walked along the pier for a bit."

Mrs. Morton nodded at Emma for a moment. "Oh, okay. Great! Anyone else?"

"Damn, that was a crazy story. God, please tell us another one, Emma." A girl laughed.

"Now, Megan, don't say things like that. You don't know what the other person could take from …" Mrs. Morton said as her voice disappeared in Emma's mind.

Emma looked down at her lap and twiddled her thumbs. She was trying to focus on anything else in an effort not to cry. Emma pulled out her notebook and wiped her eye right as a tear had nearly fallen out. Her hands fumbled for a pencil, and she began to draw a forest. The trees stretched across the whole paper, and birds sung to one another between branches.

In the middle of sketching a waterfall, one of the trees spoke to Emma. "I went to the pier over the holidays too." The oak tree spoke from the notebook page.

Emma looked down at the paper and stared at the tree. There was no mouth on it, and it wasn't talking to her. She felt a tap on her shoulder and looked to the right.

"I went to the pier over the holidays too," Shaun said, apparently trying to strike up a conversation.

"Oh, cool, Shaun," Emma responded.

Emma had known Shaun since the third grade. He had always been off to the side. Shaun was never much of a standout person in the class, and in that, he and Emma were the same. Although Shaun never said much and was never part of the happening group, he was there nonetheless. He was there when Emma's father left her family in sixth grade. Shaun was there when a star football player was diagnosed with leukemia in eighth grade. Shaun saw everything happen and never said much about it.

Although she was usually weirded out by how little he said, she also appreciated it. Shaun was one of the few kids who didn't care to spew his opinion on everything that happened in San Mateo. This was the first time he had spoken to Emma in over a year.

"Yeah, sometimes I just skate up there when I need a breath of fresh air, you know?" Shaun whispered to Emma.

"Sure," Emma answered, giving a slight grin.

"Either that or I go see like a horror movie or something alone. Guess I do a lot of things alone." Shaun laughed awkwardly. "You like horror movies? I mean, I doubt you would. Not because you're a girl and not that that would even matter. Most girls just get scared too easily. Not that girls are wimps, but like …"

His voice trailed off as Emma slipped into her thoughts. She was ecstatic that someone had asked her about horror movies. For the longest time, she was always the weird, awkward girl who liked violent and scary movies and books. She knew she didn't necessarily follow the societal norms when it came to hobbies or things to do on the weekends. If someone brought up the most recent Disney movie, the only thing on her mind would be how great the twenty-fourth James Bond movie was.

Whenever she passed by the group of cheerleaders in the hallway, they would be talking about the most recent Fifth Harmony concert and how they got front-row seats because one of their fathers was a venture capitalist. Emma always felt like an awkward loser talking about her favorite music, which consisted of Against the Current, Green Day, Blink-182, and Radiohead. Her favorite solo artist wasn't Ariana Grande. It was the lyrically dark XXXTENTACION. Up until Shaun asked about horror movies, she was uncomfortable talking with him because she thought they had virtually nothing in common.

"Yeah, I like them," Emma finally responded to Shaun in the middle of his rambling.

"Cool." Shaun stopped talking and nodded quickly.

The bell rang, and everyone instantly got up from their seat.

"Oh, uh, okay," Mrs. Morton said, startled. "The homework will be posted online tonight! Have a good first day back, everyone!"

"Okay, yeah, bye, Mrs. Morton," replied the class.

"Peace out, Mrs. Moron." Jackson flashed a hang-loose sign at Mrs. Morton and laughed with his teammates on the way out.

She smiled and patted each of the students on the back as they left. She walked over to her desk and picked up a stack of files. Emma watched her turn around and started for the door with her schoolbag.

Right before Emma reached the door, Mrs. Morton turned around. "Excuse me, Emma?"

Emma shut her eyes and collected herself before turning to face Mrs. Morton. "Yes?" Emma said, irked.

"Look." Mrs. Morton was clearly concerned. She might not have been above the age of thirty-five, but worry wrinkles were forming in her chubby cheeks. Mrs. Morton stood up to close the classroom door. "I know how hard it's been since your sister's crash. But I think reaching out to someone would really aid in your recovery."

"Mmm, yeah," Emma said, looking away.

"Yeah, see? We have plenty of people willing to talk to you. Plenty of great resources here for you. You can talk to any of the kids or your counselor. You can talk to me if you want. I'm always here to—"

"Have you ever?" Emma asked, her eyes watering. Emma couldn't cry. She couldn't be seen like that. She held in her cry. "Do you have any sisters or brothers?"

Mrs. Morton shook her head.

"Then how the hell could you know how hard it's been?" Emma snapped.

Mrs. Morton opened her mouth to respond, but Emma was already making her way out of the classroom. Emma walked over to her locker and calmed herself down. She brushed her hair over her ear and grabbed her folder for the next class. It was labeled "Chemistry honors; Mr. Jacobs is a complete pedophile, by the way."

Emma laughed to herself. Her sister had written the latter part of the label before the start of sophomore year. Emma longed to see Christina again, and she wiped her eyes before putting the folder in her bag. She buttoned the top of her schoolbag and looked up. She was met with the face of one of the varsity field hockey players, Sophia. She was stunning. She wasn't too tall, with long blonde hair. She was skinny but not anorexic, the stereotypical idealized American teenage girl.

"You have world history with me," she said to Emma.

"Really? Huh, learn something new every day," Emma said, wandering to her next class. Emma just wanted to be alone and sad for a moment. She avoided conversation with Sophia at all costs.

Sophia caught up to Emma and stopped her in her tracks. "Hey, I'm trying to be nice," she said. Emma could see she meant it.

Sophia continued, "Given all the shit that's happened lately, Señor Douchebag Jackson Decker has been really insensitive. All of those shit-faces have been."

"Thank you."

"Yeah, name's Sophia, by the way." Sophia walked to her class.

"Ahh, the *nice piece of ass*," Emma joked.

Sophia turned around and shouted down the hallway, "You better believe it!"

Emma smiled and walked to class. When Emma had first entered the hall before her class with Mrs. Morton, she was terrified. The thought of having to talk to anyone about her sister was like a ten-thousand-pound burden weighing down on her back, which was straining underneath the pressure. Sophia had lightened the load with her brief moment of release, a relief of Emma's fear of being friendless for her second semester.

The bell rang at the end of the second period, and lunchtime was upon the students. Emma brushed her hair over her face and bolted out of the classroom as soon as she heard the first note of the bell toll. She didn't want to have to stick around so she could have another painfully awkward conversation with another painfully awkward teacher.

As soon as she stepped into the hallway, Emma could feel the eyes on her. She didn't even bother going to grab her lunch from her locker. She avoided the hallways since she would be out in the open for everyone to gossip about her. But Emma could already hear what they were saying.

"That's the girl whose sister ran from the cops."

"She died, right?"

"What the fuck happened with that girl?"

There was no hesitation in Emma's mind on where to head, and she went straight to the cafeteria to blend in with the crowd. A long line of food ranging from fried chicken to caesar salads stretched out in front of her. She grabbed a tray and walked down the line.

One of the lunchroom workers began yelling as kids poured into the food line, "Fried chicken today, everyone. Grab your beans! Grab your chicken! Grab your drinks! Fried chicken!"

Emma smiled at the older man. He beamed at her and reached across the lunch line to hand her a plate of food. Emma didn't want to yell over the clamoring kids, so she just mouthed "thank you" to the man.

She grabbed the plate of chicken tenders along with an orange soda. She walked across the cafeteria and sat down at a lunch table away from everyone else. Being around too many people made her nervous that everyone was paying attention to her. She opened up her soda and took a sip while opening up her notebook.

She grabbed a pencil and put the soda down on the table. Emma stared at her notebook, briefly trying to recollect where she was going with the drawing of the forest. Nothing came to her mind, and she started a sketch of the cafeteria.

In the middle of her drawing of Jackson Decker and the rest of the baseball jock table, Shaun came up to Emma. "Mind if I sit?"

Emma looked up from her notebook and stared at him blankly. Even though Emma liked Shaun, she did mind if he sat. However, when she noticed people watching Shaun stand awkwardly over her table, Emma knew how pathetic it would look if she turned him down.

"Umm, the table. Can I?" he asked again with a look of minor confusion on his face.

"Oh yeah. Sorry. I ... sorry," Emma sputtered out after getting lost in her thoughts.

"Thanks." Shaun put his plate down and threw his backpack down by the end of the table. He looked across at her notebook and then dug into his fried chicken. "How's the drawing coming, Alberti?"

"Who?" Emma asked.

"Alberti. C'mon, Leon Battista Alberti," Shaun repeated.

Emma raised her eyebrows at Shaun.

"You're drawing architectural scenery of the cafeteria and you don't know Alberti?" Shaun asked, astonished. "He's like one of the most famous architectural painters of all time."

"Apparently not," Emma joked.

She was surprised she didn't know what Shaun was talking about, and he impressed her. However, she didn't want to show her lack of knowledge. So she went with a dig at his comment rather than saying she didn't know who Shaun was talking about.

Emma watched as Shaun's look of excitement quickly vanished from his face. She felt pity for him because she knew he wanted so badly to talk, and ironically, so did Emma. She just didn't want to have a conversation with him. At least not at that moment.

Emma went on with her drawing, ignoring his comment completely. Emma thought Shaun would take the hint and leave, but he continued to sit on the edge of the bench and watch Emma draw. Occasionally she would look up, and he would give her a head nod. She would smile politely and look back down at her drawing.

"Don't talk much, huh?" Shaun commented.

Wanting to be nice but getting to the end of her rope, Emma quipped, "Says you?" She was praying that he would give up and go away.

Shaun snorted a laugh out, acknowledging her response. "Fair enough. Just lately I've been trying to open up more so I'm not forever the loser that sits alone at lunch." Shaun laughed and then immediately stopped when Emma gritted her teeth and scowled at him.

Emma shook her head slightly irked. "Oh, so a loser that sits alone, like me, huh, Shaun?"

"No. No, of course not. I don't have a problem with people who sit alone, not that that's bad anyway. I mean it's not. I just don't want to be antisocial. I mean, not antisocial, just not alone. I didn't mean to say you're alone. I just meant—" Shaun cut himself off. He winced and said, "I'm gonna go."

"Do that," Emma responded.

Emma watched Shaun frantically nod and grab his tray and then rush out through the glass doors of the cafeteria. Emma looked back at her drawing. Her breathing grew more intense. She gripped the pages of her notebook and slammed it shut. She knew Shaun didn't mean what he said, but subconsciously she thought he did.

She hated that she made him leave and presumably made him feel awkward for a simple mistake. God knows she said worse stuff to her own family than Shaun did to her. Emma shook with anger and turned redder than a fire truck. She breathed in heavily several times and calmed herself down.

She looked out the glass doors for Shaun and saw him sitting on the bleachers, propping his head up on his arms. Emma wanted to go up and apologize but feared it would create more awkwardness between the two.

She grabbed her pizza and downed it, and she washed it down with her orange soda. Emma walked up to the glass doors and gazed at Shaun. Maybe she should've given him more of a chance. After all, he wasn't completely wrong about what he said. Like Shaun, Emma didn't want to be alone her entire high school career. When Shaun tapped into that, Emma got angry that she couldn't admit that she understood and agreed with him. Emma frowned at Shaun from inside the cafeteria. Next time, she'd give him a chance.

The final bell for school rang, and kids swarmed the parking lot, trying to escape the traffic of amateur high school drivers. Emma watched as the jocks all climbed in their douche-mobile as she nicknamed the midnight-blue Porsche. She was starting her long, dragged-out walk to her apartment when a new white, convertible Cadillac pulled up beside her.

"Hey, pier girl!" Sophia shouted from the Cadillac.

"Oh, hey, Susan, right?" Emma said playfully.

"Actually it's Sophia." Sophia clarified indignantly.

Emma nodded. "Sorry for the mistake, Sylvia."

"No problem." Sophia smirked and nodded. "So is that walk home too fun for a quick trip to Jake's Smoothie Parlor?"

"Yeah, just about as fun as my Christmas break was." Emma rolled her eyes.

Sophia leaned back in her seat, acting surprised. "Wow, sounds like a party."

Emma chuckled.

"C'mon, hop in. Wouldn't want you to have too much fun on your walk."

"You sure? I don't wanna waste your time."

"What? No, you're fine. Let's go."

Emma jumped into the passenger side of the Cadillac and caught the belt loop on her jeans on the door handle. It tore and broke in half.

"Shit, sorry about that." Sophia reached across to remove the door handle from Emma's jeans.

"No, it's good. They're ripped jeans anyway." Emma was embarrassed that Sophia had to help her out like a mom, but she covered it with a joke. "It'll add to the stereotypical rock loner girl look."

"And what a good look that is," Sophia said, complimenting Emma.

Emma laughed. "Are we a lesbian couple now?"

Sophia flicked Emma's shoulder, chuckling. "Fuck off, pier girl."

"Hey, I don't care. Doesn't matter to me. Not a big a deal if you like to hold the bowling ball occasionally." Emma cracked up.

Sophia laughed, shaking her head. "You're not too bad, pier girl."

A loud honk came from behind them. Emma looked back and saw the same boy, Dillon, who catcalled Emma in the morning. He was wearing sunglasses and a hat inside his car. When the annoyed senior flipped them off and waved for them to start driving, a gold chain bounced around his skinny soccer-player wrist.

"Fucking hell," Emma said.

"What?" Sophia adjusted the rearview mirror.

"I just don't want to have to deal with this guy. Just drive." Emma sighed and folded her arms.

"Who? Dillon?" Sophia looked at Emma. "Dillon's chill. I've known his family for like a decade."

"Maybe to you, but I'm just someone he wants to fuck." Emma covered her eyes. She went from an encounter with Ted to Dillon, to Shaun, and now Dillon again, and she was through with boys and men for the day. "Oh my God, just drive."

Another honk came, and Emma took her hand off her eyes and glared at Sophia. Sophia raised one hand out the window at Dillon. Sophia waved at him and shrugged. She rolled the roof back onto the car and turned on the ignition. The car revved into its eco-friendly mode, and the two girls drove out of the school parking lot.

"I mean, I'm not surprised he wants to fuck you. Your boobs are huge." Sophia laughed.

Emma looked down at her chest and then up at Sophia, smiling. "What? No. I mean, yeah they are, but I'm chubby from like the boob down."

"Naw, you're not chubby. You're thick with a *c*," Sophia said. "Trust me. I know chubby girls. You're not one."

"I appreciate the compliment, but you're beautiful. You've probably never even worried about what someone thinks of you."

"No fucking way, pier girl. I would kill for boobs like yours, but then I couldn't play field hockey. I guess the trade-off to play sports is to have tennis balls for tits." Sophia laughed.

Emma cracked up. "Take the cards you're dealt, I guess."

"Exactly. So give yourself some credit. I'd rather be cute to a guy than hot. It leads to longer-term things dating-wise. Even if it's not Dillon, any guy would be lucky to have you."

Emma rarely heard compliments from girls like this and covered her mouth to hide her beaming smile. Sophia reminded Emma so much of Christina. Neither of them had a filter. Emma cleared her throat. "Thanks."

"Of course." Sophia turned to Emma and grinned.

"And like how she always wears her little righteous pink raincoat?" Sophia laughed out loud.

Emma nearly spat out her fruit smoothie. "Good lord, Mrs. Morton. Like is she even real? Like today she came up to me and asked about the … the … you know."

Sophia's raised her brows and stirred her smoothie around. She shifted in her seat, and her laugh trailed off. Emma noticed Sophia avoiding eye contact when Sophia said, "I don't know actually, but I can take a guess at what you're tryna say."

"Yeah," Emma said, looking down at her smoothie and then continuing, "Sorry. I didn't mean to like bring down the convo."

"Don't worry about it. I would be handling everything way worse than you are, given the situation. I'm really sorry."

Emma was fine with where Sophia was going before she said that word. The day wasn't even over, but Emma was already tired of people feeling sorry for her.

"I don't want to be rude, but I really hate it when people say 'I'm sorry' as if they know how it feels," Emma admitted to Sophia. "You get what I mean, right?"

Sophia leaned back in her seat. Her eyes appeared to widen

slightly before she leaned forward again. "I get it. More than you know."

Sophia's obligatory smile at Emma acknowledged the now awkward silence between the two of them. The only sound was the occasional blender chopping fruit in the background.

Emma looked around at customers coming in and out, ordering smoothies of banana and mangoes or raspberries and passion fruits. Emma rubbed her temple. She did it again. Just like with her interaction with Shaun, Emma made a situation awkward because of a simple mistake.

She hastily broke the dead air. "I wasn't really trying to. I guess I'm just a little tired of people pitying me, Soph. I didn't want to make you feel bad for showing empathy."

"Don't worry about it," Sophia said.

Emma smiled and brushed her hair back. "Ironically I'm sorry, Soph. Can I call you that?"

"No, it's a forbidden name in this town," Sophia replied.

Emma smiled and looked around again now that another silence had filled the room.

"So," Sophia said. Emma looked back at her. Sophia continued, "Got any Ryan Goslings on your horizon?"

"Excuse me?" Emma asked.

"*La La Land*, dude," Sophia responded.

"Oh, yeah. I never saw that," Emma said.

Sophia's blue eyes widened, and her mouth dropped in disbelief. Emma shrugged.

"You're kidding me, right, pier girl?" Sophia asked.

"No, never saw it. I was never a fan of those generic and unrealistic love stories between two people. Like *The Fault in Our Stars*. It has a couple good songs, but that's probably the only good thing about it."

"I can't believe you didn't like *The Fault in Our Stars* and you haven't seen *La La Land*!" Sophia flailed her hands around, emphasizing her outrage.

"I don't know. Just not my thing."

It was a lie. Emma had only ever seen people kiss around high school or on a TV screen. The fact is—Emma longed for a romance between herself and a boy. However, after seeing so many unrealistic love stories end in tragedy both in real life and on the big screen, she started to lose hope that love even existed. Emma had never so much as hugged a guy outside of her cousins, whom she hadn't seen in years.

Sophia smiled. "Okay, okay, okay, back to my earlier question. Let me rephrase. Are there any guys on your radar?"

"Oh." Emma was grinning. "Honestly, I wouldn't mind having one of the baseball guys if they weren't all assholes."

"Not Jackson Decker," Sophia said, annoyed.

"No fuckin' way." Emma chuckled. "I don't know. Just someone that's good looking enough, normal, and nice. I don't know. Someone who can prove that chivalry hasn't died yet."

Emma basically wanted a guy like Shaun but couldn't admit that she wanted a guy like Shaun. How could she? She had known Shaun for so long that he might as well have been family. Then again, they never really hung out, but no, not Shaun. He wasn't popular or the stereotypical, smooth, cool kid that Emma saw in romance movies.

Emma also couldn't see Shaun being the type of guy that could take control during a kiss or say he knew what he was doing. She always pictured her dream guy telling her what to do because he would know how to act from experience. Emma wanted someone who was nice, chivalrous, and honest, but also a guy who wasn't afraid to step up and show Emma that he wasn't afraid to put himself out in the open for her.

"Right. Chivalrous, kind, and normal. So like not a baseball guy." Sophia laughed.

"I guess you're right."

Sophia bobbed her head from side to side. "I'm always right, pier girl."

They left the Parlor at 5:27 p.m., just as the sun was beginning its descent.

"So where do you live?" Sophia asked at an intersection.

Emma didn't want Sophia to know about her small apartment on the other side of town. It was embarrassing to Emma. Before her parents divorced, they lived in a two-story house plus a basement with workout gear in it. When Emma's dad left, her mom married Ted, who was a funny, charming bartender at the local club.

Emma never particularly liked Ted, but her liking of him dropped even further when he realized that Emma's mother was a vulnerable single mom. Ted snaked his way into Emma's life, calling her mom an angel, a goddess, and anything else that would help him take advantage of her. They married after two years of being together. Her mom knew that his bartending and her being a nurse practitioner couldn't and wouldn't maintain the property tax of their current home. At the end of their first year of marriage, they moved out of the hills and into the Deepcrest apartments, or, in Emma's words, "where the upper-lower-lower class resided."

"Um, you know what, Sophia? Just drop me off here. I can find my own way home. Thanks," Emma said, smiling politely.

"Oh, is your house close by?" Sophia furrowed her brows, confused.

Emma shook her head.

"Then what the fuck would I drop you off here for? Just tell me where you live, and I'll drop you off there. It's not a big deal for me."

"No, it's not the distance. My house just isn't like that impressive to what I'm assuming yours is. I mean you drive a Cadillac, Soph," Emma said, flustered. She was already intimidated by Sophia's beauty. *Now she wanted to see my place?* No. Emma believed if Sophia saw Ted's shitty pickup in front of her apartment, that would end their brief friendship.

Sophia looked at her in disbelief. "This doesn't mean shit, pier girl. Before we moved here, I lived in a one-bedroom apartment in filthy-delphia."

Emma looked at Sophia surprised. She moved around in the car seat and leaned her back against the door. She rested her head on her hand, confused. "What the hell happened? I mean how'd you get to driving a Cadillac out here from Pennsylvania?"

"My dad invested in some small computer company, and when it went public, he made a load of cash," Sophia explained in a soft voice.

"Make it rain, girl." Emma raised her voice in excitement. She golf-clapped for Sophia.

Sophia chuckled. "Yeah, so where are we going, pier girl?"

"You know east side San Mateo?"

"East side! That's like nothing compared to what I had to live in."

"Yeah, well the people are the problem for me, and now the lack of a person …" Emma said, averting her eyes from the road and looking out the window.

"Hey." Sophia looked at Emma and then back at the road.

Emma kept her eyes focused on the side window.

"Hey," Sophia said again. She tapped Emma's shoulder. Emma turned, and Sophia leveled her eyes at Emma's. "Your sister is in a good place. Cliché as this sounds, it gets better, pier girl. With time, it at least gets easier."

Emma wiped her eyes with her finger and smiled. "Thanks, Mom."

"No problem, sweetie pie." Sophia smiled and laughed.

Sophia dropped Emma off and waited until Emma got to the front door of the apartment. Emma waved, and Sophia smiled and drove off. Emma couldn't believe that after one day she had made a new friend. She originally took Sophia's empathy as phony, but after hearing her story, Emma assumed that there was more to Sophia than a varsity field hockey jersey.

Although she knew she would soon be talking about her day to her hellish stepfather, Emma looked forward to all the days of hanging out with her newfound friend after school. It gave her some hope that she might not spend the whole year alone.

SHAUN

As soon as Shaun left the table, he was sweating harder than a NFL lineman doing sprints. He shook his head, kicking himself for having his advanced conversation skills. Shaun sat down at the top of the bleachers near the press box and started having conversations in mind with Emma that would never occur in reality. Each of the conversations ended with his asking her out, kissing her, or putting his arm around her and vice versa. Even Shaun knew that these conversations realistically would never occur, but it was nice to think so.

Shaun was never necessarily a loser or at least not as bad as he pictured himself to be. Shaun's only problem was an acute obsession and more of an insecurity with his constant appearance. Every time he got up to dress himself for school, he would look in the mirror from all angles. Shaun would flex his arms and back to see how much muscle he had gained, even if the last workout he made was just the night before. He would jut out his jaw to see if his jawline would appear more than it did the previous day.

After his self-modeling routine in his room, he would walk into his bathroom. Shaun would flip on the bright fluorescent light and turn on the faucet. Shaun would quickly put his hands into the cool water and yank them out as fast as they had gone in. If his hands were too wet, his hair gel wouldn't stick. Unfortunately for Shaun, he was not blessed with perfectly straight hair, so he would end up spending fifteen minutes on his hair in order to get it close to straight. Shaun's hair would remain straight for around twenty minutes before it became wavy again.

For the rest of the day, the only concerns on his mind were his jawline, his muscles, and his hair. This lasted from the beginning of freshman year until the first day back from vacation this year. His concerns changed. Shaun was carefully fixing his hair when his eyes fell upon Emma Walsh, the girl who had never been on his mind as a point of attraction until that day. He stopped fixing his hair and watched Emma draw her forest during class. At that moment, Shaun's obsession and insecurity with his hair was replaced by an attraction to someone whom he normally barely noticed.

Shaun sat on the bleachers imagining how the conversation could have gone. He thought about Emma and him going out on a date, seeing a movie, going back to his place, waking up together, then kissing and making out, and finally more and more. He changed the topic in his head.

"She's a nice girl, dude. Relax with that shit," Shaun thought out loud. He gestured, telling himself to cool it.

He looked out over the baseball diamond where girls swarmed Jackson Decker and his teammates. They all swooned over him, and Shaun wondered what Jackson had that he didn't. Shaun started brushing his hair around, and looking at his sides for any excess fat, he looked great. *Good build, green eyes, and square jaw. Funny?* Yeah, Shaun was funny if wanted to be.

After all this questioning of himself, a light bulb went off in Shaun's head. He propped his head against his arm and sighed. "Confidence."

Shaun rolled around in his sheets on Wednesday morning, two days after his brief conversation with Emma. He looked to his left and pressed the home button on his phone to check the time. It was 7:10 a.m., which technically meant there were still five minutes of precious sleep time left before his dad would come in to wake him up.

He closed his eyes and pulled the sheets over his head. Shaun focused on the sleep and got comfortable on his side again. His eyes fluttered for a short time before they finally began to shut, preparing for a temporary slumber. There was a knock on Shaun's bedroom door, and his father stepped in.

Wiping the morning gunk out of his eyes, Shaun heard his dad ask, "Hey, you up? Time to get ready."

"Oh my God." Shaun groaned, pulling the sheets off his face. He rubbed his eyes, which were filled with early-morning grime, and he raised his voice slightly. Shaun knew better than to full-on yell at his father, despite his annoyance. "I was literally on the brink of falling asleep again."

Shaun sat up and watched his dad kind of waddle into the room in his too-tight-for-an-older-man corduroy pants. His white dress shirt was scrunched into his pants with a brown sports coat on top of it. Shaun didn't take himself for a fashion expert but could still tell his father wouldn't be impressing anyone with his outfit. A wispy mustache took up most of the space above Mr. Baxter's upper lip, and his large nose draped the middle of his face. Shaun still saw where he got his muscle definition from though. Despite some of the fat in Mr. Baxter's belly, the man's height and bulk in his arms were still enough to make Shaun fear the badly dressed Santa Claus.

"Sorry about that. School is kind of important though, and did I hear an *oh my God*?"

"Oh, I meant *Goshhh*," Shaun said with a smug look on his face. Shaun had barely missed a Sunday's mass in his life, but not because he loved going. Shaun respected his father's dedication to his beliefs but was long tired of having him force those beliefs on Shaun.

"I thought so," his dad said, smiling slyly as he left Shaun's room.

Shaun snorted a short laugh out. He started his routine muscle check in the mirror and made sure his jaw was still in good shape. Not surprisingly, his jaw was right where he left it.

"Why couldn't you just grow facial hair?" Shaun spoke to himself. "Hide that fat side."

There was no fat side on Shaun's face, and if there were, it would be nearly impossible to pull it from his face. Nonetheless, Shaun rolled his eyes and swung his body to one side to inspect his abs. They were visible, but only just. Shaun widened his eyes in horror.

"This is why you can't do more than one cheat meal," Shaun said in disgust. "I knew I shouldn't have gone out with them last night."

Shaun went into his room, grabbed his phone, and walked back into the bathroom. He opened his phone and went into a calorie-counting app and input the calories into his phone. It came out to twice the amount that the supposedly all-knowing app allowed him to eat for a day. He looked up bodybuilders online and compared himself to their insanely toned bodies.

"I guess it's just 'cause they're like five years older, right? I'll get there soon." Shaun tried to tell himself so he'd stop worrying about his image. He stared at the abs on the bodybuilders and the weights they were lifting. "Just have to eat less and work harder, and I'll get there soon."

Shaun hopped in the shower and stayed there for as long as possible without having to shampoo himself and eventually exit the bathroom. He finally hopped out of the shower and threw on some jeans, a T-shirt, and hoodie. He grabbed his backpack and a carton of muscle milk from the refrigerator. He made his way around his house to the backdoor.

"All right, I'll see you tonight, Dad!" Shaun shouted through the house.

Shaun's dad aggressively swallowed his cereal to say, "All right. See you. Did you say goodbye to Mom?"

Shaun rolled his eyes and yelled, "Bye, Mom!"

No answer.

"Oh, she's still in the shower. Sorry," Shaun's dad commented.

"Great. So can I go?" Shaun shouted.

"Yeah, get out of here!" Shaun's dad joked and threw the remainder of his cereal down the drain in the sink.

Shaun closed the door behind him and walked over to his skateboard. He ran into the street and threw down the board. Shaun put his headphones in, turned on Pressure by *Muse*, and skated to school. The cool winter breeze flowed through his hair and hoodie. He hit an intersection and stopped. The car waiting to make a left turn onto his street waved at him. Shaun waved for the lady to just drive through. She waved again, getting impatient. Shaun insisted that she go first.

Fed up, they both went at the same time and then just as quickly screeched to a halt. They were back at square one. Shaun couldn't wait any longer to get to school so he just pushed the board as fast as he could through the intersection so as to not inconvenience either of them further.

Shaun rode onto the campus and picked up his skateboard. He took off his backpack and strapped the skateboard onto it. As he was putting one of his arms through the strap hole, he was punched lightly in the shoulder. Shaun turned around and was met with Jackson Decker's face—undercut with a fade, pointy noise, and blue eyes like a movie star. Without having pounds and pounds of muscle, he was exactly what Shaun wanted to be. The baseball pitcher Jackson Decker had come up to Shaun with his platoon of jocks from the baseball, football, and basketball teams.

"Hey, Baxter," Jackson said with a light grin after punching Shaun.

"Oh, what's good, Jackson," Shaun said in an effort to stand tall, despite being shorter than the jock.

Jackson shrugged with a smug look. "Same damn thing every day. Hey, there's gonna be a party at my place on Saturday. You should come, kid."

"Kid?" Shaun didn't like being talked down to. Anything that was remotely childish like kid, sport, or chief, Shaun would ignore. Shaun might not have had the confidence that Decker did, but he didn't want people to know that. Ironically, getting so easily angered by a nickname revealed his lack of confidence faster than anything.

"Fine, you should come, twinkle toes." Jackson laughed. "Look, just come all right. When was the last time you had a girl's ass on you longer than bumping into one in the hallway?"

Shaun shrugged. He could only imagine Margot Robbie or Emma fitting that image in his mind, and although they weren't terrible images to have, he didn't believe they could ever occur.

"Yup," Jackson said, patting Shaun on the back. "See ya there, Baxter."

"Oh ... uh, okay ... I ... uh, see ... see you ... dude!" Shaun stuttered out.

Shaun rolled his eyes for not being able to form a complete sentence at the end of his conversation with Jackson. He put his other arm through the backpack strap and went to his first period.

Lunchtime rolled around by the end of Mrs. Morton's world history class, and Shaun kept his hand on his notebook to make it seem like he was still writing. Once he saw Emma get up from her seat and leave the room, he threw the notebook in his bag and walked out of the door. Shaun came into the hallway and looked left. The baseball players were all laughing, trying to pick up some poor cheerleaders who didn't know any better.

He shook his head and looked right. Shaun saw Emma's long brown hair bouncing in time with her step, and he walked after her. He was so nervous, as though the sweat on his hands might cause a tsunami down the food line. Once he grabbed his tray of food, he entered in his PIN at the cashier and walked into the cafeteria.

Shaun scanned the area for Emma. When his eyes landed on her, she looked up at him. Shaun smiled awkwardly, and she returned a polite grin to him. *Holy shit? A smile?* Suddenly hope filled Shaun.

Shaun pulled out his phone and went into the camera to make sure he looked good. He nodded to himself and closed his phone. The nerves in his body were on edge the whole walk over to Emma's table. Shaun exhaled, gathering himself before opening his mouth to speak to Emma, but she spoke first.

"Hey, Shaun." Emma greeted him without looking up from her lunch.

Shaun stood over her. "What's good, Emma?"

"Definitely not this. I think it's salmon." Emma dangled the piece of fish from her fork before forcing down a lamentable bite from it.

"Got that right. Personally I would suggest just eating the optional pizza they serve every day," Shaun said, observing her reaction while still standing over her. She nodded in approval of his sentence. *Finally.*

He asked, "Mind if I sit?"

Emma gave him a thumbs-up as she swallowed the rest of her orange juice. Shaun smiled, dropped his bag down underneath the bench, and set his food tray down. He almost bit into the pizza and remembered the advice he gave Emma.

"Hey ... you, uh ... you want this?" Shaun offered the slice. "I promise it's better than whatever the hell you're eating."

Emma laughed, looked at him, and looked at her fish. "You sure?"

"Yeah, no problem. This pizza slice didn't cause the Great Depression in my wallet. I'll just get another one," Shaun joked.

Emma laughed and stared at the pizza. She hesitated and then took the slice from Shaun. "Thanks," Emma said, smiling.

Damn, her smile is perfect.

"Yeah," replied Shaun.

Emma's smile stayed on her face as she and Shaun continued to sit at the table in silence. She finished the slice of pizza and wiped her hands on her torn jeans. Shaun opened up his milk carton, and it nearly sprayed across his whole hoodie. Emma shook while smiling, presumably holding in a laugh. Shaun laughed off the event while cleaning up the milk that had spilled onto his lap.

"So there's a party at Jackson Decker's house this Saturday."

Emma rolled her eyes. "God, I hate that guy, but go on."

Shaun was relieved. He didn't want to have to act like Jackson's friend for a night just so he could have Emma grind on him. Shaun wanted every moment with Emma to be perfect and without some drunk kids at a party spewing liquor across the floor.

"Thank God. I was going to ask you to go with me, but personally I think he's a little too full of himself, too mean, and just ridiculously cocky and—" Shaun cut himself off. "Sorry. I kinda ramble sometimes."

"Noticed," Emma said.

"So … so, what … uh … what are you?" Shaun stuttered nervously, trying to ask her out.

Emma raised her eyebrows at him and watched him struggle to get out the sentence.

Shaun stopped talking and then abruptly asked, "You said you like horror movies, right?"

"Yeah, they're great."

"Cool cool," Shaun said, trying to finish his statement. "Well, there's this horror movie coming out on Friday called *Hereditary*, and I was thinking maybe we could go see it."

"I'm for sure down. Ooh, wait. Is it rated R? Because if it is, I can't go. Ted, my stepdad, would go ballistic if he found out that I saw something above PG-13."

"We can still go. I'll pay for the new Marvel movie, and we can just sneak into the theater for *Hereditary*," Shaun explained.

Emma bit her nails. Shaun thought she was going to turn him down, given how long she was taking to decide. Shaun went into a state of anxiety. He wondered if she were trying to find a polite way to let him down. *Maybe she's just going to say no straight up. Maybe I don't look good enough. Damn, I shouldn't have skipped that workout. Is my hair fucked up? What is taking so long? Maybe she would yell at me and get up and leave.* So many scenarios played out in his head, and his mind was racing.

Emma looked down at her nails and quickly wiped them on her

shirt. She folded her hands on the table and responded to Shaun's query. "All right, yeah. I'll go."

"Oh, okay. Cool." Shaun was both relieved and filled with excitement. "So, umm, I actually don't have a car. I just take a skateboard to school. So you wouldn't mind walking like half a mile, would you?"

"I take a sidewalk to school. So yeah, no big deal." Emma was smiling.

Shaun didn't want to sound too excited. His heart was pounding from the simple success of getting a yes from Emma. "All right, so I'll grab tickets for like a seven o'clock showing and come by your place at like six fifteen?"

Emma shoved out a question that made Shaun pause before she rambled, "Uhhh, how 'bout I come to your place and then we can walk to the theater from there?"

Caught off guard, Shaun answered, "Oh. Uh, okay then. Isn't that kinda a far walk for you?"

Emma sighed. "Oh, you know where I live?"

"Well, no. I just live kinda out of the way of anyone. My house is right next to Vernon Park. You can just come to my place, I guess. Yeah, actually yeah. Just come to my place at like six on Friday. 3985 Needue Lane." Shaun saw Emma staring past him and looked behind him. When he looked back at her, she blinked a few times. "So does that sound good?"

"Sorry?"

Shaun realized she hadn't been paying attention, so he summed up his spiel. "Six on Friday. My place. 3985 Needue Lane. Sound good?" Shaun asked again.

"Oh, oh. Yeah, cool." Emma's face perked up.

"Okeydoke, then. See you, Emma." Shaun got up from the table before lunch ended.

Emma gave a half wave and stood up with her bag to go the opposite way.

Shaun repeated what he had just said to himself. "Okeydoke. What the fuck are you? Seven years old?"

He shook it off, put the food tray in its appropriate stack on the lunch line, and went into the boy's bathroom. One of the boys in the marching band was carrying a trombone and held open the door for Shaun. Shaun smiled in thankfulness, and the boy nodded. Shaun went over and stood at the urinal.

The boy with the trombone wrapped up and ran out of the bathroom when the bell rang. Shaun flushed the urinal and went over to the sink to wash his hands when it hit him. He had managed, at all odds, to scare up a date with Emma. He looked around the bathroom, pumped his fist, and jumped up and down in excitement.

"Fuck yes!" Shaun shouted.

A teacher walked in as he said that. Slightly embarrassed, Shaun recollected himself and walked out of the swinging bathroom door.

It was Friday, and Shaun's mom was folding his laundry twenty minutes before Emma would arrive at his house, just as Shaun requested so he could choose his outfit.

"Hey, Shaun, are you wearing your khakis or jeans?" his mother shouted through the house.

"Oh, you know what? I'll wear the jeans. I'll be right out."

"All right. Because if you wanted to wear the khakis, I think it would still look fine."

"I already said jeans," Shaun shouted, irritated.

He wondered if his mom ever heard him. *Did she think she was helping by asking and repeating the same thing over and over?* Normally she was okay, but sometimes her annoying comments struck a chord with him.

"I know, but if you want your khakis, they're right out here!" his mom shouted.

Shaun yelled back, "Mom! Jeans!"

His mom shook her head. "Okay, okay, okay, Shaun! Okay, okey. Okeydoke. Okeydoke artichokie."

He could hear her talking through the door. *So that's where I got the okeydoke from.* His mom's strange vocabulary was plaguing the way he talked around Emma. There was a very prissy knock on the door and then the sound of something hitting the floor.

"One second," Shaun said through the door.

Shaun opened the door a crack to see his mother standing in front of it with his clothes on the floor. "Great. Thanks."

He grabbed his jeans, underwear, and a gray shirt, and he closed the door in his mom's face. It closed louder than he intended, so it really came out to be more of a slam.

He closed his eyes and winced at the sound. "Sorry, that wasn't supposed to be so loud."

"It's all right. You know I can help with your clothes if you want."

Shaun rolled his eyes and cranked up the music in his bathroom.

His mom knocked on the door again and asked, "Are you sure you're okay?"

"Mom, I'm fine. I'm just shav … I'm just getting changed right now!" Shaun lied.

"Oh, okay okay. Oh, I'm so excited for your first date. I can drive you guys if you want," his mom said, walking away.

"No! Wait, Mom? Mom?" Shaun sighed and pulled his pants on.

Shaun rolled his eyes, annoyed with his mom's invasiveness. He knew she didn't mean to be so in his face about everything, but she was nonetheless. Shaun stepped out of the bathroom, but not before checking his hair in the mirror one final time. He brushed it back and forth and stared at himself from all angles before nodding in acceptance. He grabbed a stick of deodorant and put it on his chest and underarms so he wouldn't smell like a dirty gym bag around Emma.

The doorbell rang. It was happening. Shaun was sweating, and he exited the bathroom wiping his face with a towel. He walked through the kitchen and stopped behind the wall leading up to the door.

"Ooh, she's here, honey." Shaun's mom grabbed a glass of wine. "I got the door-or!"

"Oh God." Shaun put his hands over his face.

Shaun's mom licked her lips and put down her glass of wine on the countertop in the foyer. He peered out from behind the corner so he could see his mother talk with Emma. His mother was wearing jogger sweats and a T-shirt with a sweatshirt over it. *Really?* Given how concerned she was over what Shaun wore, he couldn't believe she didn't even try to dress up. *Great.* Shaun's first date with a girl, and he was already worried that she would think his mom was a slob.

She opened the door, and Emma stood there on the welcome mat.

"Hi, Mrs. Baxter," Emma said with a polite smile.

"Well, you must be Emma!" Shaun's mom stretched out her hand, all her bracelets jingling.

Emma shook Mrs. Baxter's hand. "Nice to meet you."

"And you, you know you're just as pretty as Shaun said, with those cute skinny jeans," Mrs. Baxter said, beaming. "Shaun, Emma is here!"

Shaun quietly tiptoed back a few feet from the wall and acted like he was just walking down to the doorway in the middle of putting on his leather jacket.

"Hey, Emma," Shaun commented.

Mrs. Baxter's eyes dotted between Shaun and Emma before landing on Shaun's shirt. "Oh, honey, your shirt tag is sticking out." Mrs. Baxter reached on his neck to push the tag back into the shirt.

Emma folded her lips back into her mouth, and she rocked back and forth on her heels. She looked up at Shaun and raised her brows. He gave an awkward grin. Emma held her mini-purse in front of her waistline, and Shaun looked up and down her body. *Wow, she looks good.*

"Yeah, okay, Mom." Shaun moved his eyes back in forth, trying to signal for his mom to ditch the scene.

"Oh, okeydoke." Shaun's mom put her hand on Emma's shoulder. "That's my cue, Emma. Off I go."

Shaun watched Emma stifle a laugh as Mrs. Baxter walked away in a bouncy manner, winking at Shaun. Shaun was embarrassed out of his mind, pushed the gel in his hair back, and walked down the steps of their house with Emma.

"Looking good, Bon Jovi," Emma joked.

Shaun laughed, and the two started their walk to the movie theater. The silence that was present for fifteen minutes of their walk was broken by a question posed by Emma. Shaun heard Emma open her mouth when her lips separated loudly. He turned to her, and she seemed to nearly talk. Whatever she was going to say made her hesitate.

Emma resumed with her question, which came out rather blunt to Shaun, but he respected the honesty. "Hey, just out of curiosity, this date isn't like ... like I don't know ... it's not like a I'll-take-advantage-of-the-depressed-girl type of thing, is it?" Emma shivered, folded her arms, and continued, "Because if it is, just tell me, and I'll walk home right now."

Shaun turned away. "What do you mean?"

Emma shrugged her shoulders, pushed her hair back from her eyes, and explained, "Like since you know like the whole thing with my sister, I just feel like a lot of people that I wouldn't normally talk to have been coming up to me and talking with me. And it's all completely out of nowhere."

"Oh." Shaun continued to stare at the sidewalk ahead of them. He didn't intend for the date to seem like a pity gesture, but given Emma's comment, he almost regretted asking her out.

Emma looked up at him and then back at her folded arms. They walked underneath a pine tree, and it shook in the cold wind. Pinecones fell down around them, and Emma started kicking one that landed between her feet.

"I mean, it just seems like everyone's saying, 'Oh, let's make friends with Emma because her sister died and I wanna look like a good sympathetic person.' They all act like fucking idiots around me too, like I can't tell that their hugs and patronizing comments are bullshit. Like sorry if that were too forward, but it's just been getting on my nerves. I mean, so if that's what this is, then the better thing for both of us would be to just leave me alone."

Shaun squinted and focused on the movie theater that was just coming into view as they entered downtown. He wracked his mind for an answer to Emma's question that wouldn't seem like an actual pity gesture. "Yeah. I mean, no. That's not why I asked you out. I just said yeah because I get it. I mean, I don't get what you go through with all the bullshit and fake pity, but it makes sense to me." Shaun checked Emma's face but couldn't discern her expression. "By the way I hate that patronizing stuff too. Like if I get shit from guys at school or, as usual, I get a shitty grade on one of Mrs. Morton's tests, my mom always races into my space to inject her vials of patronization into my brain."

Emma laughed for second. "Right? Especially parents. In fact, parents are worse."

"Worse than a bunch of guys faking emotions to get in your pants?" Shaun smiled at her. "I don't know. That's pretty hard to beat."

Emma snickered. "Trust me. You have no idea. You know Ted?"

"Ah, yes. Your idol, right?" Shaun commented sarcastically.

"Pfff right. The only person idolizing Ted is himself," Emma continued venting to Shaun.

He looked at her long brown hair and the way it cascaded past her shoulders. He snuck a peek at her butt and smiled to himself. He did good.

Shaun didn't want to creep himself out, but he loved her level of vulnerability when talking with him. Most girls didn't talk to Shaun, period. At least not voluntarily. He enjoyed being trusted enough by Emma to be a person to divulge information to.

He couldn't believe the conversation hadn't gone to shit yet. He was so surprised he couldn't formulate a sentence long enough that he could comment on Emma's venting.

"That guy thinks he actually saved my mom from crippling depression after my dad left rather than worsening it. Plus, these past few weeks haven't helped, and he's just been 'standing by me and my mom in our time of trouble.' Standing by? My ass. That slimeball couldn't even pull himself to come to the funeral for Christina." Emma's eyes watered. "He always acts nice around my mom and feeds her bullshit because she's vulnerable. As soon as Ted talks to me, the conversation turns into a competition of who will cry or yell first."

"And I'm assuming it's usually you, huh?" Shaun inched over on the sidewalk to try to comfort Emma.

"Yeah." Emma took a long sniffle and wiped her face. "Sorry, everything's just been real shit lately. I bet I look really attractive right now, huh?"

Shaun wanted to say something like "You look beautiful" or "Don't worry. You always look attractive." He wanted to say how much he cared about everything that was happening with Emma, and he wanted to hug her. Shaun thought better of it and told himself to be realistic. He didn't want to fall under the category of another patronizing asshole in Emma's mind.

"You look great. Also, fuck Ted." Shaun wondered if he went too far with the comment.

Emma smiled, looking away from Shaun as they entered the movie theater. Emma seemed to collect herself though because of what Shaun said. She affirmed him. "Fuck Ted."

They bought tickets to *Black Panther* and walked to the snack bar. Emma grabbed an ICEE, a sirloin hot dog, and a box of Whoppers. Shaun bought a Coke and a tray of nachos.

"You're not gonna have more?" Emma asked.

"Naw, I'm good. I gotta stay in shape, you know?" He couldn't even afford to eat nachos, but he figured he'd indulge himself.

"You look fine, like really fine." Emma smiled. "Just buy something else. It won't destroy your body."

Shaun struggled not to crack a smile, and his eyes darted between Emma and a mountainous stack of candy options back in the food line. "Aight. I will."

"Yeah, live dangerously." Emma chuckled.

Shaun walked back to the food and grabbed a box of M&Ms. He couldn't believe what he'd heard. *I looked good? To a girl? To Emma?* Even from that one compliment, he felt like he was standing on top of the world.

Emma offered to pay, but Shaun waved her wallet away and gave the cashier the amount due. And with that, Shaun and Emma checked the halls of the theater and snuck into *Hereditary*.

In the middle of the horror flick, Shaun looked over at Emma to see how she was reacting to the movie, and her eyes were glued to the screen as she threw Whoppers down her throat. He made a toothy smile, looked back at the screen, and leaned back in his chair. A character in the movie suddenly got decapitated, and the entire audience jumped, including Shaun who rocked Emma's seat.

Emma laughed out loud. "And you were saying girls are usually more scared? I barely jumped," Emma whispered.

Shaun raised his hands in resignation. "My bad," Shaun said, embarrassed.

Emma playfully patted his thigh and continued watching the movie. Shaun looked down at her hand and then back at the screen. He let out a sigh after puffing his cheeks like a blowfish.

After regaining his masculinity and confidence, Shaun looked at Emma and slowly inched his arm around the back of her seat. He assumed Emma hadn't noticed yet as his arm came to a rest on the top of the chair, centimeters from her neck and shoulders. Shaun looked back at the screen, trying to remain cool.

Nervous as a virgin in a prison shower, Shaun held his breath, closed his eyes, and tensed his muscles as he slowly lowered his arm around Emma. Shaun opened his eyes and exhaled a sigh of relief that she didn't move away. He knew he probably looked like a deer in the headlights.

Emma looked over at Shaun and grinned with a short laugh. Shaun watched Emma from the corner of his eye as she slowly lifted up the armrest separating them and scooted into Shaun's shoulder.

Emma let out a shaky breath. Shaun felt her body shake and then relax as she leaned into his chest and shoulder. Toward the end of the movie, Shaun fell asleep from the exhaust and stress of his small move on Emma.

"Hey, Shaun," Emma said, tapping him on the thigh.

Shaun blinked once and barely moved.

"Shauuuuuun," Emma drawled, continuing to tap him on the thigh.

Shaun jerked awake, and his eyes opened. He realized he was drooling and wildly wiped his mouth. He leaned forward, wiping his eyes. "Sorry. Was just resting my eyes." Shaun yawned. "Why are we waiting around? The credits are rolling."

Emma shook her head and chuckled. "Suuuure resting your eyes. Yeah, let's go."

When they arrived at Shaun's house, his dad opened the door and let him in. Shaun squinted at his father, wondering why he didn't just ask Emma to come inside too.

"Hey, Emma, you sure you don't a bottle of water or something?" Shaun's father asked.

Emma shook her head. "No, it's fine, Mr. Baxter. Thank you though."

"All right. Also if you want, I can give you a ride back to your place."

"Dad, she already said it's fine."

"I know. I'm just trying to be polite, Shaun, a new concept to you."

Shaun and Emma both laughed.

"Okay, but seriously she's fine. You're fine, right, Emma?"

"Oh yeah, definitely. I walk around at night all the time." Emma validated Shaun's comment. Shaun nodded at his father.

"Okaaay, okay," Shaun's dad said, smiling. "Nice meeting you, Emma."

"You too, Mr. Baxter," Emma said. "See you Monday, Shaun."

"Oh, aight. See you, Emma." Shaun waved as his dad shut the door.

"Seriously would it kill you to be polite?" Shaun's dad bent down toward his son and waved his arms.

"She said she was fine. I was just expediting her trip home." Shaun grinned.

"Yeah, okay, kid. Time to go to sleep." Shaun's dad laughed and rubbed his son's shoulder before walking to his bedroom.

"Night, Dad," Shaun said.

"Ditto." Mr. Baxter yawned.

The bedroom door to Mr. and Mrs. Baxter's room shut, and a click of the lock was made. Shaun walked around the end of the hallway and into his bedroom. He undressed himself down to his briefs and flopped onto his bed. A smile grew onto Shaun's face, and he went to sleep, filled with the joy of knowing that he had just managed to turn Emma's perspective of him to an attraction.

EMMA

"Oh, aight. See you, Emma." Shaun waved as his dad shut the door.

Emma smiled and walked back to her apartment. She beamed as she walked down the street in the pale moonlight. A few couples on their evening strolls passed by her, and she waved politely and watched them hold each other's hands.

Emma stretched out her arms. *Damn, that was great.* It had been so long since Emma went out with someone, especially someone she liked as much as Shaun. She wondered how much he liked her. She thought maybe he was thinking about her at the same time she was thinking about him. Maybe the reason she couldn't stop thinking about him was because he couldn't stop thinking about her. She wondered when he'd ask her out again. *Or should I ask him? No, the girl never asks. What the fuck, Emma? Yeah, Shaun would think I'm desperate.*

Emma crossed the street as she approached her apartment complex. She wondered if Shaun had seen *The Gift*, a classic horror movie. She realized Jason Bateman was in that movie. He was also in *The Kingdom*. She remembered Jamie Foxx was in *The Kingdom*. She found him extremely sexy. Emma also realized Jamie Foxx played the piano. *A musician and an actor ... so hot.*

She wondered if Shaun played piano. Shaun could play Emma's piano any time. *What the hell are you thinking, Emma?* Emma bet Shaun liked rock music. *Likes Billie Joe Armstrong. Green Day too maybe.* Emma's stream of consciousness ended when she opened the door to her cigarette-reeking apartment.

Emma was smiling and in one of the best moods she had been in in weeks when her eyes fell on Ted. Her smile turned upside down, and hate filled her. Ted was watching 10:00 p.m. *Wheel of Fortune* reruns with a Marlboro cigarette in his left hand and two beers on the coffee table. The remote in his right hand clicked, and the TV paused Pat Sajak in the middle of his sentence.

The cigarette ashes fell from his hand and onto the carpet, leaving a gray mark in the middle of the green floor. Ted took his feet off the coffee table and leaned back, exhaling smoke through his nostrils. He squinted his right eye on Emma and itched the middle of his bare chest. More ashes from the Marlboro fell as he lifted the cigarette to his mouth to take a hit. Emma stood ten feet away from him, shaking with anger.

"You're late." Ted sighed through a puff of smoke. "I thought we had an agreement of a ten o'clock sharp arrival time."

"Well, it was ten about five minutes ago when I came in. Of course maybe if you were sober you would be able to check the time without your vision blurring."

"Whoa!" Ted shouted then in a calmer, still drunk tone. "What happened towower discussionszuhbout respect on Monday? Or the rules I talked … talkkkeduhbout last year?"

"I broke one of them. Oh no," Emma said carelessly. Ted was too drunk to take seriously for that moment. "I talked back. Whoops."

Ted nodded, slurring, "Youuu're damn rightcha did. Do you need to be reminded of the other rules?"

"No, I really don't think—"

Ted's greasy voice interrupted Emma. "Shut up. They were along the lines of, of, of no talking back, no dates unless I met the … unless I met the kid firsssst, no swearrring, and respect. Is that sssoooo harddo sunderstand?"

"Yeah, well respect goes both ways, Ted!" Emma snapped.

"See that's … that's sh-what I mean. You already broke rule

number one and number four and why?" Ted asked, grinning malevolently.

Emma walked past him and lied, "I was just out with my friend Sophia, Ted."

"I don't give a shit who you were with." Ted laughed.

Emma rolled her eyes and turned away from him.

"Hey!" Ted yelled and stood up to finish his statement. "You don't fucking roll your eyes at me, Emma Walsh. I'm the part of the reason to uhh … to keep this roof over your head! So don't you fucking roll your eyes at me!"

"Well, I didn't think it was part of the rules." Emma started her walk up the stairs to her room and then stopped. She turned around. "Oh and by the way, I think putting this roof over my head would require you getting off your lazy ass more than twice a day!"

Emma closed her mouth as fast as she opened it when she realized she had just sworn out loud at Ted. She couldn't help herself. The word just came out in her fit of rage. Ted stood at the bottom of the stairs and then slowly made his way up the stairs to the one Emma was standing on.

He leaned in, encroaching on her personal space. She turned her head away and started to cry when he grabbed her by the bottom of the neck. "Say you're sorry." Ted breathed into her eardrum.

"I'm sorry," Emma cried out. Emma clearly didn't mean it, but she just wanted to get away from the disgusting bartender.

Ted turned his ear toward her, grinning. "Sorry, I didn't catch that. Can you repeat yourself?"

"I'm sorry … Dad," Emma cried as tears streamed down her face.

"Music to my, my ears," Ted whispered and turned to go down the stairs.

She was met with the face of her mother. Emma breathed hard and gagged on her tears, relieved.

Cynthia Walsh nodded for him to go to her room. Ted smiled and kissed Cynthia on the cheek before leaving Emma's line of sight. Emma couldn't stand to see her mom so blissfully in denial and nearly threw up in her mouth. She couldn't understand how her mother acted like Christina never even existed.

"Do you even care that she's gone?" Emma asked her mother.

Cynthia bowed her head. "It's just better if we move on."

"Move on? She's barely been gone a month, and you want to move on." Emma raised her voice at her mother.

"Well, what do you want to do? Hmm? Christina isn't coming back, so move on." Cynthia wiped one of her eyes with the back of her hand.

"I want you to admit that it's Ted's fault she's gone. I want him to act like a man and take responsibility," Emma pleaded.

"It's a hard thing to accept, Emma."

"Then make him leave. Why can't you just make him leave?" Emma pleaded again. She held onto the wall for support as she shuddered. She couldn't accept what her mom was saying. They had been together for a couple of years, but not a lifetime. How hard would it be for Cynthia to just kick Ted out and call child support?

"It's complicated. He does miss her. As much as we do," Cynthia said.

"That's not true. He's the reason she died," Emma sputtered out and covered her mouth.

Cynthia looked up at Emma from the ground. She pointed at Emma and pursed her lips. "Go to sleep now, Em." Cynthia walked into Ted's room.

Emma watched horrified as her mom walked away, locking the door behind her. The tears had stopped pouring from Emma's eyes, and her eyes went dry with only a soft cry still emitting from her throat. She'd seen her mom in denial since she met Ted. She saw her in denial when they moved into the Deepcrest, when they struggled to pay bills, and when Christina left. But now? Emma couldn't understand it. Christina was her mother's own daughter and Ted's stepdaughter, and her mom was just like okay with her being gone?

Emma was desperate for an escape. It had only been fifteen minutes, but she missed leaning against Shaun already. She dried her face off and brushed her hair over her ear. She walked into her room and slammed the door.

SOPHIA

"A sixty-four, great." Sophia sighed while looking at her first world history test, which was just handed back.

Sophia glanced around the room, trying to catch what other students might have gotten or, like herself, what they didn't get. The only grades she could see were As or Bs, and she strained her eyes trying to see the grade the person next her, Jackson Decker, had received. Sophia's eyes began to shake and throb as she stared at Jackson's paper, trying to see the number written at the top. She needed to know if at least one other person in the room did as poorly as she did.

The second digit, number one, came into view from Jackson's paper. Sophia was on the edge of her seat, quite literally, antsy to see his grade. She knew that the one, as a second-digit placeholder, automatically moved Jackson to the lower end of whatever grade he had. When she finally saw his grade, her heart sank. He had a ninety-one.

Jackson looked up at her as she was looking at his paper. "Yes?" he asked, suspicious of Sophia.

Sophia lied, "Oh, sorry. Just wanted to see what you got for number thirty-two."

"Oh, I got B. It was completely wrong. Fuckin' hate this class." Jackson groaned.

Sophia smiled and looked back at her paper.

The conversation was over until Jackson spoke abruptly. "So

did you get that one wrong too?" Jackson looked at Sophia's paper. "Because judging by your score, I'd say you got a lot more wrong."

"Wow, thanks," Sophia said, rolling her eyes.

Jackson chuckled slightly but said, "Hey. Hey, I'm sorry. I was kidding. I got a forty on the one before this, so you still did better than my last one."

"Why'd you get so high on this though?" Sophia queried.

"Uh, I temporarily borrowed the correct answers from the kid next to me." Jackson grinned.

"So you cheated." Sophia sighed.

Jackson took a sip from his water bottle, waving his finger at her. "Ah, ah, ah." Jackson's water dribbled from his mouth. "Temperrarorhy bahrowwed."

Sophia smiled slightly. "Fair enough."

Despite Jackson's stupidity and troublemaking, he was still a little cute. He sure was attractive, but his dumb personality made him seem more like a gentle giant. Jackson was looking around the room, appearing anxious. He seemed desperate to keep the conversation going.

He turned around and spoke to Emma. "Hey," Jackson whispered.

Emma didn't look up. Sophia could still hear him. His whisper was more like a yell-whisper.

"Hey!" Jackson whispered louder.

Emma continued to write on her notebook.

"Emmaaaa," Jackson drawled.

"What?" Emma looked up, annoyed.

"What sport does Sophia play?"

"Uh, she does cheerleading, but field hockey is the sport she does, I think? Why?"

"Do they play in the spring?"

"No, it's a fall sport. Why though—"

Jackson ignored Emma's questions. "Thanks." He turned back

around and folded his arms behind his head. Sophia could see his reflection in the window near her. His toned pitching arms bulged.

"So field hockey. You any good?" Jackson smirked.

Sophia looked over at him, confused. "Didn't know you even knew that existed?"

"Yeah, well, I mean I'm not a fanatic. I can enjoy a good game though."

"Oh, yeah." Sophia grinned. Jackson was being ridiculous. Sophia tested him. "How many players per team?"

"I think it's—" Jackson paused and leaned back in his chair.

"Eleven," Emma whispered without looking up.

"Eleven!" Jackson declared.

Sophia cracked up after hearing Emma answer. She found Jackson's cheating a little impressive. She was surprised he even wanted to talk to her seriously. She nodded in approval and spun her finger in her hair, smiling at him. "Not bad, baseballer."

"Like I said, I enjoy a good game." Jackson grinned. "Maybe we could talk about this more over a smoothie at Jake's Parlor sometime."

"Maybe." Sophia looked back down at her paper, blushing.

"All right. Well, here's my Snapchat in case that maybe turns into a yes." Jackson wrote his info at the top of her test.

Sophia beamed.

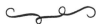

Emma swirled her smoothie around with her straw, and the sound of the drink slowly mixing was blared out by the blenders simultaneously blending in the background. She stuck her tongue up into her gums, licking the plaque off her teeth.

Sophia glanced up and cringed at Emma's teeth cleaning. She looked down at her phone and texted Jackson. Both girls were waiting for the other to talk first, but neither wanted to initiate a conversation until Emma yawned. She winced as her jaw locked during the yawn and quickly popped it.

"Shit, that hurt." Emma grunted.

"Yeah, I heard it from over here." Sophia was pulling her hair while typing a text out.

"Yeah." Emma nodded. "So, uh, not to like to call out the elephant in the room … er … the elephant that's not in the room, but what was with you and Jackson today?"

"What do you mean?" Sophia lied. She knew exactly what Emma meant. Even Sophia couldn't tell how she had gone from hating Jackson's sleaziness to being seriously attracted to him. She supposed that, for once, Jackson sincerely acted like he wanted to talk for the sake of talking. It didn't come off as a conversation, so he could get in bed with her.

Regardless, Sophia didn't want Emma thinking she and Jackson were just going to have a casual fling. Sophia wanted a relationship like Emma, so she just told her, "He changed, I guess."

"How?" Emma questioned Sophia. "I mean, like just two weeks ago when we first came here you were telling me how much you hated that baseball douche."

Sophia put down her phone and began to bite her nails. In between bites, she said, "I don't know. He just seemed genuine today."

"Why? Just because he gave you an answer to your field hockey thing?" Emma asked.

Sophia could tell Emma was annoyed that she wasn't being given credit for providing Jackson all the answers for Sophia's questions. Sophia couldn't have cared less because to her, Jackson was just making a sweet gesture to get to know Sophia better.

"Like anyone could have just told him those answers. He also could have guessed it. I mean he plays football too, and eleven players are also on the field too in football."

"No?" Sophia looked at Emma in disbelief.

"Actually yeah. It is eleven players in football." Emma pulled up a page from her phone to prove her point.

"Oh." Sophia looked down, embarrassed. "Well, either way he was nice today."

"Look, I just hope you know what you're getting yourself into." Emma calmed down, and she put her hand on Sophia's wrist as a sign of compassion. "Decker's kinda got a rep you know?"

"Are you jealous?" Sophia was partially trying to rile Emma up so she'd leave her be, but a light bulb also went on in Sophia's head.

Maybe Emma was prodding so much because she was dating someone far less popular and well known. Yeah, that made sense to Sophia. Emma was probably jealous over Sophia, succeeding instantly with a guy rather than not knowing how to even talk with one.

"You're kidding, right? No. No way in hell. I'd rather lose my virginity to a homeless guy than to Jackson."

"What is your deal? Is it Shaun?" Sophia did not take kindly to Emma's beating Jackson, the dead horse. Sure, they both had disliked him in the past, but Sophia wished Emma would take her side and give Jackson a chance.

"You've been going out with Shaun for like three weeks, and he still hasn't kissed you. Don't you think that's odd? Like maybe he's not into you anymore? Just a thought."

Emma's arms tensed. Sophia saw through Emma's fake grin.

"Whatever you say to make yourself feel better. I don't get it. You live in a mansion. You have parents who could pay for anything you want and are like the most popular girl in the sophomore class at BRHS. What could you possibly gain by insulting someone like me who has jack shit compared to what you got? Like you could do so much better than Jackson-fucking-Decker. Why him?" Emma implored.

Sophia shrugged. Sophia didn't understand what Emma was saying. Jackson seemed like a great fit for Sophia now. He might not have been as smart as Shaun, but Jackson was confident, cute, and funny, and he seemed sincere. Sophia just wanted one ounce of an agreement from Emma.

"Just be careful all right." Emma stood up and walked out of the smoothie parlor.

Sophia looked down at her phone to text Jackson as a tear sneaked out of her right eye and slowly walked down her cheek to the bottom of her neck. "Because maybe he's the right guy for me," Sophia muttered under her breath as a late response to Emma's inquiry.

Sophia drove home, her hands gripping the steering wheel so hard that it winced underneath them. She was completely solid with and frozen with anger at Emma for being so intrusive into her life. *What does Emma know anyway? She's just some pathetic, friendless loner that I'm being nice enough to, to take under my wing.*

Sophia pulled up to her house and opened her car door after grabbing her purse. She slammed the door behind her and ran up the steps of her front porch. The doors of Sophia's home opened, and a cool breeze rushed in as the wooden frame smacked the walls. Sophia took her jacket off and hung it on the coat rack so she could close the double wooden doors behind her.

She turned around, and her mother was facing her from the back of the foyer with a paper in her hand. Sophia leapt back, surprised by the dark silhouette of her mother in the dark shadow of the entrance to her house.

"Oh my God." Sophia laughed nervously. "You friggin terrified me."

"Oh sorry. I was a little shocked myself." Her mother's voice rose to a yell, so loud her gold hoop earrings swung around. "When I received this email from your world history teacher!" Mrs. Milverton stood with one hand on her hip over her perfectly tailored black work suit. The other was outstretched, waving the printed email at Sophia outstretched.

Sophia averted her eyes. "Look, Mom, I'm not tryna be rude, but I really don't wanna have to deal with this right now."

"That's what you say every time, so you know what?" Sophia's mom raised her eyebrows and put her hands on her hips. "You're gonna deal with this right now."

Sophia rolled her eyes and began to walk to her room. *What an intrusive bitch.*

"You come back here right now, Sophia Milverton!"

"Why? So you can tell me that I need to fix my grade? That I need to talk to my teachers because they like a student that cares? Or I need a tutor because they can help me overcome my struggles?" Sophia yelled, coming back into view of her mother.

Her mom folded her moms and closed her mouth.

"You know only eighteen percent of high school students need tutors." Sophia's pointless argument went down the drain and did virtually nothing against her mother's authoritative pose and strong factually intact reasoning. "I don't wanna be the loser dumb girl that needs to be tutored, Mooooom."

"You wouldn't need to be tutored if you did better in class. And, honey, who cares if you have a tutor?"

"My name is Sophia, Mom. Remember? You gave me that name so don't patronize me with stuff like honey or sweetheart. I'm not ten years old," Sophia retorted.

Mrs. Milverton stepped back, clearly baffled. "Oh my God, I'm not patronizing you, Soph. I'm just trying to—"

"Yeah, you're just trying to help, right? You wanna help me right now? Leave me alone!" Sophia ran into her room and slammed the door so hard that it nearly bounced back open.

Sophia hated being undermined by anyone. She knew she wasn't as smart as the other students in her class, but she knew damn well that no one could top her popularity. Sophia wiped her eyes in order to prevent a black line of liquefied makeup from running down her face. She knew how pathetic she looked and how pitiful it was to be crying over such a pointless argument with her mother.

Every time she argued with her mother, it always ended in one of two things: Sophia would leave the room on the brink of tears and never let them show or she would cry and continue to argue until someone got tired and went to sleep. Most of the time, that person would be Sophia.

Sophia went onto her phone and made a post to her 2,093 followers on Instagram about the fight with her mom. She took a picture of her looking down at her nails longingly. She placed a black-and-white filter over the image and captioned it: "Some kids want freedom from school; I want freedom my parents."

The reality was that compared to other kids, her freedom outmatched theirs tenfold. She drove a Cadillac, lived in the hills just west of San Mateo in a mansion, and could go wherever she wanted with whomever she wanted at any time.

The only freedom Sophia lacked was that of not having parents who were constantly breathing down her neck. Sophia always felt under constant scrutiny based on her choices of friends, her grades, her choices on what to wear, her haircut, and anything else her parents would look for to criticize. She felt like her life was a continuous game of I Spy played by both her mother and father.

With the notion that nothing was unseen by her parents, she was under constant paranoia of disobeying them. She never felt comfortable enough to tell them anything about her life and therefore had to be as vague as possible about anything she was planning on doing during the week. The absence of trust between Sophia and her mother also left a void of love and connection, waiting to be filled by any attraction she held to a boy and any friend Sophia made.

Sophia scrolled through the hundreds of likes on her picture and the numerous comments that said phrases relating to "I'm so sorry, hon. Your mom sounds like a total bitch. Hang in there!" followed by countless heart emoticons and thumbs-up tags. The comments, left by all her friends, filled the void of connection in Sophia's family.

However at some point, the void would eventually empty itself, and no matter what the comment read and regardless how many followers Sophia gained, she would be in a state of numbness and feel an emptiness lasting in perpetuity.

Sophia kept scrolling through her notifications of comments

when a notification for a private message came through. She went to the top of her phone and clicked it. Jackson Decker had messaged her.

"Hey, you wanna hang out at Sheridan Park? Saw your post. I bet you could use some company."

Sophia hesitated. Jackson might not be the safest boy to hang out with alone, given a certain reputation of being a one-night-stand kind of guy. Still she needed something better than an Instagram post as a way to vent, so she responded, "Yes."

She grabbed her coat and opened her window. She crawled out and fell into the surrounding oleander trees below it. A car came down the street, and she hid her face from any familiar faces that might be watching from the car. Sophia looked up when the car had driven passed her house, and she made her way down to the local park Jackson had told her to meet him at.

Sophia came to a stop on the edge of the play structure and saw Jackson sitting at the bottom of one of the slides. She saw him holding a brown paper bag, and the top of a bottle of liquor was protruding from it. Sophia had a sudden urge to leave and go back to her home to just cry. She didn't want Jackson to see her so pathetically sad.

However, the part of her that was lonely and missing a connection with someone who cared for her desperately wanted to stay. She stepped on an oak leaf, and it cracked with a deafening snap. Jackson turned and saw her standing near the playground, her breath exiting her body in a foggy cloud. She smiled and walked over to the dual slide attached to his. Jackson took off his jacket and reached out to her with it. She politely waved it away.

Jackson sighed. "Just take it. You're shivering, and I can see your breath."

Sophia smiled and nodded, and she put the jacket on her shivering back. Jackson looked down and fingered the bag of liquor around in his hands. He turned the bag around and took a swig of the liquor, breathing heavily.

"You know the first time I came down here was after ..." Jackson paused. "You remember that kid Isaiah Porter who died during your freshman year?"

Sophia nodded. "Yeah, kinda. I wasn't there when the principal told everyone."

Jackson licked his gums and looked up, staring at the horizon, north of Sheridan Park. "Yeah, he was my best friend," Jackson said in a gravelly wet voice. "I remember I was just coming out of English when I heard the principal come onto the loudspeaker and tell all sophomores to go to the basketball gym. I turned to my friends, and they shrugged. We walked into the gym. I went in, and there were around four hundred chairs lined up with a podium at the front of the audience. I sat down next to that redhead kid in our world history class. You know him? Dude's name is Kevin."

"Yeah, I know him," Sophia said, looking into Jackson's eyes. "He doesn't talk as much as he used to freshman year."

"He went to middle school with me and Isaiah, so take a guess why." Jackson looked back, darting between Sophia's eyes. "Anyway I started talking to Kevin. I asked him why we were here. He said he didn't know. The announcement only said that all sophomores needed to be in the gym. I asked if someone got expelled or suspended or something. At this point, I figured it was just some procedural thing for the school, or someone actually got expelled. Kevin asked, 'I don't know. What if someone died?' There hadn't been a death here in like five years, so I took it as a joke. 'Yeah sure,' I said sarcastically. 'You never know, dude.' Kevin laughed, shrugging his shoulders. I said, 'True, but they wouldn't get everyone together to tell them about a—' But I was cut off by a voice speaking through a microphone on the podium. It was the principal."

Sophia watched Jackson move around uncomfortably, and he tapped his fingers on the side of his temple. He looked like he was about to cry but smiled instead. Sophia could tell where the story was going but wasn't about to cut Jackson off from spilling his guts. He yawned a quivering yawn and continued the story.

"He said, 'It is with a very heavy heart that I bring you this news. One of your fellow classmates passed away in his sleep last night. Isaiah Porter was a good friend to many and a—'" Jackson stopped talking.

"You good?" Sophia asked, knowing perfectly well that Jackson was not good and that her futile attempt to distract him did virtually nothing.

Jackson looked at her and nodded once. "You don't realize how much you care for someone until he's gone. I'd known Isaiah for a while, and when I found out he was gone, I don't know. I just wish I'd told him how good of a friend he was to me."

Sophia opened her mouth to speak and then withdrew a pointless "I'm sorry for your loss" from her thoughts, remembering what Emma had said. "That sounds like it was hard. Can only go uphill though, right?"

"It was. And yeah, yeah, that's true. Real true." Jackson wiped his eyes on his sleeve. "It's just stupid."

"What is?" Sophia asked.

Jackson began to ramble. "Like when I found out about Isaiah, I thought I was going to pass out."

Jackson put the bottle down on the ground and shook himself out. He folded his arms on his knees. Sophia could see him grit his teeth. She could see him holding his emotions in.

Jackson continued, "Well, no. Not pass out, but I felt my soul go cold. Well, not cold. I just felt like there was like something missing. Well, not missing. Just like—"

"Like part of you was empty." Sophia finished his sentence. "It's a shared feeling."

"Yeah, and that's not even what's stupid to me. What's stupid is that I couldn't show it. Do you have any idea what it's like to lose your best friend and not being able to cry because you know that people will look at you differently? I'm the best pitcher this school has seen in maybe twenty years, but I can't fucking cry over my friend? Because I'll lose the respect people give me?" Jackson threw his arm up like he was trying to swat a bee.

Sophia could see the anger inside him, the fury he used to cover the sadness.

"I knew I'd lose the respect. I'd be looking like a pussy, whatever you wanna name. I woulda lost it if I cried. It's such fucking bullshit, not like I think guys should spill out their thoughts into fucking diaries and shit, but like it's stupid." Jackson groaned.

"Yeah, that's ridiculous. And parents don't help because they don't know what to say, but how can you blame them? Society has changed a bit since they were younger."

Sophia wanted to help Jackson but wasn't sure what to say. She barely knew what to say to Emma when she brought up Christina. What do you say to someone in mourning? Sophia didn't know. She tried to show Jackson that she was attempting to be sincere rather than responding in three-word sentences.

"Exactly, I don't blame my parents, but they seriously need to pull their heads out their asses to even see a bit of what I go through." Jackson laughed, wiping his nose and eyes.

Sophia laughed along with him, and they sat next to each other laughing until Jackson's tears dried. Sophia's laugh slowly died out, and the playground was silent again.

"You wanna hear my petty story? Well, compared to yours," Sophia asked with a nervous laugh. "Since we're getting deep, I figured, 'Why not?'"

"Well, if you want to get deep, nighttime is the time to do it." Jackson took a swig from the paper bag.

Sophia nodded in agreement. "I'm lonely, the end," Sophia said, smiling awkwardly.

Jackson laughed uncomfortably and cocked his head to the side. "I feel constantly alone because my parents are retarded and can never see how I actually feel."

"Lemme guess, empty?" Jackson smiled back.

"Wow, how'd you know?" Sophia joked. "Seriously though, I've fucked like eight times, but it's the same each time and actually probably a bit worse each time because—"

"Because the guys' dicks get smaller and smaller?" Jackson laughed.

Sophia chuckled, which distracted her from tearing up. "That too." Sophia looked away and stopped laughing. "But mainly because I've had sex eight times. What the fuck is wrong with me? Like I'm sixteen and I'm the town hoe. Isn't the normal thought of a sixteen-year-old how her winter dance photos will look? Not which basketball player is going to join her extending list of hookups."

Sophia couldn't believe what she was saying, but holy hell, it felt good to let out. She kept these thoughts to herself until she told Jackson. She'd waited for someone to trust enough to fully rant to without worry of them spreading rumors.

"And that's what my parents don't see and don't give a shit to ask about. I'm lonely and, more importantly, alone." Sophia sighed.

"You're not alone." Jackson smiled. "Not anymore."

There was a silence. Sophia couldn't tell if Jackson were faking it, but she saw him look at the ground to hide a smile. She knew he was sincere. A guy wanted her for more than sex. *What a feeling.*

Jackson took the bottle of whiskey out of the brown paper bag. "You know after Isaiah passed away, I came down here the week after with this massive bottle of brandy and got drunk outta my mind. Now whenever I feel like shit, I just come down here, bottle of something, and drink it all."

"That's not good. You could die if you drink too much." Sophia considered taking a sip though. Her parents had raised her to be completely straitlaced, so even at parties she rarely drank more than a beer. Besides, she assumed she wouldn't become an alcoholic after one swig of liquor.

"I realize that," Jackson sputtered through a sip of whiskey. "It just helps to ease the pain."

"Jackson, alcohol isn't a prescribed painkiller." Sophia shook her head.

Jackson put the bottle down and averted his eyes from Sophia. "Yeah? Well, it should be. Works wonders for me."

Sophia felt him building up some anger and was worried what he would say if she didn't drink. Jackson looked back at Sophia and offered her the bottle with an outstretched arm.

"No, I can't. My parents already hate me enough for my shitty grades." Sophia pushed the bottle away.

"Who said your parents will find out?" Jackson grinned.

Sophia looked up at him, pursed her lips, and took the bottle. "All right. Can't tell no one though."

"I wouldn't," Jackson said.

Sophia could feel Jackson's eyes on her. Under pressure, she finished off his bottle of liquor.

SHAUN

Shaun was having a late dinner with Emma at a burger joint. She sat across from Shaun, sluggishly stirring her soup around with her left hand, her head propped up by her right hand. Shaun bit into his cheeseburger, and grease dribbled out of his mouth. He watched on as Emma slowly lifted the spoon to her mouth, swallowed the sweet tomato blend, and placed the spoon back in the bowl to stir the basil around once again. Shaun placed his burger down on the table and forced the large bite down his throat, grease coating his esophagus.

Shaun spoke in a greased-up, phlegmy rumble. "Everything good?"

Emma looked up with a tiny smile. "Yeah."

Shaun accepted the comment of affirmation.

"Well, yeah," Emma repeated in a more somber tone.

"No, it's not," Shaun commented. "What's the deal?"

"Do you not like me?" Emma asked with a frown.

This caught Shaun off guard. "What?" Shaun stared in disbelief and then joked, "Yeah I hate you. I'd rather be gay."

Emma laughed slightly. "Sorry. I was just talking to Sophia the other day, and she kinda like insinuated that since you haven't made a move yet, you didn't like me. I mean, we have been going out for a couple weeks, and we're still going out and—"

Shaun thought that he probably should've kissed her. *Duh. What the fuck am I doing?* Then again, most teen movies take the whole movie for them to kiss. Shaun tried to reason why he hadn't made a *real* move. Shaun assumed he'd waited enough. He considered kissing her right then and there.

Shaun started to lean in, and Emma stopped talking.

"Shaun, you paying attention?" Emma asked, confused.

Shaun nodded and leaned back. Shaun started a conversation with his conscience. *What the fuck was that? I don't know. I just thought maybe she was trying to clue me in to kiss her. Right, so if a guy mugged you and then apologized, you'd say, 'No problem?' No, I just thought I should like fix the problem of not kissing her by kissing her.*

"So you get what I said, right?" Emma asked.

Shaun stared at her blankly. "Mmm."

"Shauuun," Emma drawled his name. She snapped her fingers in a Z in front of his face.

"Sorry. Yeah, I get it," Shaun said with no knowledge of what she'd said.

"Oh." Emma grinned. "So you've just been trying to find the right time then?"

"To?" Shaun faked a grin and laughed playfully.

"To make a move, dumbass." Emma laughed playfully along with him. "Because the guy *has* to make the first move, at least to me. This won't go anywhere unless you do something."

Shaun didn't know what to say. He decided to just roll with it. Maybe he'd actually make a move if he went with the flow of the relationship.

"You'll have to find out." Shaun faked confidence.

"Ooh, okay." Emma blushed. "Hey, sorry for like questioning you like that. I was just getting the vibe that you weren't into me."

Shaun chuckled, embarrassed. "You know that you're literally the first girl I've gone out with, right?"

"That's sad," Emma joked. "Even I went out before you, except it was like one date. But once is more than nonce."

"Touché."

Shaun snorted a laugh and bit into his burger again. *Touché?*

Really, Shaun? He sounded like his mom. He knew it was a dumb line, but everything before it was working fine.

"Hey, once I finish this soup, you wanna go back to your place and chill for a bit?" Emma asked.

Shaun nodded and smiled once again. He was amazed at where the night was heading. He knew that something was going to happen, and he couldn't wait for it, even if it were just a kiss. His hormones were raging. Shaun didn't want to come on too strong and just invite her back to his room when they got home. He knew that would come off too creepy. He told himself to just relax and go with the flow. Whatever was going to happen would happen.

"I'm about done with this burger. What about that tomato basil?" Shaun asked Emma.

"Well, it's not getting any hotter, and I'm already kinda full so ..." Emma trailed off.

"Sooo you wanna head back to my place?" Shaun asked.

Emma nodded while swallowing her last slurp of the soup. Shaun caught the eye of the waitress and waved her over. She put the meals down at the customers she was serving and came over to Shaun and Emma smiling.

"Check?" Shaun asked.

The waitress pulled out the check binder and laid it down on Shaun's side of the table. Shaun tipped her 20 percent. The young waitress smiled, mouthed the words "thank you," and hastily brushed her tip into her pocket. Shaun nodded and stood up from the booth. He held the door open for Emma, and they started on back to Shaun's house.

Shaun's father sat on the couch near the coffee table with a bag of potato chips next to him while he read the newspaper. The door to the house opened, and Emma walked into the home first. Shaun couldn't let his father talk to Emma for more than thirty seconds before his father embarrassed Shaun. He closed the door behind both and softly pushed Emma along past his father.

"Helloo," Mr. Baxter said without taking his eyes off the newspaper. "So the date went less than average, huh?"

Emma walked into the living room, grinning. "Hey, Mr. Baxter."

Mr. Baxter glanced back, and when his eyes met Emma's, Mr. Baxter shot off the chair.

"More than average I'd say, Dad." Shaun rolled his eyes and went to lock the door.

"Sorry, Emma. I just thought that Shaun had … Well, you know I thought that nothing had hap … Shaun didn't tell me you came home with." Mr. Baxter cut off his rambling and smiled politely at Emma before turning to Shaun.

Shaun was staring at his dad wide-eyed, darting his pupils toward the kitchen. Mr. Baxter mouthed the word "sorry" to Shaun and booked himself around the corner toward the fridge.

Emma snickered and leaned into Shaun's ear. "I see where you get the nervous rambling thing from."

"Just kill me, please." Shaun was so astronomically embarrassed by his family that he could barely joke about them with Emma. "He's a weird guy sometimes. I guess he just wasn't expecting you."

"I got that part." Emma laughed.

Shaun smiled, and the skin near his eyes wrinkled. "Yeah, Imma go talk to him. Can you gimme a sec? Then I promise we can be alone."

"Sure." Emma plopped down on a chair opposite of where Mr. Baxter had been sitting.

Shaun walked through the house to find his dad. He wanted his dad out of the area when Emma was around. Shaun couldn't believe his dad's weirdness around Emma. How could he possibly have married Shaun's mom? Well, Shaun's mom was Shaun's mom, but marrying someone takes a lot of not being awkward around girls. Shaun saw his dad in the kitchen and tripped over his shoelaces while power-walking into the kitchen. He hit the wall as he entered, glaring at his dad.

"Well, I guess we're not all smooth today, are we?" Mr. Baxter said.

"Ha!" Shaun leaned up against the counter. "Like … what like … what the hell was that back there?"

"I don't know. I just thought you weren't going out with her like *that* anymore. I just thought you hadn't like done anything." Shaun's dad unbuttoned his business jacket. Fumbling with the buttons, he slapped his hands down at the edges of the counter and gave up.

"Why not?" Shaun raised his voice and lowered it again, whispering, "Why not? All Emma said today was that she thought I was not into her."

"And why would that be?" Shaun's dad folded his arms, the answer already in his mind.

"Because I haven't done anything." Shaun sighed, looking around awkwardly.

"Look, Shaun, girls like to know they are wanted, and whether that's through chocolate, jewelry, or whatever, just let her know she's wanted and you're home free until she changes her mind at a dance, leaves with the star quarterback named Frankie, and goes home in *his* BMW." Shaun's father spoke with a gruff voice.

"Old wounds, huh?" Shaun chuckled.

His dad's admission relieved Shaun's anger toward his father. *So that's where the awkwardness came from.*

Mr. Baxter snorted. "Aaanyways, just give her attention and love, but not too much love. Otherwise I'll need to remove this house from your inheritance."

Shaun laughed. "Fair enough. Thanks for the advice, Dad."

"No problem. Back to my awkwardness now and you to your girlfriend? Is that what she is now … er … yet?" Mr. Baxter raised his eyebrows at his son.

"We'll see." Shaun smiled and fist-bumped his dad before going back into the living room with Emma.

Emma was lying down on the couch with her hoodie pulled over her head as she scrolled through her phone.

Shaun sat down next to her and extended his hand. "Wanna go hang out in my room rather than where Mr. Awkward lounges?"

"Sure." Emma laughed and grabbed Shaun's hand, sitting up. "When's your mom back?"

"No fuckin' clue." Shaun pulled Emma off the couch and laughed. "In fact I think she's in Oregon."

"You just thought your mom disappeared?" Emma joked.

"I guess so," Shaun said, nodding.

He wasn't sure what to expect when they entered his room. Were they going to tear off their clothes *Fifty Shades of Grey* style and have at it? Would it be smooth, like James Bond smooth? The James Bond thought was the ideal scenario, but Shaun's minimal confidence led him to think that maybe they would kiss and then he'd take her home, and that would be the end of the night. He was praying more would occur.

Emma smiled and walked along with Shaun. He held Emma's hand softly and gently before she changed her hand's position and interlocked their fingers. Shaun grinned and looked forward. *Oh my God. I'm holding Emma's, a girl's, hand tightly.* He could feel himself blushing hard. Shaun guided her down the hall and opened the door to the room.

"Ladies first." Emma grinned and gestured at Shaun to go through.

"Ha ha. Just go in," Shaun laughed.

Emma walked into the room and jumped onto Shaun's queen-sized mattress. Shaun was closing the door and heard his dad coming down the hall, so Shaun stepped into the hall. He held the door ajar behind himself.

"Can you please not come in?" Shaun drawled while leaning against the hallway's wall. "I don't need a repeat of your weirdness from earlier."

"Fine yeah." Shaun's dad kept walking. "Just think about your inheritance when you're doing whatever you're doing."

"Oh my Lord, Dad." Shaun laughed to himself, went back into his bedroom, and closed the door.

Emma was fiddling with her sweatshirt's tightening strings when Shaun flopped down on the bed next to her. Shaun scooted himself back to his pillows and propped himself up. He turned off his phone to avoid incoming calls and text messages and threw it on the carpet. If his mom called him to tell him good night in the middle of this, he would scream.

Emma turned off her phone and put it in her sweatshirt's pocket. "Mind if I—" Emma started pulling her sweatshirt off.

Shaun raised his eyebrows and nervously spat out, "No, no, definitely not. Naw, we are good. Good, good, good."

Shaun wanted to punch his own face in. There went the James Bond smoothness. But in all fairness, he wasn't used to her or any girl in his bed besides his mom. He figured he better get used to it and stop being so weird. He just needed to relax. *Cool, calm, and collected.* All he had to do was to keep it three hundred. *Three. Hundred.*

"You good?" Emma threw her sweatshirt across the room.

"Yeah yeah, chillin." Shaun took off his jacket. "Hot in here, isn't it?"

What the fuck kinda question was that? Hot in here, isn't it? This isn't a sitcom. Shaun closed his eyes and rolled them to himself.

Emma shrugged, grinned, and looked up at him. "Not that bad. Could get worse."

Shaun smiled, trying to act natural like I've-done-this-a-thousand-times natural. He lay back down on his pillow, and Emma pulled herself up next to him. She turned around and pressed her back against Shaun's shirt so they were spooning.

Shaun, more relaxed than in the movie theater, put his arm across the front of Emma's chest and pulled her closer to him. He exhaled a sigh. He wasn't sure what to do with his other arm so he just sort of forced it underneath the pillow. That wasn't any more comfortable than before, but hell, he was lying in his bed with a girl. He wasn't about to complain.

They lay with each other for a couple of minutes before Shaun leaned up again. Emma looked back at him and pulled her hair out of her band.

Shaun stood up off the bed and walked over to the mirror in his room. "One sec."

He began to fidget with the buttons on his shirt. He reminded himself to remain cool, calm, and collected. Shaun took the shirt off, and the muscles in his back tensed. His nervousness was virtually explosive. Shaun walked over to the hamper, opened it, and put his jacket and shirt inside.

Shaun glanced up at the mirror and saw Emma take off her bra. He'd only seen a girl without a bra on in porn. She was perfect. Her tanned, brown skin was stunning. She wasn't as skinny as a supermodel. She looked strong. Emma's undone hair fell over her chest, and Shaun looked back at himself in the mirror. He couldn't believe what was happening.

At that point, he didn't care how he looked. He knew if she were comfortable without a shirt in the same room as him. He must've looked damn good. Shaun realized he wasn't some overweight, beefy wrestler or a scrawny track star. He looked fucking good, and he accepted it.

Shaun fumbled with his belt, and he heard the cushion squeak as Emma got off the bed. He turned around and nearly jumped out of his pants when he was face-to-face with her. Emma gave Shaun puppy eyes while staring up at him. He grabbed her hand, and they walked over to his bed again.

"Damn," Shaun said, looking Emma up and down.

"What?" Emma asked, following Shaun.

Shaun climbed onto the bed, and Emma crawled over him. She lay down face-to-face with Shaun, and Shaun leaned his head on his elbow.

"You just look really beautiful right now," Shaun commented.

Emma blushed heavily. "That's the first time someone's said that to me."

"Well, you are. I've been tryna to say that for a while. You're beautiful." He repeated himself.

Emma blushed and pulled her hair back from her face. "Thank you. Also good choice on the Calvin Klein's. It's hot."

Shaun felt his chest get warm as his nervousness evaporated from him. Confidence overcame him, and he put his arm around Emma's back and pulled her against him. His chest pressed against her boobs.

"You know I really, really did not take you for a, like, this kind of guy." Emma exhaled inches from Shaun's face.

"Neither did I," Shaun joked. "And you're right. It did get hotter in here."

Emma smiled, biting her lip. Shaun looked down at Emma's lips and up at her eyes. He stopped smiling, and he put his hand on Emma's neck. Shaun adjusted the pillow behind his head with his other hand. The bedroom lamp caused a glow reflecting off Emma's wavy hair. Shaun closed his eyes as Emma pressed her lips onto his. Shaun reciprocated, and his eyes opened out of surprise that she had kissed him first.

He knew one of the rules of kissing is that you shouldn't open your eyes, but he felt like he had to take in the moment at least a little bit. He looked at Emma's small cheeks and her eyes, and Shaun closed his eyes again. He consumed Emma's lower lip and continued to pull her body close. Shaun's lips pressed back against hers, and then they retracted.

Shaun exhaled through his nose. "Was that like your first?"

Emma nodded, smiling. "You?"

"I mean, one other time, off a dare in like third grade ... yeah." Shaun laughed.

Emma laughed too. "Was this better?"

Shaun exhaled. "Much. Wanna try it again?"

"Mmm-hmm," Emma said, sitting up on the bed. "One sec though."

Shaun cocked his head to the left in curiosity of what Emma was doing. She pulled her black tights off, and the only thing left on her was her thong. Emma put her left leg in between both of Shaun's legs. He wrapped his legs around hers, and she layered her right leg on top of his.

"How's that?" Emma chuckled.

Shaun nodded. "Def better than third grade."

They kissed again and rubbed their feet together. Shaun decided to try the ol' french kiss. Even though he'd heard girls generally didn't like it, Emma nearly swallowed Shaun's tongue.

Shaun pulled back, and Emma chuckled. "Too hard?"

"Lil' bit." Shaun laughed and kissed her again, minus the tongue. This time Emma stopped kissing and leaned back. Shaun opened his eyes.

Emma smiled from ear to ear, grabbed Shaun's back, and flipped him on top of her. Shaun twisted his body around and bit her neck softly. Emma moaned in Shaun's ear, and she grabbed Shaun's back as he maintained a soft bite on her neck before switching to her mouth. Emma pulled Shaun's left hand off the edge of the bed and placed it on her chest. Shaun stopped kissing her and widened his eyes.

Emma opened her eyes. "Was that too much?"

"No, definitely not." Shaun very much liked what had just occurred. He was more annoyed that Emma was just making all the moves for him rather than the other way around. "Just paranoid about my dad. He's a bit … religious."

"Oh, so should we stop?" Emma asked, surprised. She appeared somewhat worried to Shaun.

"Well, I mean, how far were you thinking we were going tonight?" Shaun inquired.

"I don't know. What did you want?" Emma flipped the question back to Shaun.

"To be honest, I thought we were like … we were gonna … we were gonna go all the way."

Emma laughed. "Wow, you're a little proud. Uh, I wasn't planning on that, but at some point, I would like that."

As slightly disappointed as Shaun was, he was fine with everything that had gone down already. He was happy to hold out until Emma was ready for sex.

"Oh, then we're good." Shaun put his hand back on Emma's chest.

"I mean, I'm winding down anyway," Emma said between kisses.

"Then let's make the most of this. Usain Bolt gets tired, but you don't see him stopping, do you?" Shaun joked playfully.

"True." Emma giggled and kissed Shaun again.

Shaun squeezed Emma's chest, and she scratched at his back, forcing him completely on top of her. Shaun exhaled a breath of relief that, for the first time, his constant state of self-consciousness had vanished. He didn't care about his hair, his appearance, or his words. Rather the only point of focus on his mind was on the passion and tenderness of this with Emma.

Just twenty minutes later, Emma was spooning with Shaun again, this time asleep. Emma had put her shirt back on, and Shaun had his jeans, albeit unbuttoned, pulled back onto him. Mr. Baxter knocked on Shaun's door and got no response. He knocked again. Still no response. Mr. Baxter opened the door and stepped into the room.

He was looking down at his phone when he asked, "Hey, Shaun, it's like nine fifty-seven."

Mr. Baxter looked up and saw Emma asleep and Shaun with his hand wrapped around Emma's waist. Mr. Baxter started toward them, stepped back, and finally walked toward Shaun and Emma again.

"Shaun!" Mr. Baxter yelled.

Shaun and Emma both jerked awake. Shaun looked down and saw he forgot to put his shirt back on. *Shit.* Emma's eyes stretched across her face. She looked away from Mr. Baxter.

"Dad, please just leave. We can talk about it in the morning," Shaun begged.

"I'm not mad at you, Emma. But Shaun and I agreed he wouldn't have any girl sleep with him until he was married." Mr. Baxter folded his arms in the middle of the room.

"You did?" Emma whispered.

Shaun shrugged and rubbed his face. Shaun couldn't remember the conversation, but given the rule in the Bible about no sex before marriage, he wasn't surprised that his father extended the rule to "no sleeping with girls before marriage."

"No, I remember the discussion. Trust me on that." Mr. Baxter huffed. "Now I don't want to know what happened—or if anything happened—but I won't allow you two to sleep together in this house. My house. My rules. Get your shirt on!"

"Fine." Shaun hoped a short response would get his dad to leave quicker.

Emma added, "Yeah, I'm sorry, Mr. Baxter. I hope you know I don't sleep with g—"

Mr. Baxter put his hand up, "Ah-ba-ba-ba-ba. No. I told you I'm not mad at you. Heck, your parents might have no problem with this, but I do. Shaun, get your damn shirt on. Emma, I'll drive you home if you—"

The doorbell rang. Mr. Baxter gave a sigh that took all the air out of the room. He looked around the room and at Shaun's alarm clock. Shaun and Emma looked at each other, confused. Shaun thought it might be his mom, but she wasn't due back for a couple of days.

"Ten o'clock? Who the hell?" Mr. Baxter said. "You know what, Shaun? I'll talk with you later. Just get some clothes on, and I'll be right back." A tired and annoyed Mr. Baxter left the room.

"Let's go see who it is." Shaun pulled Emma by the arm.

"What? No, your dad can't see me in a thong. He'll think I'm a slut," Emma said.

"My dad hates me, not you. Besides there's a wall near the door where you can peek around to see whoever's at the door."

Emma leveled her head at Shaun. "So is that how you came out so fast during our first date?"

Shaun smirked. "Let's just go see all right."

Emma grinned, shaking her head. "Fine, let's go."

Shaun led Emma out of his room and behind the wall near the door. They watched Mr. Baxter peer out the glass at the top of the door. He cocked his head, unlocked the door, and opened it, and his face was met with a puff of cigarette smoke. Mr. Baxter waved the smoke out of his face.

"Hey there," a man with a thick goatee said to Mr. Baxter.

Emma gripped Shaun's arm. He looked back at her and shook his head, confused. He pointed back at the door, and he turned back around.

The man was dressed in a gray, beer-stained, button-down shirt with stretched-out sagging jeans.

"Hey. Sorry, do I know you?" Mr. Baxter asked the man.

The man pushed back his greasy hair with his hand and then outstretched his other. "Name's Ted," Ted said with a fake grin. "Ted Walsh."

Shaun gulped and turned back to Emma. She nodded, and Shaun was shocked. He pulled Emma behind him and continued watching his father interact with Ted.

"Derrick Baxter." Mr. Baxter shook Ted's hand

Ted held onto Mr. Baxter's hand a little too long, so Mr. Baxter retracted.

"Ted Walsh? Sorry, don't believe I've heard the name," Mr. Baxter lied.

Shaun had told his father Emma's full name multiple times, so either his father didn't remember, which was quite possible, or he was covering for Emma.

"Oh, well good to meet you. Anyways I have a daughter named Emma, and she hasn't come home yet, and I like her in her bed by around now, ten o'clock," Ted said to Mr. Baxter.

Mr. Baxter nodded, and he looked down at Ted's left hand. Shaun followed his dad's gaze to Ted's hand. There was a ring on each finger, and there was a thick residue of crusty blood on his knuckles. Shaun tried to think of an excuse as to why his hands were bleeding but came up with none. Emma gripped Shaun's arm, and Shaun reached back to hold her hand.

"Everything all right?" Ted asked, sliding his hand into his pocket.

Mr. Baxter looked up at Ted. "Yeah, yeah. Sorry, I was just looking. I mean my eyes were just getting a little tired. Long work day."

"Oh yeah. I understand that." Ted chuckled insincerely. "So about my daughter."

"Yeah, you know where she is?" Mr. Baxter carefully blocked the doorway with his arm. Shaun understood that his dad *was* covering for Emma. Shaun thought that maybe he wasn't actually so bad to be around.

Ted leaned on his back foot, dumbfounded. "If I would, I wouldn't be here, would I?"

Mr. Baxter chuckled slightly. "Suppose you wouldn't."

"Yeah, well I was just driving around tonight, and I saw her walking down this street with some kid, and I thought I saw them turn into this nice, cozy place." Ted smirked and puffed out a cloud of cigarette smoke into the Baxter residency. Shaun could smell the odor from the wall and wafted the scent away.

Mr. Baxter paused and looked down at Ted's left arm, which was pressed into his side in an effort to hide the blood. Mr. Baxter glanced at Ted's wrist and saw more blood.

"Just wondering if she came by here. I just don't like her going out with some guy I haven't met yet, you know?" Ted laughed.

"Oh yeah, definitely. Definitely understand." Mr. Baxter stalled.

"Yeah, I know if my son were out with someone's daughter that I hadn't met I wouldn't be too happy."

"Oh, so you do have a son?" Ted asked incredulously.

"Yeah, just found him asleep though on his desk chair. Late night for him too, I guess," Mr. Baxter lied.

"Oh yeah. I remember those days. Definitely don't have as much energy as I did when I was sixteen," Ted commented.

"Amen to that," Mr. Baxter said.

"Yup, driving with my girl till two in the morning. Hanging with friends till three. You remember doing stuff like that, right?"

Mr. Baxter snorted a laugh. "Yeah, doing dumb stuff, but I always tried to have a limit. Going out too much leads to an unhealthy lifestyle, you know? Don't wanna end up like someone on the streets."

Ted smirked. Ted looked up and down the street, taking in another puff from his cigarette and exhaling it in Mr. Baxter's face. "Well, I guess wherever Emma is she's safe, huh?"

"I'd say so yeah," Mr. Baxter replied. "Night, Ted."

"Cheers, Derrick," Ted said, walking toward his silver pickup truck.

Mr. Baxter squeezed out a smile and closed the door. He turned toward the wall, and Shaun ushered for Emma to go back to the room. They made it back in and onto the bed before Mr. Baxter came lumbering inside. He saw them lying in bed, practically unmoved from where he left them.

"Somehow I knew you guys wouldn't move." Mr. Baxter sighed. "Okay, here's the deal. Emma, you can stay the night, but Shaun, if I come in tomorrow morning and you're within a foot of Emma's body, it's gonna be a rough day, boy."

Shaun nodded and made an A-OK sign with his hand.

"Thanks, Mr. Baxter," Emma said. "Who was at the door by the way?"

"Oh, just some drunk guy. He seemed like he was a little off, so I just alarmed the house," said Mr. Baxter.

"Gotcha," Emma replied.

Shaun nodded at his dad and then at the door. Shaun was dying for his father to leave the two of them alone again.

"Right, so I'll see you both in the morning. Goodnight, Emma." Mr. Baxter waved.

Emma waved back, smiling. "Goodnight, Mr. Baxter."

Mr. Baxter smiled back and then frowned at Shaun. "Shaun."

He pointed two fingers at Shaun and then back at his own eyes. Mr. Baxter left the room. Shaun finally breathed out. He felt like he'd been holding his breath, but he'd just been taking quick ones.

"Why the hell was your stepdad here? That's weird, Emma." Shaun was seriously concerned for Emma's home life and wanted to do something. He thought better of it because he assumed Emma would tell him if she wanted him to interfere.

"I honestly don't even want to think about it." Emma looked away from Shaun and at the wall next to the bed.

"Oh, sorry," Shaun said. "I just hope you're okay. If you're not okay, you can always just tell—"

Emma leaned over, grabbed Shaun's face, and kissed him. They finished, and Shaun chuckled. "That was a shut-up kiss, wasn't it?"

Emma nodded. "Can we just go to sleep?"

Shaun didn't want to prod any farther into Emma's feelings than he already did. He decided to quit while he was ahead and just go to sleep.

"Sure." Shaun lifted his arm, completely ignoring what his dad ordered him to do.

Emma grinned and slid underneath his hand, and Shaun pressed his chest against Emma's back. He turned around briefly and turned off the desk lamp. Shaun kissed Emma on the neck, and she turned back, smiling at him. She leaned up, and they kissed several times before Emma turned around and shut her eyes. Shaun could barely stand how cute Emma looked, but he lay his head down and closed his eyes too.

Emma gripped Shaun's arm, and she pulled it across her chest so he was holding her shoulder. Shaun had done it. He had a girlfriend. He never thought he would even have another kiss with a girl before college, let alone be in bed with one.

Apart from Ted's abrupt stop by their house, Shaun was more than satisfied with lying in bed with Emma and with how the night went in general.

EMMA

The rising sun shone through Shaun's blinds, and Emma began to stir in his bedsheets. She looked down and realized her tights had been off the whole night. The radiant sun blinded Emma in the warm bedroom. She blinked a couple of times and wiped the morning dirt out of her eyes. She crawled off the edge of the bed, grabbed her tights, and pulled them over her legs.

Shaun flipped over and saw Emma walking over to the mirror. "Sup," Shaun said, standing up from the bed. He blinked his way through the bright sun.

Emma grabbed her hair band off the ground and began to put her hair back through it. She looked back at Shaun. "Oh, hey."

"Had a good time last night," Shaun said, grabbing a shirt out of his closet.

"I've had better," Emma joked.

"That was a *Liar Liar* reference, right?" Shaun asked, hopeful.

Emma looked at him in the reflection of the mirror. "No shit it was. By the way, you might wanna wash your pillows. You were drooling across the whole bed."

"Oh, don't worry about it," Shaun said, stumbling around with the new, clean shirt over his head. "I haven't washed my pillows in like a month."

"That's disgusting. All guys do that?" Emma asked, her face winding into a cringe.

"Prolly, I dunno know, but a couple of my friends don't wash their sheets for like three or four weeks."

"Ugh. Unreal … Oh shit!" Emma exclaimed while grabbing her sweatshirt. She remembered that Ted had come by the house the night before. Sleeping had stalled her mind from thinking about it, but Ted became front and center in her thoughts once again.

"What? What's up?" Shaun said.

"Oh my God, Ted is going to kill me," Emma said anxiously.

"Oh, fuck." Shaun rubbed his eyes. "Shit, I completely forgot about that."

Emma grabbed her schoolbag quickly. "He was already pissed last night. Fuck, what am I going to do?"

She was in panic mode. She thought about just running home, but that would be too obvious. Maybe she would just call him, but she never called Ted. That option was out too. Emma couldn't believe that she spent the night at Shaun's house even with Mr. Baxter covering for her.

"He could've just been worried, you know? Like, my dad would be worried if I were missing and hadn't come home without telling him."

"You can't be serious." Emma threw her bag on and dropped her hands, amazed by what Shaun said. "Ted doesn't care about my safety. He's not even close to being a normal dad. He just likes to control me."

"You can't know that for sure," Shaun said, pushing his boundary.

Emma's mouth dropped almost into a laugh at Shaun's ignorance. "I can't know that? I've lived with that sack of shit for years. You've never even met the guy."

Shaun raised his brows and rolled his eyes. "Someone woke up on the wrong side of the bed."

"What the fuck are you talking about? You're being so dismissive of me. You have no idea what Ted is like. Didn't you see his hand last night?" Emma questioned Shaun, trying to have him back her up. She was shocked that Shaun was opposing her.

"Yeah, it was a bit weird, but maybe he like cut himself or something. Maybe he dropped a glass. He's a bartender, right?" Shaun suggested, offering his hand up.

"Because he wouldn't hide it! Why would he hide it? Look, I don't know what he was doing or why he was bleeding, but don't act like you know more about my family than I do. You don't." Emma finished her point and folded her arms. Her breathing had escalated, but when Shaun failed to come up with a response, she calmed down. She knew Shaun was smart enough not to push her further into an argument.

Emma continued getting ready for school. She turned on her phone and grabbed her sweatshirt.

"What's the rush? I live like what's about a five-minute walk from BRHS," Shaun said.

Emma's mood was lightened by Shaun's attempt to change the subject. She assumed Shaun wanted to forget their pissing match had happened as much as she did.

"Oh really? All right, it's like seven thirty-five. Leave in fifteen minutes then?" Emma asked.

Shaun nodded and flopped onto his bed again. Emma sat down next to him, pulled a file out of her bag, and began shaving down her nails. She looked down at Shaun, smiled, and rubbed her hand across his back.

"Knock, knock," Shaun's dad said through the bedroom door.

"Come in," Shaun gave a muffled shout through the bedsheets. He leaned up and moved away from Emma.

Mr. Baxter walked into the room while tying his teal tie. "Ah, good. I don't have to kill you today, Shaun."

"Thank goodness." Shaun sighed.

"Hey Emma, can I ... can I talk with you for second?" Shaun started to get up. Mr. Baxter glared at Shaun. "Privately. I'm sure you can survive without her for five minutes."

Shaun raised his hands and dropped them on the bed.

"Yeah, sure, Mr. Baxter." Emma stood up and followed Mr. Baxter out of the room.

Mr. Baxter turned to leave, and Emma followed behind him, leaving the door ajar.

"Uh, so last night after you and Shaun ..." Mr. Baxter nodded at Emma.

Emma felt awkward discussing what she and Shaun did, and she didn't know if Mr. Baxter wanted her to complete his sentence so she just stared blankly at him.

Mr. Baxter nodded again. "After you and Shaun ..."

Emma assumed he did want her to complete the sentence. As awkward and painful as it was to tell him what they were doing, she assumed he wanted to know, given his religion.

"Oh, okay," Emma started. "Well, after we finished like making out and Shaun stopped grab—"

Mr. Baxter shook his head hard. He raised his voice sharply. "No! I wasn't even going to bring that up. I just wanted to make sure you were following where I was starting."

Emma blushed, and Mr. Baxter was sweating.

Emma continued, "Sorry. I thought you wanted to know because of like a commandment or something. Like I don't know. Just keep going with what you were saying. Sorry."

Emma had never felt so awkward. She just told her boyfriend's dad that she was making out with his son. Geez. Why didn't she just nod along like he assumed she would? She wanted to crawl into a corner and cringe her mind out. She shifted uncomfortably on the hardwood floor, twiddling her thumbs. Mr. Baxter must've felt the same because he folded and unfolded his arms several times for no reason.

"God in heaven." Mr. Baxter looked up and shook himself off. "Anyways, after you and Shaun woke up, I left the room to get the door. Well, the man at the door said he was related to you."

"Ted?" Emma asked, even though she knew the answer.

Mr. Baxter nodded lightly. "He said he was looking for you, but

I told him I didn't know where you were. I hope that was okay with you. I know you probably would've wanted to go home or at least talk with me, but I just wasn't getting a very safe feeling from Ted. I know I wouldn't want Shaun going home with someone like that. You see what I mean?"

Emma bit her cheeks hard and looked down at the floor. She couldn't admit that she and Shaun had overhead the entire conversation. Nor could she say how screwed she would be since she would be coming home a day late. However, she wanted Mr. Baxter to know how much she appreciated the cover.

"I rarely feel safe around Ted, so I'm thankful for what you did, Mr. Baxter."

"It's no problem at all." Mr. Baxter waved his hands.

"No, seriously. Shaun's told me that you are a very devout … you're a deeply religious person, so for you to see me and Shaun like that last night and then vouch for me …" Emma's eyes started to water. Mr. Baxter was the kind of father she wished Ted was minorly like. "What you did for me was extremely nice. I like Shaun a lot, and that was the first time I'd ever been in a bed with a boy. I just … I just hope you don't think that's how I normally act with guys."

"I would never assume such a thing." Mr. Baxter smiled. He joked, "If it happens again though, I might start to wonder."

Emma sniffled and laughed.

"Hey," Mr. Baxter said, leaning down to Emma. He was trying to be quiet. He whispered, "If you ever think something might happen with Ted at your house, don't hesitate to text Shaun. I know he'll come running to me. I can pick you up as soon as you feel unsafe, okay?"

Emma was astounded by the offer, but she didn't want any more drama with Ted. So she decided to play it safe. "That's really nice of you, but I think I'll be fine. I've lasted this long, right?"

Mr. Baxter leaned back up. "Yeah, of course, just an open suggestion."

Emma gave a smile out of formality. "Thanks. If something really bad happens, I will text him, fa sho."

Mr. Baxter raised his eyebrows at her.

Emma explained, "It means 'for sure.'"

Emma enjoyed Mr. Baxter's aloofness but thought he was one of the sweetest fathers she'd ever met. His goofiness always made her laugh, especially if he and Shaun were arguing.

Mr. Baxter nodded. "Ah, the cool-kid lingo."

"Not cool when you say lingo," Emma joked.

Mr. Baxter grinned. "I'm old. Okay, well regardless of my offer, you should at least call the police. I don't know what your father was doing last night, but he came by with a bloody hand. Now I'm not sure if he cut himself or, you know, God forbid he hit someone, but it looked like a serious wound."

Emma stared past Mr. Baxter, trying to think of any possible targets besides her mom that Ted would go after. She could only assume that he got in a bar fight, but that wouldn't make sense because Ted would lose his job.

"I don't know who he would have hit, but I'll keep that in mind." Emma nodded. She didn't want to discuss the matter of Ted anymore, no matter how nice Mr. Baxter was being. Thinking about who Ted hit was making Emma nauseous. "I really should be going to school now, Mr. Baxter."

Mr. Baxter took the hint and let up. "Oh yeah. Well, of course, yeah. I'll let you and Shaun go. Hope everything works out at home."

"I hope it does too," Emma said, walking toward the bedroom door. She stopped because she felt like she hadn't gotten her point across about how much she liked Mr. Baxter. She was so jealous of Shaun. She could tell Shaun was constantly embarrassed by his father's social ineptness, but Emma liked Mr. Baxter.

"Mr. Baxter, I just want to let you know that if Ted were different, like if he acted like someone else, I'd want him to act like you. You're a good dad. Shaun's luckier than he realizes."

"Well, anyone who has a daughter as nice as you is a very lucky family," Mr. Baxter said, walking away.

Emma smiled to herself, and her eyes watered. She wiped her eyes and went into the room with Shaun to drag him off the bed.

"What was that about?" Shaun asked while he put his socks and shoes on.

"Just asking about Ted, but we're done talking about that. Fair enough?" Emma asked, hoping Shaun would understand.

Shaun did and didn't bother responding. "Can you skate?"

"Like skateboard?" Emma asked. *Stupid question. He obviously meant skateboard. Why would he mean ice skate?*

"Uh, duh." Shaun laughed.

Emma punched him playfully. "Yeah, I used to all the time before high school."

Shaun stood up and yanked his backpack onto his shoulders. "I usually skate to school, and I have an old long board if you wanna use that."

Emma lit up and jumped into a question. "I'd love to, but what about when I have to go home?"

"Just give the board to me when we get to school. I'll ride it back and put my other board on my backpack. Don't even worry about it. It would be cool to skate with my girlfriend to school." Shaun smiled strongly. "Felt weird saying that."

Emma walked up to Shaun and kissed him passionately on the lips. "Felt good though, didn't it?"

"It did." Shaun nodded and smiled coyly. "We should get going."

"Right," Emma responded. She hadn't heard someone say the word *girlfriend* in reference to her, and she was pleased by the sound of it. Emma was content with her place in life, and Shaun's presence made the thought of Ted escape her mind for a moment.

Shaun handed Emma his long board, and they left the house.

Emma walked around the corridors of the high school during the last period of the day, her free period. The noise of teachers lecturing or kids asking questions echoed throughout the halls and clanged through the lockers. She walked around the corner to the girl's bathroom and opened the creaky door.

Emma heard panting and felt the walls for the light switch. The panting grew louder as she walked farther into the bathroom. The sound of a boy grunting overpowered the girl, and Emma found the light switch. She flicked it on. Jackson Decker had his hands down Sophia's pants, and he was shirtless. Sophia looked up at Emma and hastily threw her shirt back on.

"Oh, how lovely," Emma commented, disgusted.

She wasn't surprised that Sophia had rejected her advice with Jackson but was more grossed out by the fact that they were already physical so quickly. Emma assumed it was because of Sophia's and Jackson's higher levels of experience. However, unlike Jackson and Sophia, Emma ended up enjoying the wait for her night with Shaun. She couldn't stand seeing such a despicable guy with a girl whom Emma thought could do better.

Emma insulted the couple. "Most popular girl with the scummiest boy."

"Em, wait," Sophia called after Emma as she bolted from the bathroom.

Emma left the bathroom in a hurry. She was walking along the lines of lockers when she was grabbed and turned around by Sophia. Sophia was still pushing her earrings through when Emma shoved her off.

"Emma, you don't get it." Sophia tried again.

"Don't get what?" Emma asked, waving at Sophia. "I told you. Be careful. Jackson's an idiot. He'll use you."

"And you would know?" Sophia returned.

Emma put her hands on her hips. "My sister did. She told me all about him. They used to go out sometimes, but she ended it. Trust me. You have no idea what you're getting into."

Jackson skidded out of the bathroom, buckling his belt and straightening out his hair.

"I think you should shut the fuck up." Jackson pointed at Emma. He strode up to Emma quickly, looming over her. Emma backed up, genuinely scared of him. Jackson boomed, "You don't know what the hell you're talking about!"

"Jackson, relax." Sophia turned back to Jackson.

He opened his mouth to speak and gritted his teeth. Jackson closed his mouth, shaking his head. Emma and Jackson stared each other down. She grimaced; he smirked.

"Look, do what you want, Sophia. Just don't be an idiot." Sincerity filled Emma's eyes. She turned to Jackson, scowling at him. "Fuck you, Jackson."

"You too, Miss Walsh," Jackson said with a peace sign.

Emma quivered with anger. She looked up at the clock in the hall, 2:42 p.m. Emma slowly slogged down the halls after witnessing a sight she could not wipe from the windshield in her mind. She pressed the handle and walked through the double doors leading into the school's parking lot.

The doors slammed shut behind her, and a car engine revved outside. Emma was looking down at her shoes when a silver pickup truck pulled up in front of her. She looked up and jumped back to avoid being hit. Ted was at the wheel and was smoking another cigarette.

Ted smirked at Emma. "Hop in?"

Emma's mouth dropped a bit, and she looked around for anyone else to take her home. The fear that Ted brought to Emma was tenfold that which Jackson brought. The school bell rang, and she instantly turned toward the double doors of the school, looking for Shaun. She looked for Mr. Baxter or her world history teacher, Mrs. Morton, but no familiar faces appeared in her field of view.

"C'mon, let's go!" Ted demanded and banged on the side of the truck.

Emma bowed her head and brushed her hair in front of the left side of her face. Emma didn't have much of a choice, but she didn't feel safe getting into the car. *Should I text Shaun? No, Ted would see me pull out the phone and subsequently take it from me.*

Emma didn't really know what Ted was capable of, but she didn't know whom else to go home with. She unwillingly walked around to the other side of the truck and hopped into the passenger's seat. Emma grabbed her seat belt and pull it around her until she heard a little click. She lay back in her seat while gripping the handle of the door.

"So, Emma," Ted said, taking the cigarette stub out of his mouth and throwing it out the window, "where were you last night?"

"Oh yeah. I'm sorry, uh." Emma struggled to force out the word, "Sorry … Dad. I was at my friend Sophia's house and just fell asleep on her couch," Emma lied and looked out the window. "Just lost track of time, I guess."

"I thought we had an agreement on a set of rules." Ted prodded. "One being that you be back in *my house* by ten o'clock."

Emma coughed. She nearly muttered the word *shithole* but held off. She wanted to at least make it back to her house before Ted tried anything.

Ted glared at her. "So if you were at your friend's house, what was going on with that guy a couple streets past our place?"

"Oh, his name's Shaun. We were studying at the diner downtown for a huge chemistry exam today." Emma lied throughout her explanation. She looked up at Ted, who was fuming; however, she maintained a collected state of mind. "It wasn't a date, if that's what you're wondering. So relax. I know you're just being protective, but relax."

She didn't believe that he was being protective and always wondered if there were more to Ted keeping guys away from Emma. But Ted never tried anything sexual toward her or Christina. She ignored the hypothesis and focused more on getting Ted to just calm down so they wouldn't be screaming at each other by the time they arrived at the house.

"Good, good. Well that's ... that's good," Ted commented, slightly skeptical of her story, but ultimately he dropped the subject.

Emma looked at his left hand steering the car. It was wrapped in medical tape and several layers of gauze.

"Damn," Emma said, switching topics. "What happened with that?"

Ted looked down at his hand and clenched it, making a fist. He winced from the pain. "Yeah, got in a fight with a customer last night. The guy didn't tip me after I served him and his whole damn group for most of the night, and on top of that, he gave me attitude through the goddamn roof. Funny thing is his buddy ended up tipping me out of fear that I'd take him on too."

Emma cracked a smile. In a weird way, she thought Ted's toughness was bad ass, and she almost felt bad agreeing with such a messed-up person. "Don't mess with Ted, huh."

"Damn right." Ted laughed.

For a fleeting moment, Ted and Emma shared a laugh over something they both found humor in. No matter how weird or odd the topic seemed to Emma, it was one of the only times she had seen Ted smile over something she added to the conversation. Although Emma presumed the moment wouldn't last and that Ted was most likely using her, she wanted to believe his emotion was sincere.

Ted nodded and continued driving. "Not trying to kill this, but I, uh, I just wanted to say that uh ... I didn't ... didn't know her as well as you did, but I miss your sister Christina too."

Emma's blood started boiling. *How dare Ted act like he missed Christina. He was the reason she was gone.* Ted finished speaking and gave his full attention back to the road. He licked his lips and placed another cigarette between his teeth. The moment of happiness in Emma's family vanished just as she unbuckled her seat belt as her line of apartments came into view.

Ted opened the door and walked in ahead of Emma. He walked over to the couch, turned around, and fell into the crevice his body had created from sitting in the same spot time and time again. Emma watched Ted flick through the channels on their TV before stopping on the weekly UFC fight. Ted held up his fists as his favorite fighter threw punches at the opponent. Ted swung his fists as the fighter swung his. The opponent fighter dropped to his knees and face-planted on the bottom of the fight cage.

"Wooooh!" Ted threw up his hands, applauding the fighter. "Let's go, baby. Let's go! Two more fights left. Here we go." His eyes landed on Emma, who was watching Ted take his victory lap from the couch. "Whatchu looking at?"

Emma shook her head and sighed. *New Ted out. Old Ted in.* She walked up the stairs to her room. She missed talking with Mr. Baxter.

Emma opened the door, and her mom was sitting on the bed. When Emma entered, she stared at Cynthia, who was wearing slippers and a bathrobe. It was barely three thirty. Why couldn't her mom just dress semiwell? Not like she wanted her mother to be dressing up like a banker every day, just not dressing down.

"Hey," Emma said, confused.

"Hey, yourself." Emma's mom grimaced at her and waved a sheet of paper at Emma.

It was a printout of Emma's grades from BRHS's online website. Emma squinted. *What now?*

"What's up?" Emma asked, annoyed with her mom's breach of privacy into her room.

"What's up?" Cynthia interrogated Emma. "Ted and me work our asses off to provide for you, and this is how you repay us? Only two As and four Bs? What happened to all As? Hmm?"

"It's actually *Ted and I*, Mom, which is why my English grade is higher than everyone else's, and as for the Bs, I'm working on it, all right?" Emma explained in a huff.

Cynthia rolled her eyes, tightening her bathrobe. "What do you think Ted would have to say about your world history grade? An eighty-four! What the hell is that?"

"It's a number, and I would be genuinely surprised if Ted even knows how to spell world history." Emma was enraged. She was the only person she knew who tried as hard as she did given her family life. Her mom didn't understand that kids with perfect lives, like Sophia, were getting Cs across the board.

"Don't get smart with me, Emma." Mrs. Walsh raised her voice. "You live in this house; you live under our rules."

"Oh my God, Mom! It's a friggin shit apartment in San Mateo. And maybe if you didn't choose such shitty husbands, we wouldn't be living in this hellhole!" Emma shouted.

Mrs. Walsh's eyes went wild, and her teeth gritted so hard that she ground off the plaque. "Ex-cuse me." Mrs. Walsh said each syllable on its own and stood up from Emma's bed.

Emma thought maybe she took her words a step too far. She stopped escalating and attempted to settle things down to a simmering dispute. "I'm sorry, but it just seems like Ted is the reason everything's so off right now. You have to at least admit that."

"I will not. Sure, everything isn't perfect, but can you blame Ted? The way you talk to him is embarrassing. He's a good man." Cynthia turned her attention to the ground. Emma could see the denial written across her mother's furrowed brows.

"You know I'm right." Emma walked over to her bed and lay down on it, running her fingers through her hair. She straightened her hair out and wiped off the sweat from her brow, which had formed during the argument with her mom.

"You don't know how I feel," Mrs. Walsh started.

"Please just leave," Emma said. Why wouldn't her mom just take a fucking hint for once in her life? She wanted her mother out of her room as soon as possible. "Leave!"

"No, you don't get to order me around. You don't get to talk to me or Ted like that. I am your mother. He is your father!" Cynthia shouted.

Emma blew a fuse. "Just leave me alone and stop coming in my fucking room!"

A vein on the side of Cynthia's forehead was pulsating. Cynthia shook. "I wish your sister lived just long enough to see how badly you treat me."

Emma stopped talking. She could feel pressure build around her eyes and throat. She felt her mouth and eyes water. Her mom didn't know what she was talking about. She just brought up Christina because she knew Emma wouldn't be able to handle it. But what if her mom were right? Emma knew Christina hated Ted as much as Emma did, but not her mother. Christina knew her mother was in denial but never talked to her like Emma did. No, she knew her sister better than her idiotic mother did.

"She would've agreed with me," Emma said quietly.

"Well then maybe you should take what he says differently than I do!"

"I do!"

"Then frickin show it!" Mrs. Walsh roared and slammed the door shut.

Emma rolled off the bed onto the floor and onto her back. She was breathing heavier than a wrestler after winning a match. Emma wanted to go down after her mom and yell at her for being such an unfair, stupid bitch. How could she seriously tell Emma that Emma messed up something as minute as her grades when she messed up her family's life by marrying that disgusting, lazy, piece of shit, Ted? Her mom should be through the roof ecstatic that Emma was able to pull off any grade higher than a C.

Emma's abusive stepfather killed her sister just weeks ago, and her mother was making her feel ashamed for grades. *Fuck her.* Emma wanted to go into the living room and rip out the cords from the TV. She wanted to watch Ted stumble around drunk while she punched him in his rows of dirty, yellow teeth. She wanted to see him sprawl out on the ground and crawl out the door. Emma just wanted to leave and never come back. She wanted her mother to worry about her for the rest of her life and feel responsible for her abrupt departure. Maybe then she'd realize how badly she fucked up as a parent.

Emma grabbed her schoolbag and her sheets from her bed. She placed the bag underneath her head and wrapped the bedsheets under and around her body. Emma set her alarm for 2:00 a.m. to remind herself to start doing homework in the morning. She took the pillows from her bed, put them under her back for support, and finally went to sleep.

Emma woke up. She was being shaken awake by her sister. Emma looked around and realized she was downstairs sitting on the couch in their apartment. She looked at her sister confused and felt her sister's arm. She grabbed her sister's legs and touched her face.

"You're actually here," Emma said.

"Of course I'm here, you idiot." Christina laughed. "C'mon, grab your bags. I have the GPS on my phone set for the Marriot near that water park we used to go to with Dad."

Emma looked around the room and felt the couch. "You're here." Emma repeated to herself.

Christina looked around the room and squinted at Emma. "Yeah, duh. Can you stop acting so weird and just grab your bags so we can go?"

"For sure, let's go." Emma grabbed the duffel bag near the front door.

"All right, just be quiet. Don't want Ted coming out now. He just came back from the bar hammered," Christina whispered.

"Too late," Ted said and stumbled out of his bedroom. "Where y'all be going off to?"

"Away," Christina said, holding Emma behind her.

"It's late like, like, like 9:50 p.m. or a.m.? No, no PE-EM," Ted stuttered out.

"Ted, you're drunk. Again. I don't think Emma should be staying here with you. I don't think it's safe for either of us, so I'm taking her south, and we're gonna find a place to stay. I saved my money from working at the smoothie parlor, and we're just gonna go right now." Christina pulled Emma with her. "C'mon, Em, let's go."

"You're leaving me and your mother!" Ted shouted and threw a beer bottle at Christina. She dodged it, but when it smashed on the door behind her, a piece of glass embedded itself into her kneecap.

Christina clutched her knee and fell to the ground. She tried pulling the glass out, and the skin tore around the shard. She strained to stand up and looked Ted straight in the eye. "We're going," Christina asserted.

Ted stumbled over to the two sisters and grabbed Christina by the arm. She tried to swat his stronger forearm away, but he had a firm grip, and he slapped her in the face. "You're not leaving me!" Ted shouted. "This is my house and my family. You leave me. Where the hell will you go? Huh! You got nothing without this place!"

"Let me fucking go, dick!" Christina threw a punch. Ted caught it and slammed her against the wall. "Emma, get in the car!"

"No, you stay right here! This won't take long!" Ted growled.

Emma unlocked the door to the house and ran outside. She threw her bag in the trunk and opened the passenger side door and the driver's side door.

Christina grabbed one of the shards of glass from the broken beer bottle and stabbed Ted in the shoulder with it. He howled in pain and let go of her. She grabbed her backpack and purse and sprinted out the door.

Christina threw the bag and her small purse into the trunk and slammed it shut. She hopped into the car and slammed the door shut. Emma reached for the passenger side door, and Ted grabbed her arm and pulled her out of the car as Christina accelerated.

"Emma!" Christina shouted as the car pealed away. "I'll come back!"

Emma started crying as she watched the car drive away. Ted

dragged her back inside the house and slammed the door shut. Emma stopped her tears, fell onto the couch, and waited for her sister. Ted walked back into his room and crawled into bed with Mrs. Walsh, who was passed out after a round of Ambien. Emma sat up and watched the door, waiting for a knock.

Ten minutes passed. Twenty minutes passed. Thirty minutes passed. Forty minutes passed. Emma's eyes began to close when she heard a knock on the door. She jumped up and ran over to the door, ready to hug her sister and get into her red Camaro. Emma unlocked the door, and her smile fell from her face.

A police officer was standing with his back to her. He heard the door open and turned around. "Hey there. Are you related to Christina Walsh?"

"Uhm, yeah, yeah. I'm her younger sister," Emma said, nodding anxiously.

"Well, is a parent around?" the officer asked, looking around and behind her awkwardly.

"No, I mean yeah. They're both asleep," Emma said. She was getting worried.

The officer looked through the house. Emma stood tall to block his view. She didn't want Ted talking to the police. It would go on so much longer. She just wanted to know what was going on immediately.

"Miss? Miss, I need to speak with an adult." The office nodded at her politely.

"Just tell me what happened, please," Emma begged. She leaned against the door. She assumed Christina had gotten pulled over for speeding. *Damn Ted. He shouldn't have made her drive so recklessly.*

The officer sighed. He took off his cap. "Your sister was driving fast in the rain, and well, I guess too fast. She crashed. She didn't make it."

Emma laughed nervously. "She sent you here to say that, right? Because she just left. Like forty minutes ago. You're messing with me, right? Because she was gonna come back to get me."

"No, uh, I'm sorry." The officer bit his lip and looked at the ground.

"No, she's sitting in the back of your car, right? She said she was gonna come back." Emma repeated herself as her laugh began to fade out. "She's in the back of your car, right?"

"No, she was speeding. Her body was ejected from the car when it hit the concrete divider on Highway 280," the officer explained again.

"Oh." Emma began to shake.

Christina dead? It couldn't be. She didn't die. No, I just saw her leave. She wouldn't be driving fast enough to crash. She was a good driver. She couldn't be dead. I don't believe him.

"Well then, we gotta go check on her. Yeah, we gotta. We gotta go make sure she's okay. If she fell out of the car, she's probably hurt. We gotta. We gotta go."

The officer shook his head, looking down the street. "I'm sorry, but she's gone, miss."

"She's not gone. She's not!" Emma shouted. A tear hit the entryway into her apartment. "She said she was gonna come back. You don't understand. She was gonna come get me. She was ... We gotta go help her. Where is she?"

"Miss, please." The officer tried to control Emma.

"Where is she!" Emma shouted.

The policeman sighed and put his arms on his belt. "In an ambulance on her way here. I assume your family would like to see her."

"Oh no, no, no, no," Emma said quivering as the event began to sink in and everything leading up to it. "No, she can't ... She was just ... Oh. God. Oh my God. She was ... Oh."

"You wanna sit down, miss?" the officer offered.

"Mom? Mom!" Emma cried out.

The door opened to her mother's bedroom, and she walked out slowly. Mrs. Walsh blinked her eyes from her drowsiness.

"Christina! There's something … something happened to her!" Emma shrieked and reached out to the officer.

Emma hugged him and began to cry again. She might have waited for her mom, but in that moment, she didn't see her as a source of support. She just wanted to feel, to be in touch with someone who could show empathy and nothing else. Shocked by the embrace, the officer slowly put his arms around her and patted her on the back.

"It's gonna be aight. Gonna be aight. Let it all out," the officer said, trying to comfort her.

Mrs. Walsh walked up to the officer and Emma. He let go of Emma and walked toward Mrs. Walsh.

"Are you the mother of Christina Walsh?" the officer asked.

"Yes, what's wrong?" Mrs. Walsh asked in a panic as the ambulance pulled up in front of the apartment.

"Your daughter passed away at ten seventeen tonight. She was in a car crash, and she—" The officer was cut off.

"Christina? Christina!" Mrs. Walsh shoved her way past the officer and out to the ambulance.

Emma was in a daze, and then the ambulance and officer disappeared. "Drive" by Incubus was playing somewhere in the house. She ran up to her room and found that the noise was coming from inside. Emma slammed on the door and burst into the room.

Emma awoke from the dream on the floor of her room. Emma was panting and dripping in sweat. She hit the snooze button on her radio's alarm. She looked around for Christina and her mom. They were nowhere in sight.

Emma sighed and picked up her schoolbag from under her neck. Emma opened her bag and grabbed her homework. Emma reminisced on the night her sister died but shook the thoughts out of her head. She stood up, climbed onto her bed, and began typing away on her schoolwork.

SOPHIA

Sophia grabbed her lunch from the long line of food in the cafeteria. A riot of clamoring teenagers followed her, trying to grab their beef and potatoes. She reached for a chocolate milk and retracted her hand. She looked down at her body, which was nearly in perfect shape, but there was that one damn spot on her hip that looked a little too fatty. Despite her figure, she put the milk back and grabbed Vitamin Water instead.

Sophia paid for her meal and drink and walked outside to sit on a slab of granite overlooking the sunken soccer field. A girl, Clara, looked up when she saw her coming over and waved and smiled. Clara wasn't necessarily a friend of Sophia, but she was a friend when she wanted to be. Sophia just used her as part of her way of maintaining her image. She had to have some popular people to hang out with. And because Clara was just as rich as Sophia, Sophia could complain about all her petty problems to Clara without worry of judgement.

She opened her bottle of water, placed her tray on the granite slab, and sat down next to her friend Clara. "Claraaaa," Sophia drawled out her friend's name. "Whatcha doh-en, Claraaa?"

"Jesus, stop with the stupid New Yorker accent all the time. I hear enough of that shit from my stepmom." Clara smirked, rolling her eyes.

"That's the point. I know you love her." Sophia grinned.

"Yeah, as much as vegetarians love pork." Clara shook her head, slightly amused by Sophia's joke. "But to answer your question, I'm eating lunch, genius."

Sophia laughed and bit into her steaming beef.

"What's up with you these past few weeks?" Clara asked.

Sophia smirked at Clara and spoke through a mouthful of pulled pork. "Few weeks? What about since like Saturday? You know the last time I saw you?"

Clara shrugged her shoulders. "I don't know. I just say few weeks because you've made, um, a couple *improbable* alliances lately."

Sophia's felt her forehead crease, and she hurriedly relaxed it. Last thing she needed was wrinkles as a teenager. She racked her mind as to whom Clara was referencing to, although subconsciously she knew the answer.

"Who are we talking about again?" Sophia asked.

"C'mon, Soph," Clara said, wincing as she swallowed a chunk of pork. "You and Decker? Gotta be honest. Didn't see that one coming in a million years."

Sophia rubbed her hands over her face, irked by the question Clara posed, the question that everyone at BRHS had been dying to ask. And the subject of the question had been shoved in Sophia's face by Emma numerous times.

"Why? Because of his reputation or something? Because he's a jock? Because he seems hot-headed." Sophia went off. "Ever occur to you that Jackson's a nice, more sensitive-than-not kind of guy?"

"Geez Louise, Soph." Clara raised her eyebrows at her friend. "Just didn't take you for the Decker type. Even though he is kinda hot."

"It's just so annoying that every person on campus acts like they know better than I do about Jackson. Like I'm the one who's blowing him, not you." Sophia defended herself. She was offended by the constant judgment of her relationship with Jackson.

"Okay, okay, I get it. I just personally wouldn't date him. He's attractive and stuff, but I don't know about him in general. Can't figure him out. He just always seems kinda off. Not like mentally insane off, but just like he's always hiding something or always has a plan in mind." Clara divulged her opinion.

Clara the know-it-all. Why did she think she knew better? What gave her more knowledge than me? Nothing. That's what. But Sophia trusted Clara's opinion. Clara rarely steered her wrong, and she wouldn't have anything to gain by doing it to Sophia now. So what if she were right? I mean, besides the one night in the park, Jackson never opened up that much again. She wondered if he were taking advantage of her vulnerability that night. She nodded in response to Clara's comment.

"Look, if you say he's nice, right now you know him better than any of us, so Imma go with him being nice." Clara put her hand on Sophia's thigh and smiled. "Don't worry about it. No one thinks you're a hoe or anything like that."

"Thank God," Sophia added in a sarcastic joke.

"Well, I mean you're close to being a hoe, but not there yet," Clara joked.

Sophia cracked a smile. "Thanks, hoe."

"No problem, slut." Clara chuckled.

Sophia sat up straight on the granite slab to deliver a brief spiel to Clara. "I heard everything you been saying to me, but now I'm indifferent. I came over here half-expecting you to talk about Jackson anyway, but like I had my mind set on not letting Jackson go. Except after hearing what you said, it fits in with someone else's advice."

Clara cocked her head to the side, opening up her water bottle she had brought from home. "How so?"

"Well, like how you said, he seems like he constantly has a plan in mind. One of my friends is just skeptical of his motives," Sophia answered, her eyes looking heavenward. "I just don't know what to do now. Like I can't figure out if I should stay with him and roll with it. I can't figure out if I should just leave him and say it was nice while it lasted. I just don't know."

"Look, your gut feeling is to go for it, right?" Clara inquired.

Sophia looked back at Clara, nodding.

"Then what's holding you back from rolling with it?" asked Clara.

Sophia's jaw clenched. "Just … just like the thought that you could be right. Like I dunno, I guess I'm afraid to jump in cuz I have an inkling feeling in the back of my mind that it's the wrong move."

"How 'bout this, Soph?" Clara turned her body around on the slab of granite. "What do you like about Jackson Decker?" Clara emphasized his name.

"He's cute. He's nice and fun to be with, but the most surprising and maybe the most intriguing aspect of him is that I can tell deep down he aches. I know there's something that's kept him from opening up, and if I could be that person that helps fix it, I just wish I could be that person."

"So what don't you like?" Clara asked.

"Why doesn't he just open up? He already has to me about something way too deep to share with someone on a first date or hang out or whatever. Why wouldn't he just tell me? He knows I care about him."

"That's what I'm saying," Clara drawled.

Sophia slumped her shoulders. "Yeah, yeah, maybe you're right."

"I usually am," Clara added. A ringing sounded from the school. "Oops, the lunch bell just rang. See ya around, babe."

"Bye, hun." Sophia hugged Clara and hopped off the granite slab with her food tray.

Shit. She heard what Clara said and was inclined to agree, but maybe she should just take the leap of faith. For all she knew at that time, he was a perfectly normal guy who just wasn't comfortable divulging his life to Sophia. She rationalized his not telling her everything to just being a guarded person. Sure, that made sense. Sometimes she wouldn't share things with Clara that were too close to the bone. *What did Clara know anyway? Did she have any proof of Jackson being manipulative? No.*

As of right now, Sophia knew more than anyone. She also didn't want to ruin the first real relationship she'd had in months. She loved being wanted by someone for more than a one-night stand at a house party. She wasn't ready to let that go.

JACKSON

Two Years Earlier

Jackson slogged through his kitchen, picking up beer cans and paper plates to throw away. The guests from his parents' Fourth of July block party had left, and Jackson's mother had gone out to buy more trash bags for Jackson to put leftover debris into. Jackson's father sat in the office working on his computer.

Jackson was beyond bored but was promised that he could relax after he cleaned up the house. Normally there would be hundreds of more tasks for Jackson to attend to, but his parents were being lenient given that two hundred people were just in their home. Jackson threw food into a trash bag and sat on it, bouncing multiple times to compress the garbage. He quickly flipped around and tied up the bag before the contents could expand again. He let out a sigh of relief and cracked his neck. Jackson walked into the kitchen again and stared at the towers of silverware and glass plates that sat on the countertop. He had already been cleaning for nearly two hours. *Why couldn't I just take a quick break?* His dad was always so quick to call him lazy.

"Oh my," Jackson's father said.

Jackson turned to look at his father leaning back in the office chair. Jackson slowly walked over while his father covered his face. Jackson was confused. He'd seen his father reading emails earlier and was briefly worried that he got one saying someone had passed.

Jackson turned his focus to the article that was on the screen. It read, "'Equal Dignity' under the law. High court legalizes same-sex marriage nationwide." Jackson smirked and snorted out a laugh.

His father uncovered his face and looked up at Jackson, his eyes widened with anger. "I know. Can you believe this shit? All because that guy didn't wanna bake a cake."

Jackson's father had no idea he wasn't angered by the decision. He was ecstatic. Jackson nearly cracked up out of joy, but he kept his cool. "Crazy."

"Really crazy. This ruins the point of marriage." His father straightened his arm out at the article.

"How so?" Jackson enjoyed seeing his father angered by this. Jackson loved seeing some of his beliefs win for once.

"How so?" Mr. Decker sat up, staring at Jackson dumbfounded. "How so? Marriage is between a man and a woman. That's it."

"I didn't even think you cared about that rule from the Bible," Jackson said.

His father shook his head in a rage. "Well, you thought wrong. Now there'll be kids growing up confused with their two moms or two dads. This is the destruction of a normal-marriage society. Soon people are gonna be marrying their nephews."

"People in Louisiana already do that," Jackson joked.

"But now it will be normalized, just like this shit is." Mr. Decker stood up and walked away from the computer. Jackson let him storm past him into the kitchen. "I mean if you're gay, fine. Be in love or whatever. Why'd they have to ruin marriage?"

"Gay people were already getting married, Dad. I mean just not legally." Jackson was getting fed up with his dad saying gays "ruined" this and "ruined" that. "Like just because it's legalized now doesn't mean dudes are gonna start having sex all around you. This barely affects you."

"So you agree with this, this abnormal bullshit." Mr. Decker put his hands on his hips and leaned his ear forward.

"Sure." Jackson wanted to see how many buttons he could push.

He was enjoying seeing this. "I mean if I were gay, would it still be abnormal?"

Without hesitation, Mr. Decker responded, "Yes! Men aren't supposed to have sex. It goes against natural law. Men and women make kids. Men and men or women and women don't. Why do you think that it was normal for only a man and woman to be married for the past ten thousand years? Because only a man and woman can have kids."

"Okay, fair enough, but where's the harm in letting people marry the same sex? It gets normalized. Who cares? As long as Uncle Jessie doesn't come down with his boyfriend and get married on our front lawn, why do you care? Why would you care either way? He's not marrying you." Jackson fanned his arms out. He was sweating. His enjoyment had turned into anger at his father's beliefs. "It's funny how dumb this argument is."

"I think it's funny how much you disagree. If you're a fag, just come out and say it. That's the brave thing to do, right?" His father laughed. "Actually no. If you were a fag, you'd know better than to tell me."

Jackson grunted, trying to yell at his father, but he shut his mouth. He was in awe of his dad's ignorance. *What an idiot.* He thought given his dad's enormous salary he'd be smart enough to understand Jackson's point of view. *Apparently Ivy League schools don't teach you the skills how to be a good person.*

"I'm gonna go clean up the backyard." Jackson walked away from his dad.

"Fine, don't argue. Be a wimp. I need to decompress. I can't believe this shit." His father slapped the countertop quickly and walked over to the liquor cabinet. Jackson had no intention of cleaning up. He needed to decompress as well, and he lay down on a lawn chair to take a nap.

The decorations from the Fourth of July party hung down in front of Jackson, waving back in forth in front of him, carried by the afternoon wind blowing from the south. The cups, plates, and food from the block party were strewn across the pool deck and under the lawn chair Jackson was reclining on. Jackson spun his phone around in his hand and contemplated posting something on social media, something that would change his identity and everyone's view of him.

After the argument with his dad, Jackson was going to prove just how brave he could be. Jackson was no wimp. He raked his fingers through his hair and turned on his phone. He scrolled to Instagram and made a post about something that had been on his mind for months. Jackson's fingers shook through the whole typing of the post. He finished the confession, and his finger hovered over the "post" icon on the bright screen held between his hands.

Jackson read the post repeatedly to make sure it was how he wanted it to sound. "So this is mad random to everyone reading this, but just bear with me thru it. About four months ago, I came to the realization that I am bisexual. With all the confessions about coming out lately on tv and shit and the Supreme Court ruling, I figured u guys can add me 2 that list haha. But for real, this is a weight lifted off my back. I haven't been able to tell any of u guys this b/c I'm too afraid y'all will look at me differently. I was also too afraid to tell my parents because as u know, they hella religious. But I'm not afraid anymore. I, Jackson Decker, am bisexual, so either deal with that hard-hitting truth or get the fuck outta my life."

Jackson Decker held back the only tear trying to run out the corner of his left eye, and he hit the post button. He exhaled with the force of a thousand hurricanes and threw his phone aside. Jackson lay back in his lawn chair and took in the sun, the day after America's holiday of independence.

An hour later, Jackson awoke and leaned up. The lawn chair snapped as the straps peeled from his back. He blinked his eyes. The brightness of the sun blinded him, and he looked around for his phone. Jackson found it off to the left of him on the grass where he had thrown it before his impromptu afternoon nap. He turned on his phone, took a deep breath, and scrolled through the comments on his post.

The dullness inside his mind faded, and a release of dopamine filled him with ecstasy. A smile grew upon his face. The expectation to see anger and disgust piled on top of each other through the comments section was a false expectation of Jackson's. Not one negative comment surmised his phone screen.

The comments included:

"You're such a brave, brave person, Decker. Yo I was scared asking Ally out last year, and now you do this. Always one-upping me."

"I love you, Jackson. You're such a sweet guy. Be proud ~ laycie."

"Jackson bro, you already know I got hella respect for you. This don't change anything, bro."

"And I thought you couldn't get any better ;) hmu sometime Jackson – Chris Stellanar."

Jackson was beaming. He was relieved by the response from his friends and Chris. Jackson copied Chris's username and DM'd him a message, "I'll take you up on that meetup offer. Free for a coffee in like fifteen, downtown? Denny's?"

The words "Chris is typing …" came up on the screen, and Jackson tapped the sides of his phone anxiously. He thought of all the worst-case scenarios. He could be rejected or, worse, rejected and find out some of his friends were pranking him with a fake account. He hadn't even checked Chris's account. *God, what if it were a fake account?*

Jackson quickly scrolled to Chris's account. It had a few hundred followers, nothing next to Jackson's proud couple thousand followers. Still, this confirmed that Chris's account was indeed real. A message came down from the top of the screen, and Jackson opened it in the Chris's DM.

"Didn't think you'd respond so fast hahahah. Sure, lemme get changed, and I'll b down," Chris replied.

Jackson shivered with euphoria, and he scrolled back to his own post. Jackson read Chris's comment again. He couldn't believe someone already wanted to go on a date with him. He wondered how long Chris wanted that. He thought about their going out on dates during the year, and he hadn't even met him yet. Jackson knew his dad would be angry but couldn't imagine he was serious about what he said he'd do if Jackson weren't straight.

Jackson walked into the house shortly after reading the notifications on his phone and walked through his kitchen and hallway into his bedroom. He put his phone on the charger and walked back through his hallway into the kitchen.

"What's good, Dad?" Jackson beamed.

"Mmm?" Jackson's dad replied, his attention on the dishes he was cleaning.

"You're not paying attention, Dad." Jackson rolled his eyes.

Mr. Decker put the dish in his hands down and turned off the water. He turned to Jackson and sighed. "What is it?"

"I'm gonna go out downtown and get some coffee with a friend. Want anything for when I come back?" Jackson said, still grinning.

"I'm fine without it. You realize it's like five o'clock, and you're having coffee, right?" Mr. Decker leveled his head at Jackson.

Jackson was annoyed with his father criticizing his actions yet again. "Yeah?" Jackson said, looking around the room.

"All right then. Just making sure you know you'll be bouncing off the walls for a bit," Mr. Decker said, turning back to the dishes.

"I'm good, Dad," Jackson said.

"Not that you need it," Mr. Decker mumbled.

"What, Dad?" Jackson questioned his father.

"I said 'not that you need it,'" Mr. Decker joked. "I can tell you're already packed with energy, though you hide it very well."

Jackson laughed and strutted to the door, high on confidence.

"So what's her name? You know this girl you're obviously swooning over," Mr. Decker shouted through the house.

Jackson racked his mind for any names to use as a lie. "Chris—" Jackson blurted out, adding on, "Stina!"

"Christina, cool, cool. Well, have fun buying her coffee!" Jackson's dad shouted over the noise of water and sponge hitting utensils in the sink.

"All right, bye!" Jackson yelled and walked out the door.

He locked the door behind him and started his walk downtown. Jackson was shaking his head. He was pissed he couldn't tell his dad about the post; nor the fact that the girl he was seeing was actually a guy named Chris who commented on said post. He couldn't stand that his dad might have been right. Maybe he wasn't brave enough to hear people's reactions. He wondered if he were right in posting what he did. Oh well, it was too late for that.

Jackson muttered to himself, correcting his dad. "Him. Have fun buying *him* coffee."

"Ignore everyone else. Ignore everyone else. Ignore everyone else," Jackson talked himself through meeting Chris at Denny's.

Jackson shook himself around before entering Denny's in attempt to loosen himself up. He walked through the swiveling doors and sat down at the booth closest to the door in case the situation got uncomfortable. A young waitress with scarily long nail extensions came up to Jackson, smacking her mouth with chewing gum. She moved her dark goth hair out of her face several times.

"Double espresso, please," Jackson said, turning around to look out the door.

"Any cream or milk?" she asked, pressing her pen to her pad. Jackson didn't hear her.

She walked around him to block his view. "Milk or cream?"

"Oh." Jackson blinked his eyes and glanced back at her. "Sorry, milk. Please."

The waitress nodded and moved away from blocking Jackson's

line of sight, and Chris came into view as he was entering the coffee shop. Jackson whirled back around to face the other side of the booth even though he knew Chris had seen him. He rapidly tapped his fingers on the table. Jackson gazed down at the ground as two feet came to stand next to him, and he looked, staring at Chris's face.

Chris smiled. "Cool if I sit?"

Jackson nodded slowly and then quicker. For being so confident around girls, he had no idea how to act around a guy he was interested in. Chris sat down and leaned back with both arms on top of the booth. Jackson smiled back and avoided looking at Chris in the eyes. He stared at his full lips and then his muscular chest. Chris was toned, and the cutoff shirt underneath his plaid revealed his muscles. Jackson glanced up at the ceiling because he was *definitely* not checking out Chris.

"First time going out with like not a girl?" Chris asked.

"Obvious?" Jackson laughed nervously.

"Well aside from your shaking hands and looking like you're about to shit bricks, no." Chris laughed and held out his hand. Jackson looked at it and then calmly reached out and shook it. "I've seen you around at school but didn't really know you. You were just a cute baseball jock."

Jackson snorted. "I think you were in my comp sci class, but I barely remember anything I learned from that. So sorry I don't remember you."

Chris snickered. "That's facts. Damn, that class was a snooze."

Jackson nodded a few times. *Couldn't the waitress make that coffee any faster?* Jackson jerked his head toward the kitchen and then back at his fingers, which were still tapping. He stopped tapping them and cracked his neck. Jackson was astonished that awkward silences were worse with guys than girls.

Chris broke the silence. "Believe it or not, my dad doesn't know I'm gay either."

"Honestly kind hard to believe," Jackson said. "I thought the stereotype was ripped dudes with good style and like if I looked that up your face would pop up."

Chris laughed. "I guess. I don't know, man. This plaid shirt with a wife beater underneath isn't something you'd normally see on the cover of *Time* magazine, so I can relax. You get used to hiding it though. If you at least hang out with guys and go out with girls, you can keep a low profile. Although broadcasting it on Instagram might not have been the best idea."

Jackson shook his head, grinning. "Now that is something to relax about, bro. This is like the most liberal city ever. People wouldn't even bat an eye if I walked down the streets in a dress."

Chris chuckled and looked out the window. Jackson followed his gaze and watched all the high school kids walking around in their cliques, driving cars so decked out that they would get stolen in a matter of seconds in Compton. The waitress came over and dropped off their coffee.

"That's kinda true." Chris looked back at Jackson and outside again. "But see all these rich assholes out here?"

"Chris, we're rich assholes," Jackson joked.

"Yeah, but not like that." Chris pointed out. "Those are the kids you gotta look out for. If they find out about your emotional sexuality vent post, the fuckin' governor and his sister will see it in about an hour."

"That's true, but people have never messed with me, I bench like 205, and I'm almost a sophomore," Jackson explained.

"All the more reason they'd go after you dude," Chris responded. "You're telling me I'm the most stereotypical gay kid out there? People won't care that you are bi, man. The only part of that they see is the I-like-guys part."

Jackson sighed. "I got enough people to protect me, enough friends that I know got my back."

Jackson didn't know how much of that was true, but he was confident that the baseball team would have his back at least.

"You sure about that, Jackson?" Chris asked, turning away from the window and looking at Jackson face-to-face. Jackson watched him brush his pompadour back and bite his lip. Jackson's mouth watered, and he swallowed while staring at Chris's long, sharp jawline.

Chris went on, "Think about it, one of the most popular guys in the freshmen soon to be sophomore class decides to come out and posts it on social media. Everyone that knows you knows you constantly go to the gym, hang with chicks all the time, and hang out in the locker room before practice."

Hearing someone else say it made the thought sound far worse to Jackson than when he even considered it. There was a ringing in Jackson's ears, and he could have sworn he felt his heart stop beating for a moment.

"And you're saying I look gay." Chris snickered.

Jackson took a sip of his coffee and then pushed it away. He cracked his knuckles and neck in anxiousness. "Holy shit. I fucked up."

Chris nodded. "Yeah. Definitely. But give it a couple weeks or so before you talk about it again with anyone."

"Why?" Jackson was on the edge of the seat to hear what Chris was going to advise.

"If you talk about it soon, it will cement the new image people have of you. If you wait a couple weeks or a month and then bring it up, people won't be as inclined to think of you as the bi kid in town," Chris raised his brows at Jackson, offering his hands toward him in suggestion. "Right?"

"All right, okay." Jackson's heart was still beating fast, but the advice made sense.

"Also when you do bring it up in a month or so, whoever you're speaking with, make it blatantly obvious that you're not actually bi and that you were just going through a rough patch or something along those lines. And repeat that process with whoever saw the post. Trust me on that. Also delete that post right now." Chris kicked Jackson's pocket from under the booth.

"My phone's at home charging." Jackson cupped his hands over his mouth and nose. He thought that maybe his parents had gone through it. No, they hadn't done that since sixth grade. But what if they had? Jackson was getting scared. He didn't know exactly what his dad would do and started thinking he might lose the relationship. He might be disowned.

"All right, well delete it when you get back, aight?" Chris tapped the table for emphasis.

"Mmm-hmm." Jackson gripped the edge of the table. All he wanted to do was show people he wasn't scared of being himself, and now he was worrying about losing a relationship with his father and all his friendships. *How could I have been so idiotic? I should've just stayed in the closet.*

Jackson cocked his head to the side. He was curious about Chris's motivations. "How do you know all this shit? And why do you suddenly wanna help me, dude? We literally just met."

Chris shrugged. "Just wanna be a good person. I get the struggle."

Jackson wondered if someone had put Chris up to this. He didn't know why anyone would, but why would he trust Chris, a virtual stranger? What if he wanted to screw over Jackson more?

And then it hit Jackson. He remembered making fun of Chris's makeup in class with the baseball team. He only did it because he was trying to fit in with his friends, but he didn't know if that hit a nerve with Chris. Chris might tell everyone throughout the city.

"Why are you helping me? For real," Jackson demanded. He was in hysteria. Chris stared blankly at him. "Is this about the makeup thing?"

"What?" Chris chuckled. "What are you even talking about?"

"I used to talk shit about your makeup in class. I remember how embarrassed you were," Jackson spat out.

"I mean yeah, but that shit kinda went over my head. It didn't matter that much. Why?"

Jackson grit his teeth and settled down. Maybe Chris was just trying to be nice. He looked up at Chris, who was beginning to turn red. Jackson realized his mistake. He just wanted to take out his anger on someone. The only person he could take it out on was himself.

"Sorry. Never mind."

"Are we good because you seem like a nice guy and—" Chris shook slightly. He folded his hands on the table, close to his body.

Jackson nodded. "Yeah. No, we're fine. I'm just not feeling. I need to go. Yeah, I need to go home right now."

Jackson stood up, ready to shake Chris's hand, but was met with a hug. Jackson wasn't prepared for the new custom when saying goodbye to a guy. He felt incredibly awkward and tensed up. Despite how warm the embrace felt, Jackson was cracking up mentally. Jackson was not prepared for a hug, especially from a guy. A hug was the last thing Jackson wanted right now. He shoved Chris away and looked around to check if anyone were watching.

"Um, okay then," Chris scoffed. "I guess you weren't expecting that."

"Yeah well, I'm not in the best state of mind right now." Jackson took out his wallet.

Chris shook his head and started walking out. He turned back to Jackson. "Do you want to meet up again or—?"

"I don't know. I'll just … I'll text you at some point." Jackson paid the bill for the coffee before running out of Denny's, past Chris.

The lock clicked, and Jackson stepped into his house. His mom was standing in front of the doorway holding up Jackson's phone in her hand, the screen displaying his post. Jackson's heart rate shot through the roof, and he looked around the room and saw his dad pacing back and forth. He racked his mind for an escape route excuse, but his mom spoke first.

"What the hell were you thinking? Do you know what this could do to your reputation?"

She waved the phone violently at Jackson. He reached for it to delete the post and missed. Jackson started tearing up. He could feel his dad's anger from across the room.

"Mom, it was just a dumb mistake. I can delete the post. I … I can tell everyone that someone took my phone. I …" Jackson sputtered.

"You're damn right it was a dumb mistake. It was idiotic! How could you do something like that?" his father roared.

"Hey, Dad, it's the twenty-first century, like people get over stuff like that faster and—" Jackson tried to make a case for himself.

"And they keep what they really wanna say inside themselves," his mother joined in.

Mr. Decker shook his head. "Now I know why you went downtown. You weren't seeing a girl. You were just downtown hanging out with one of your newly made faggot friends or boyfriend."

He rushed over to Mrs. Decker and grabbed the phone out of her hand. Jackson held up Chris's comments.

"Yeah, I'm sure he does think you get better and better now that he knows you'll be giving out blow jobs for free. Right?"

Jackson said nothing and looked away. Humiliation swept over him like a heat wave.

"Hey!" Mr. Decker yelled at Jackson. He ran up to him and got face-to-face with Jackson. "You look at me when I'm talking to you. I will not have a family relationship with a faggot and certainly not with a disrespectful, arrogant prick. So you look at me when I'm talking to you."

"Hey, honey." Mrs. Decker walked forward, trying to deescalate the situation. She tapped her husband's arm. "We can figure out what to do with him tomorrow. Just let's just go to bed."

Mr. Decker shook his wife's hand off, dropping his mouth to the floor. He pointed hard at Jackson. "Go to bed? Why? So he can sneak out and butt-fuck every guy on the block. No, he can go to bed. I wanna make sure Jackson understands that he disrespected us, our religion, and my family name."

Mrs. Decker looked at Jackson and sighed. She walked to her bedroom, leaving Jackson's phone on the counter, and slammed the door shut. Jackson continued to look away, his muscles tensing and face sweating.

"Look, Jackson, if you wanna be gay, fine. I'm okay with that. If you really want that, you can leave my house, or you can stay here, delete that post, and then tell everyone you know that it was a mistake. I will not have my family name die here tonight." Mr. Decker leaned in. "You're pathetic, you know that? A pathetic disappointment. You hear me?"

"I heard you, but I wasn't listening." Jackson clenched his fist. His breathing was quickening. His whole right arm flexed. He was prepared to punch his dad in his stupid, fat mouth. He was going to knock him out with one punch.

"What kind of gay love quote is that?" Mr. Decker spat at Jackson. He drawled out his words. "Did Chris tell you that?"

"No. You did. Remember? Or are you too old now?" Jackson asked through closed teeth.

Mr. Decker inhaled a deep breath and opened his mouth to talk, but Jackson beat him to the chase. "You said, 'If you're ever in a situation where you don't want to talk to someone, you can just hear what they're saying, but you don't have to listen!'" Jackson shouted. "Remember that?"

"I meant for you to use that against a bully." Mr. Decker jerked forward.

Jackson flinched. "And who's saying you're not one?" Jackson couldn't hit his father first. He wanted for his father to hit him so he'd go to jail. Maybe he'd stay in jail for life. That would be ideal. *That's what he deserved.*

"Your mom and I gave everything to get you here, to get you to the school you'll be going to, to get you to live in a house I dreamed of as a kid, and to give you everything you need to live a successful, happy life, and you're throwing it all away." Mr. Decker used up all his breath and coughed violently

"I still deserve all of that. Me liking guys shouldn't change that. You're my dad! What's wrong with you?" Jackson started crying.

Crying was not what Jackson needed to bring the point home to his dad. He had to show he was tough, but he couldn't control it. Tears flowed, and Jackson relaxed his fist. He couldn't understand how his father didn't think Jackson deserved his parents' love.

"You're crying now? I thought you were brave and tough." Mr. Decker rolled his eyes, doing air quotes to Jackson.

"I am tough!" Jackson said through a mouthful of saliva and tears.

"Well, you're gonna be tough by the time you're on your knees begging for our help, and we won't be giving anything to you because of your selfishness," Mr. Jackson breathed out and nearly laughed.

"Ever occur to you that maybe I didn't want to be rich or privileged or whatever? Not like I had a fucking choice, but maybe I didn't want to be known as the rich kid on the block and just as a normal nonaffluent kid." Jackson watched his father's wrinkled eyes widen.

Jackson couldn't tell if he'd finally broken through to his father or if he were preparing to scream at Jackson. Either way, Jackson kept talking. He had to finish his point. "And maybe if your mind were a little more open earlier in my life, then maybe I wouldn't be avoiding my faith like a disease. Maybe I wouldn't be arguing with you all the damn time, and maybe we wouldn't be in the situation we are in right now," Jackson said, wiping his tears. "You're calling me pathetic? What kind of dad threatens to kick out his own son just because he made a post on social media?"

Mr. Decker looked at the floor and wiped sweat off his face. "Go to your room right now."

Jackson was caught off guard by the reaction. He thought he had made progress, but now he was furious. His dad was too stupid to be a good person, to be a good dad.

"Or what? You gonna insult me some more? It's gotten old. Make up something original, not reuse the same insult over and over.

I thought your Harvard law degree would teach you good debate skills. Maybe you could have spent some of the money you put into this house into going through graduate school again." Jackson's sadness turned back into anger. He was going to be brave. He wasn't willing to back down now.

"Go to your room right now, or I will split your phone in half and remove you from this house myself." Mr. Decker now clenched his fists.

Jackson saw this and closed his hands again. He shook with rage; his blood vessels pumped rapidly. Adrenaline coursed through his body, and he was getting ready to fight. Jackson had never felt more useless, more of a worthless kid, more stupid in his life. He was ready to tackle his father when he looked past him and saw his mother in the other room. She was crying with a hand over her mouth, and she shook her head.

Jackson looked at her, his father, the floor, his mother, and his father, and he took a deep shaking breath. He unclenched his fists and relaxed. He had never seen his mother look so worried, and he felt helpless. He saw his father relax as well, and Mrs. Decker slowly trudged back into her room.

Jackson sighed out a cough, and he covered his mouth. He was ashamed that he made his mother cry. He wanted to go back on everything he said to his dad, but also wanted to keep those memories fresh to stay angry. He couldn't stay angry. He was exhausted.

"Phone's on the counter if you want it," Jackson said as he walked away from his dad. He shuffled into his bedroom and closed the door.

Days passed since the great debate between Jackson and his parents, and Jackson had found himself in the middle of a social crisis. He had been trying to hang out with people he thought he could trust, mainly boys from the baseball team, and found himself being rejected every time he texted or called someone.

He left his friend Hunter so many messages that he stopped counting and gave up on phone calls. Jackson knew the kid wasn't really a fan of the whole gay thing, but he'd known Hunter since like third grade. He couldn't believe he'd left Jackson's side too. Jackson texted a girl he had taken to homecoming, Riley, to see if she wanted to hang out at his place.

She had just posted on Snapchat, "bored asf, hmu for plans."

He remembered talking with her at dinner before homecoming about politics, and she leaned far into the left. Jackson figured Riley would be the person to be there for him given how liberal she was, and he went into their conversation on Snapchat.

"Ay, Riley, I'm bored outta my mind too. U wanna come over? Haven't talked for a hot couple months hahahha." Jackson sent the message and stared at his phone, awaiting the response. He didn't blink once until he saw the "Riley is typing" message pop up.

"I can't. My friend just hmu, and we're going to Jake's Smoothies." Riley's response came back almost instantaneously.

Horrible liar. Jackson pounded his forehead with his phone and grunted. He was officially an outcast, which meant he had nothing to lose if he called her out. "There is no way in fuck that someone made plans w u that fast. You posted your story at 1:58pm & I huu at like 2:01pm. Literally, there's no way someone huu faster than me."

Riley opened his chat and didn't respond. Jackson threw his phone across the bedroom and punched the pillows on his bed. He didn't want to be bothered by anyone. For once, he wanted everyone to leave him alone. He couldn't stand the hypocrisy of everyone he knew. They went to feminist marches and pride parades, but when he came out, that was where they drew the line? *Unreal.*

Since his unrefined post about his sexuality, people had turned their backs on him, and Jackson had begun to realize that not only was Chris right in his understanding of the situation from experience, but so was Mr. Decker in his goal to keep Jackson from entering an increasingly burdensome position. Jackson began to recognize as more people stopped replying to his texts and hanging out with him that his town was not as accepting as he thought or at least pretended to think it was.

Later that day, Jackson walked out of his house to go to a Labor Day soiree his family friends were hosting. It was the most stress he was forced to put on himself in weeks. Tons of his former friends and social clique were going to be there. His parents wanted him to approach each of them individually to deliver a fake apology for being so weird and making the post. He had to deny himself.

Although most people in the town had claimed to be progressive and accepting of every person, that ideology left as soon as the truth came out, the truth that one of the most popular young men in town had come out as bisexual. No one wanted to accept him, so they abandoned Jackson, leaving him alone, in the isolated position he thought he would never experience.

He stood in his front yard, staring through the metal gate thirty yards in front of him. He hadn't prepared anything to say, in particular, and was getting stressed as to what he would tell everyone. He cracked his neck and heard the front door close. Jackson turned around to see his father.

"Get in the car!" Mr. Decker ordered Jackson.

Reluctantly Jackson made his way over to the Mercedes-Benz, which beeped and unlocked once his fingers gripped the handle of the door. He slowly pulled the silver door open and sat down on the leather inside the car. Jackson's parents followed suit, and his dad turned on the car with a rev. They drove into the hills, Mrs. Decker finishing her makeup, Mr. Decker silent, and Jackson gazing out the window.

"Isn't this counterproductive because of what you believe? Like shouldn't I just stay at home? I feel like showing up at a party with me would quote unquote taint your guys' reputation." As much as he wanted his friends back, he couldn't fathom having to apologize to each person at the party, one by one.

His father glared back at Jackson in the rearview mirror. "There's two reasons why this is productive. One, because you taking responsibility can fix the situation that *you* got yourself into. Two, because people won't be expecting you to show up and therefore might not think you're that much of a wimpy queer after all."

"This is going to go so badly though. I'm gonna get more hate than I already have." Jackson sighed and pressed his face against the glass.

"Darn." Mr. Decker dismissed Jackson. "You dug your own grave already. Might as well lie in it."

Jackson could feel his heart beating out of his chest in anticipation for the party. He had sweat running down his neck, soaking into the material of his white, collared shirt. Jackson adjusted his collar, allowing him to take in a deep breath to keep himself collected. He had skipped out on putting gel in his hair that night, based on a suspicion that his friends would see his "new" self in action.

The car pulled up to the front of his friend's house. Jackson got out of the car. Mrs. Decker walked to the front door with a bottle of wine and cookies for the younger kids at the dinner.

Mr. Decker held Jackson back for a moment. "Quick reminder, this is your chance to fix or *not* fix the image people have of you." He patted Jackson on the back, smirked, and walked up to the door with his wife and Jackson.

The door opened, and the father of Jackson's best friend, Isaiah Porter, greeted each of Jackson's parents happily and Jackson with just a quick handshake and no words spoken between them. Jackson awkwardly wandered through the house and out into the backyard.

When he got outside, Jackson tried to relax, but he could feel eyes on him from all angles. All the parents were drinking or talking about the latest news in politics and would occasionally peek at him. He saw his friends on the far side of the outdoor pool and expelled a large breath before cracking his neck and shaking out his hands. The lights hanging over the patio illuminated the marble-covered ground with a scintillating shine. His black dress shoes opposed the colors, and his cologne spread through the air like a light mist.

Jackson grabbed a soda out of the outdoor fridge and popped the can. The pop was deafening, and Jackson looked around to see his friends watching him. Jackson smiled and waved awkwardly. They turned back around and began whispering to each other.

"Great." Jackson sighed. He strode over to the mini congregation of his classmates near the pool chairs, and the whispering stopped.

"Hey, man," Jackson said through a fake smile to Isaiah.

Isaiah nodded, and his brown man-bun bounced around. He had braces and square glasses, but still gave off more confidence than Jackson did. Jackson's hands were shaking, and Jackson put them into his pockets after Isaiah looked down at them. Isaiah looked away and then at Jackson, sympathy in his eyes.

"Sup, Decker," Isaiah responded and paused. "Did your parents make you come?"

"No. I wanted to," Jackson lied. Though not everything he said was false. "I wanted to fix things with all you and everyone at BRHS. I'm not bisexual."

The prima donna girls on either side of Jackson's best friend smirked, and his old friends had looked away. They coughed over what were obviously huge laughs.

"Yeah, that's fine, man." One of them laughed. "You're not bi. You're a gay kid."

The girls smiled, their bodies jerking as they covered their mouths.

Jackson nodded. "Takes one to know though, doesn't it?"

The laughter stopped.

"Excuse me?" Brock asked, squinting at Jackson from the poolside chair he sat on. "Whatchu saying? You saying I'm gay too?"

"You said it, not me, bro," Jackson retorted.

Brock stood up and stepped forward clenching his fists, squeezing so tight the pips of an orange would have squeaked. Jackson held his ground, staring fiercely into the boy's eyes. The boy towered over the six-foot-three Jackson and made Jackson feel like an ant. Still, he held his ground against the giant teen before Jackson's best friend, Isaiah, stepped in between them.

"Okay, okay, okay, Brock. Jackson didn't mean nothin' by it." Isaiah reasoned with Brock. "Right, Jackson?"

Jackson's best friend looked at him and then at Brock, hinting for Jackson to respond.

"Yeah, didn't mean anything." Jackson sighed.

"See? He didn't mean nothing, big guy." Isaiah looked up at Brock and patted him on the back.

Brock settled down, walked back over to the pool chairs, and sat down with the other teens who had gathered for the dinner party. Jackson relaxed, looking around awkwardly for what to say next.

Isaiah touched Jackson's shoulder and sighed. "Hey, you wanna go talk for a bit?"

"Sure." Jackson nodded.

Isaiah nodded back, put his arm around Jackson, and walked away.

Brock popped a mint into his mouth and chuckled. "Don't drop anything, Isaiah. If you bend down, Jackson might—"

"Do something you've always wanted to do with a guy!" Isaiah shouted back to Brock.

Jackson looked back briefly to see Brock's reaction. Brock closed his mouth, and he furrowed his eyebrows, as his less than average-sized brain worked to articulate a comeback but had no results. Jackson was satisfied with that small win. He and Isaiah walked through the adults who were talking about seemingly unimportant things like politics and the stock exchange.

Jackson drowned out the noise with the sound of blood coursing through his veins after his encounter with Brock. Jackson collected himself just as Isaiah came to a halt inside the house. Isaiah unlocked the door to the second-story balcony, and they went up into the cool night air. Jackson sat down on of the balcony chairs, and Isaiah pulled one up to Jackson, scraping the wood with the legs of the chair.

"So what's the deal, man?" Isaiah leaned back in the chair. "You good? Like mentally?"

"I mean, sort of, dude. Kinda sucks though. Like Isaiah, when I made that post, stupid as it was, those comments that came in made it seem like people liked me. Ya know? Like really liked me, like understood somehow everything I was thinkin' 'bout."

"Yeah, I saw those." Isaiah snorted. "But dawg, like that shit is just online. Why'd you take it seriously? Like you know everyone fake mad shit online. If you haven't realized already, those comments were all fake, made by fake people who enjoy fuckin' with someone else's life. They were sarcastic, my guy."

Jackson smiled. "Yeah, I kinda figured that out. But you'd at least think they'd be kinda accepting. We live in nearly the most liberal town in like the state or even country."

"Naw, I'd say New York City beats San Mateo there." Isaiah snickered.

There was a pregnant pause. Jackson opened his mouth to say something and then shut it.

"I don't know. I—"

Jackson was cut off as Isaiah tried speaking at the same time. "Look, man, if you want my ..." Isaiah stopped and waved his hand at Jackson. "You first."

"I was just gonna say that I don't know if I am bi or not or whatever, but just hope you still got me, man. I hate being left alone, man. It's been shit lately. No one wants to hang or talk or anything, just cause I made one dumbass mistake." Jackson finished rambling.

"Yo, of course I gotchu, man. I was just gonna say that if you had anything to say, you should say it, but here we are." Isaiah smiled and leaned forward. He exhaled a cloud of fog from his mouth in the air. "I just think the best thing you can do right now is to do what you just did with me to everyone you tight with. Like don't go up to someone like Sophia Milverton and be like, 'I am not bisexual!'

That would be dumb as hell. Chances are, someone like her doesn't even know. No shade, but she's kinda dumb."

Jackson laughed. "How is 'she's kinda dumb' no shade?"

"It's honesty." Isaiah wheezed and slapped Jackson on the back. They both settled down after a few more laughs. "So anyways, just say what you said to me to everyone you tight with and to everyone you not so tight with. Just pretend like nothing happened. Eventually everything will dissipate. Hunnid percent."

"Aight. Thanks, man. Sorry for you having to bring me up here to talk with me." Jackson averted his eyes so he wouldn't get choked up. The more he looked at Isaiah, the closer he got to crying out of gratefulness.

"It's all good, dude." Isaiah rubbed Jackson's back.

"You know, it's gonna be hard being friends with an outcast. You don't have to go all out for me. I'll be all right on my own if you wanna keep your rep." Jackson looked down at his feet. "Don't needa change for me."

"I already said 'it's all good, dude' stupid ass." Isaiah chuckled again and took his hand off Jackson's back. They both stared out over the backyard. "Hug it out?"

"Did my bi-ness rub off or something?" Jackson joked and bro-hugged Isaiah anyway.

"I mean, maybe I should go bi. Ain't been with a girl for months." Isaiah let go of Jackson laughing.

Jackson was cracking up and happy with where he thought his life would go. He knew, realistically, everything he had told people about himself on that post would disappear. And it did for a while.

SHAUN

Present Day

There was a ruffle of bedsheets in Shaun's room, and he had awoken from a short Thursday afternoon nap. He blinked himself awake, smacking his lips after he had gotten a hint of a metallic taste in his mouth. Shaun rolled over onto his back and grabbed his phone off the nightstand.

"Hey, hun?" Shaun's mother called from outside his bedroom. "Would you come out here?"

It was as if his mom knew exactly when he woke up. Shaun groaned and stretched out his arms and legs as he kicked off the bedsheets.

"You coming?" Shaun's mother called again.

"Yeah!" Shaun shouted back.

A long yawn escaped from him, and he rolled off the bed onto the carpet beneath it. He got up and walked out into the kitchen. The smell of crab in the air made his mouth water.

"What's up?" Shaun asked.

"The Milvertons are coming over tonight. Just thought you should know. Might want to take a shower." Mrs. Baxter smiled.

Shaun was confused. *The Milvertons?* He only saw Sophia at school, and if he saw her outside of school, it was only for one of these stupid dinners his mom would put together. The awkwardness that came from the distance between Shaun's unpopularity and Sophia's popularity was almost embarrassing.

"Wh … huh? Why?" Shaun asked, agitated.

"Because they are our friends and we haven't seen them in nearly a year. Can you believe that?"

"Mom, no."

"Well, it's too late for that."

"You don't understand. Sophia's like a thousand times cooler than me. It's gonna be so awkward!" Shaun argued, exasperated. "Why couldn't you have just asked me first? It's gonna be like Tupac hanging out with Rebecca Black."

His mom stared at him, perplexed by the analogy.

"It's like a really good rapper with like never mind." *Shaun rolled his eyes. His mother was young in the 1990s and she still didn't know Tupac? She must not have had a social life to know the trends or any life.*

"Well, like it or not, they will be here in an hour. C'mon, I'm sure it won't be that bad. You guys know each other well."

"*Knew*, Mom. The correct form of that verb would be knew." Shaun rolled his eyes. "I'm not good with girls too, like you know that."

"No teenage boy is, and you're dating Emma. You have nothing to worry about. Relax, Shaun." Mrs. Baxter tapped Shaun on the arm, and he hastily brushed her arm off. He wasn't a child.

"You relax. That's another reason this can't happen. What if Emma finds out I had dinner with Sophia? Everyone knows Sophia's literally a seventy out of ten, and she does cheerleading. But yeah, Emma won't mind. Oh, wait! She will!"

"Shaun, be careful with that tone," his mom warned sternly.

"What tone? The tone of conversation? Sophia is so not anyone I would ever even think of hanging out with. Why didn't you just ask me!" Shaun repeated all the words over in his head to make sure they sounded right.

"Because I didn't think you'd get this upset. But I'll ask next time. How 'bout that?"

"Oh wow. Thank you, Mom. You're basically Dr. Phil and solved all my problems. Ask me next time. Yeah, that'll fix this."

"You are seriously pushing it, young man." Her face went dark red, and she was speaking through a clenched jaw.

"I'm just pissed because we could have had such a good night, and yet again you found a way to ruin it," Shaun went on sarcastically. "Big surprise, you? Ruin a good night? Unheard of!"

"If I said to my parents what you're saying to me, I'd get slapped. Watch your mouth."

"Yeah, it must have been super hard growing up on a beach in Florida. Oh yeah! Grandpa owned a multimillion-dollar company, and you were spoiled out of your fucking mind." Shaun was tired and woke up on the wrong side of the bed, but even with that backing his motivation, he knew he took his insults a step too far.

Shaun's mother turned off the heat on the crab and folded her arms. "How dare you? You're really pushing your limit, Shaun." She scowled and locked eyes with Shaun. He could see her eyes glisten.

"Are you really going to do this again? You always act like you had such a hard life and then cry because of something a sixteen-year-old says to you. The shit I had to deal with even by the end of eighth grade was worse than anything I could say to you." Shaun choked on his words. He remembered being bullied by Jackson Decker in middle school.

Shaun looked down at his mother's feet and could see water pouring onto the ground. Water started spewing from all the corners of the kitchen, and suddenly he couldn't breathe. He turned back to see Jackson laughing with several other boys. Jackson plunged Shaun's head into the toilet bowl again. Shaun tried to grip the edge of the bowl and push himself out, but Jackson held his face in the water. Shaun rolled to the side and could breathe again.

"C'mon, you can get out, fat ass." Jackson grabbed a handful of fat from Shaun's side of his stomach. Shaun finally caught his breath. While crying, Shaun tried standing up off his knees. Jackson mimicked his crying. "His titties are in the way."

Jackson plunged Shaun's head into the water, and the lunch bell rang. Jackson let go and washed off his hands. He left the bathroom howling with his friends. Shaun sat next to the toilet, his face and shirt drenched with toilet water.

Shaun was tearing up when he blinked them away and wiped his eyes with his shirt. He looked up at his mother, who was still standing across from him, but she had relaxed. She had a confused look on her face.

Shaun sniffled. "I just don't like hanging out with popular people like Sophia. I got so much shit in middle school for being shy and awkward, when I was the fat loner kid. That kid Jackson Decker, Sophia's boyfriend, used to throw me up against the bathroom wall and pour toilet water over my head or drown me in toilets. Either or."

"Why didn't you tell me?" Mrs. Baxter unfolded her arms, and her forehead wrinkled with concern.

"Because you would've made it worse, kinda like you made today worse. Amazing how this all comes full circle, isn't it?" Shaun tried shaking the bad memory away from his mind, but it had resurfaced. He kept seeing himself drowned in the bathrooms at his old school. "So if you seriously think you had a hard life, you're probably lying to yourself."

"No, you're being a presumptuous brat!" his mother screeched.

"What do you even mean?" Shaun shook his head at her.

His mother looked at the ceiling as if she were pondering a thought and then back at Shaun. "I'll use it in a sentence. You are being an unappreciative, presumptuous brat for thinking I was not bullied when I was younger."

Oh, shit. Shaun wasn't expecting that. He supposed she knew how he felt, and he suddenly had an urge to apologize, but he couldn't cave that easily.

"Phone! Now!" Mrs. Baxter yelled and extended her arm.

Shaun gritted his teeth and repeated words in his head, preparing more lines to fire back, but he knew when to stop provoking his mother. Jaded from arguments over the years, he knew how far to go before his mother punished him indefinitely. He reluctantly shuffled over to his mother.

"Not like you know how to unlock it anyway." Shaun dropped the device in her palm.

He stomped like a child into his bedroom and locked the door.

An hour passed, and Shaun's emotional state had dissipated. It was six twenty in the evening, and Shaun was in the bathroom doing his routine insecurity check. No matter what the event was, whether it be a dinner such as the one he would be enjoying shortly, a graduation, wedding, or even a day at school, Shaun would make sure he looked as close to his idea of flawless as possible. Shaun stood in front of the mirror and flexed his body, checking if there were any progress from his workout the day before.

He moved on to four sprays of deodorant in the air just near his face. Shaun basked his face in the falling mist of deodorant and then rubbed a stick of deodorant on his chest and armpits. It was a formula that he learned lasted the longest without being an overbearing scent. He squeezed out a dollop of gel from its canister and rubbed it between his fingers. Shaun moved the gel through his hair and straightened out his jaw, making absolutely sure everything was symmetrical. Otherwise his image would be ruined.

The irrational fear in the past had been that a person would post a picture of how bad his face, body, or style was. Therefore, it was important there was not a blemish on his clothes, face, or body. He always compared himself to Instagram models to see if he were any closer to being as shredded as they were. By now though, Shaun had lost the fear of being picked on, and he refused to admit that the routine was an unhealthy habit fueled by these model comparisons.

The clock in the bathroom had barely hit 6:31 p.m. when the door to Shaun's house received two knocks upon it. Shaun came out of his bathroom, shaking his head at the thought of sitting in his room with Sophia for three painfully long, awkward hours.

Mrs. Baxter brushed off her jacket and pushed her hair back while staring in the mirror in the kitchen. "Oh, honey!" she called. "I think it's them. Would you get the door please?"

Shaun widened his eyes, looking at his mother, shaking his head. "No, just go. You look fine," Shaun whispered, walking up to her. He was trying to be nice to alleviate any anger that still resided in his mom.

"No, go," she instructed back. Of course she turned a nice gesture into a small dispute.

"Mom, jushtd goh," Shaun whispered back through gritted teeth.

"Shaun," she said, aggravated.

"Mom, I—" Shaun cut himself off, rolling his eyes as he walked to the door.

Click! He turned the lock on the door, and it opened. God, the Milvertons were like a stereotype of what American families look like. Mrs. Milverton was in her perfect dress and boots and had her hair curled immaculately. Mr. Milverton, the strong, providing, gristly-bearded man with a stylish jacket, even had a dope scar across his cheek. And Sophia was an innocent-enough looking girl with her perfectly straight blonde hair falling over her shoulders past her neck to her shirt's opening to her chest. Shaun looked back up.

"Hi, Shaun! Wow! I haven't seen you in forever. You've gotten so tall and handsome. I'm sure you get a lot of attention at school." Mrs. Milverton smiled, hugging Shaun on her way in.

"Mom, shut up," Sophia muttered quietly.

Her mother glared back. Mr. Milverton came out from behind Sophia. He was a tall man, built like a professional wrestler. He would be intimidating to anyone who hadn't formally met him because anyone that had would know he was also ironically the politest man in the city.

"Hello, sir," Mr. Milverton said loudly with an outstretched hand.

Shaun grasped Mr. Milverton's hand and shook it.

"Firm grip. Not many tough young men left. Am I right?" Mr. Milverton laughed, shoving Shaun's shoulder lightly.

Shaun squeezed out a fake laugh and shoved Mr. Milverton back. He laughed again and joined the frenzy of handshakes and hugs among the adults.

"So, uh, hey, Shaun." Sophia nodded.

"Hey, Sophia." Shaun nodded back and approached her with a handshake.

Unfortunately Sophia approached him with a we've-known-each-other-so-long-that-we-can-hug hug. This led to a series of awkward bumps of shoulders and each of them switching to a hug or handshake and back again until they ended up slowly fist-bumping each other. Shaun closed his eyes for a half second, thinking, *And this is where I commit suicide. Why didn't you just hug her? Stupid ass.*

"Soooo," Shaun started. "I'm like not really a fan of hanging out with four adults for three hours, so you wanna just chill in my room for a bit?"

"Yeah, let's get it." Sophia followed Shaun to his room.

Shaun crawled onto his bed and rested his back against the wall. Sophia sat opposite of him on his desk chair. She spun around in it for a moment.

"Hey, Sophia?" Mrs. Milverton called to her as she saw the teens enter Shaun's room. Shaun saw her watching them and cringed as he awaited her usual yell—"Leave the door open!"

Sophia got up, walked over to the door, left it open a crack, and shook her head. "My mom's so embarrassing."

"Not even. My mom said *sweetie pie* in front of all the baseball players," Shaun said.

Sophia chuckled slightly. "That's rough. But for me it's like a constant vortex of embarrassment, like she's probs done that to you like twice. It happens to me all the time, but not just my mom. My dad too."

"Naw, your dad's chill," Shaun said.

"No way. Are you kidding me?" Sophia's mouth dropped. "I was with Jackson downtown, and it started raining, so I called my dad to pick us up. Everything was good until my dad sang along with Alessia Cara in the car. Jackson played it cool, but I knew he was dying at my lame-ass family."

"Damn, Alessia Cara too. Of all people." Shaun exhaled a single laugh.

"Yeah, all the time too. I'm kinda tight with my mom, but when my dad's around, it's like he never talked with a kid before in his life. Like has literally no clue what to talk about."

"I mean, my mom asks me if I would want socks with bulldozers on them, like I'm four fuckin' years old," Shaun joked. "Like, 'No, Mom, I'm a big boy now.'"

Sophia giggled. "Yeah, my dad's worse. We're either completely silent, or he'll ask me about my grades, which he knows sets me off cuz I suck at school."

"Don't we all?" Shaun joked. He had not been expecting them to get along well at all. Maybe hanging with Emma changed her and she wasn't so stuck-up anymore.

"I mean, I suck like 2.8 GPA suck. I had a 2.46 freshman year."

"Sophia, I had a 2.8 freshman year. It's all good."

"What? How are your grades so good right now?"

"They're kinda not. I mean, they're fine. I have a 3.3 at the moment. Clinging on to Bs in most of my classes."

"Oh well, still a ton better than me," Sophia said, averting her eyes.

Shaun nodded, slowly leading the conversation into silence. The small connection he had made with Sophia disappeared as the talking stopped. Sophia looked around the room. Shaun followed her eyes as she looked at Shaun's pictures of himself and his family. She gazed at his schoolbooks and clothes and to the floor, where she saw a certificate reading "National Psychology Essay Competition: Third Place." Sophia looked down at her pocket and pulled out her phone.

In desperate need to keep the conversation going, Shaun broke the silence. "I just decided enough was enough."

"Hmm?" Sophia looked up and put her phone away.

"With my grades, I started trying harder this year because I decided at the end of freshman year that enough was enough."

"Back to this?" Sophia rolled her eyes. "I thought I said talking 'bout grades pisses me off."

"Yeah, but just one sec. I got some advice. Like I weighed twenty pounds more last year and my grades were, like I said, not great. And I also was super socially awkward."

"You aren't still?" Sophia laughed.

Shaun grinned politely despite her words upsetting him as he reminisced on the time. "Yeah, okay fine. I'm not exactly the James Bond of social events. I'm just saying that like something that helped me make a comeback was just admitting that I was shitty at a bunch of things. Maybe it sounds counterproductive, but I believe admitting to your own problems is a good first step to fixing them."

"I kinda have admitted. I just told you my grades are shit." Sophia laughed awkwardly.

"Well, maybe that's not your only problem." Shaun raised his eyebrows.

Sophia dropped her mouth in disbelief and scoffed. "You're saying I got depression or mental problems or something."

"You said it, not me." Shaun wanted Sophia to feel hurt. She couldn't just say how awkward he was as an insult and not expect something in return.

Sophia stared. "You must be fun at parties."

"I wouldn't know. I've never been to one." Shaun laughed.

"Yeah, probably because you're socially awkward," Sophia retorted.

"Yeah, probably. See. This is my point. I get what my deal is.

Clearly you don't get yours because you're so defensive. You don't have to tell me. Just gotta admit it to yourself."

Shaun wanted to prove how smart he was, but he also genuinely wanted to help Sophia. He had always been asked by people for relationship advice, even though he had never been in one until Emma, and many considered him a good ear. Since he never gave his opinion on anything and instead watched chaos unfold before him, he was always ripe with criticism on people whom he rarely talked to. Sophia was one such person, and he wanted to be able to connect for once in his life with someone whose name was instantly recognizable among all high schoolers in the area. He also thought Sophia was very not book-smart and saw the advice opportunity as a way to impress the most popular girl at BRHS. This would finally be his shot at popularity. He could get Sophia to like him and bring him into the popular circle.

"Well, what do you think my deal is then? Try me, Freud." Sophia smirked.

"Honestly?" Shaun questioned. "Because if I'm right, the truth might hurt."

"Try me."

"Social acceptance? Don't quite fit into one particular group, so you jump around."

"I'm a cheerleader, dude. I'm part of the quote unquote popular kids," Sophia answered with a feeling of triumph. "Wanna know what it is?"

"Go ahead." Shaun put his hands out.

"Peer pressure." Sophia nodded.

"Yeah?" Shaun could tell she just wanted to speed through the talk.

Sophia nodded again. "Yeah, peer pressure."

"Seems like a pretty quick conclusion for just starting to analyze your nature." Shaun raised his chin and looked down at her. He had the answer long before she did and was waiting to drop it so he would sound more impressive.

"Yeah, well, that's that. There. We figured it out, Shaun." Sophia rolled her eyes.

"So it was peer pressure that made you join the cheerleading team?"

"No, I've always loved cheer."

"Aight, any pressure to go to parties and hook up with every guy there?"

"Ex-fucking-scuse me?" Sophia knitted her eyebrows together. Her nostrils flared.

"Hey, don't shoot the messenger. Just know things," Shaun said.

Sophia sat back down on Shaun's desk chair and spun around. Shaun awaited the answer he knew was coming. Sophia sighed and stopped spinning the chair. During Sophia's blatant physical avoidance of the question, Shaun leaned forward from the wall, staring down at Sophia.

She came to a stop. "No, that was my choice. Never had sex. Wanted to try it. Liked it. So wanted it again. How's that?" Sophia confessed.

"All right. Pressure to date Jackson?" Shaun asked.

Sophia immediately shot down the question. Her eyes relaxed, and her lips curled into a smile. "No. Definitely not. He's the best thing that's happened to me in a seriously long time."

"So I guess peer pressure is off the list of possibilities then, huh?" Shaun said confidently.

"Guess so, Freud." Sophia licked her upper lip, which had become increasingly dry during the tense conversation. "Any other guesses?"

"I think I got it. Isolation."

There was a pause. Sophia stared off, unblinking. She went silent for a couple of minutes.

"Sophia? Sophia?" Shaun asked.

Sophia snapped back into the present. "Might be onto something there with that isolation thing, Mr. Third Place in Psychology Writing."

Shaun nodded, and he walked over to his desk. He wrote down his Snapchat on the back of a history assignment and held it out for Sophia. "If you wanna talk sometime, I provide free Sigmund Freud sessions daily."

Please take it, Shaun thought. Sophia chuckled and opened her phone. She entered his Snapchat in and added him.

"I will definitely be hitting you up. Sometimes I need this deep shit. If you go into it, you'll be a fire psychologist."

"Hopefully," Shaun commented.

She took it. Oh God, she added me on Snapchat. He looked over her hand onto her phone to see her Snap-score. "Jesus, how's your score nine hundred thousand?"

"Too many horny guys hit me up," Sophia joked, and her smile went sour. "How high's Emma's?"

"Like two hundred k or something," Shaun said.

"Sounds about right." Sophia made a straight line with her mouth and raised her brows slightly. She sighed. "Most girls are above a hundred k. You get a lot of attention for having boobs."

"That's kinda—that's like really messed up. Some dudes are fucked."

"That's the problem. Some dudes *haven't* fucked." Sophia half-smiled. "And that just gets you a toooooon of dick pics. Disgusting."

"For real." Shaun wasn't surprised by how many guys texted Sophia asking for nude pictures but thought it was repulsive. How could someone just think they were owed nudes out of principle? If he found out someone had been sending shit like that to Emma and expecting it in return, he'd split his jaw in half.

Sophia rolled her eyes to the side and frowned. "Yeah. This is completely random—well, not completely—but I was just thinking about her. You know, I've been kinda an asshole to pier girl lately. You think you could tell her it's not personal?"

"Pier girl?" Shaun waved his hand, confused.

"Emma. It's a long story." Sophia snickered.

Shaun grinned. "Sure. I'll tell her."

Sophia nodded. "You guys are a weirdly good couple." Sophia beamed. "No offense, but I didn't see it working in a million years."

"Thanks, I guess." Shaun laughed. He blinked longer than normal and shook a smile out. "I actually wouldn't know since she's my first girlfriend."

"Seriously?" Sophia smiled, moving her eyebrows down. "That's cute."

"Sure." Shaun rolled his eyes. Unless he was telling Emma how cute she was or vice versa to him, the word *cute* always made Shaun feel like he was talking to his mom. Shaun snorted and moved his hair around. "It's nice to know that not all cheerleaders are complaining rich kids with sticks up their asses and are actually real," Shaun jested.

"Thank you. Yeah, we're not. We just have depression or mental problems." Sophia winked.

"Hey, guys!" Mr. Milverton called from the dining room. "Dinner's ready!"

"That's our cue," Shaun said.

They both stood up and walked out of Shaun's room. Sophia left first, and Shaun followed, flicking the lights on his way out. By the time Shaun was leaving his room, he wasn't as concerned with gaining popularity. Granted it was still mind-blowing that he had Sophia's Snapchat now, but he was more impressed by her. He knew it was a dumb thought not to have until their discussion, but the idea that popular kids, girls especially, actually dealt with real problems was almost nice to hear. He didn't think it was nice that they were smothered with texts, from guys thinking with their dicks. However, Shaun thought their conversation was so refreshing. They were both mature enough to talk about more personal problems, and Shaun enjoyed the moment.

SOPHIA

"I think I got it. Isolation."

There was a pause. Sophia blinked away the droplets of water forming in each corner of her eyes. She reminisced on a memory from her life, a recollection of the first time she felt truly alone and isolated. The memory lasted two minutes but felt like an hour in Sophia's conscience. Her mind flashed through images, and one finally came into view.

Sophia stared into the mirror in her room and brushed her hair vigorously, yanking all the knots out. She walked around her room into the closet, picking out a leather jacket and jeans. The clothes fit tight enough so people could see the attractive features of her body. She had the ideal hourglass physique and the right amount of fat in the right places for her to stand out to guy at a party.

A text on her phone from her friend Clara went off. "Ready yet?"

She walked over and responded, "Ya, I saw ur car. I'm coming."

The makeup box clicked, the lights of her room flickered off, and the door shut ever so quietly. Sophia shuffled out of her room with her boots in her left hand. She opened the front door of her house and spent a full minute closing it. She held the hinged part of the door, making sure it didn't creak. The door clicked as the lock fell into place. The boots fell to the ground, and Sophia stepped into each one before zipping them up. Sophia tiptoed down the pathway from her house to the street. Once she hit the pavement, her gait turned into a slight jog. A black Mercedes SUV reversed down the curb toward her, and she climbed into the passenger seat.

"Hey, girl," Clara said through chews of gum.

Her red hair was damp, and her thick eyeliner highlighted the redness in her eyes. Sophia assumed Clara had gotten water in her eyes during her shower and wasn't getting high before the party. For Sophia's sake as a passenger, she was hoping it was the former.

Clara licked her pink lipstick-covered lips and looked Sophia up and down. "Damn queen. You act like you've been to a party before. Know how to fucking dress."

"This is definitely my first party. Can't wait." Sophia opened the hanging mirror to check her makeup.

Clara shook her head. "Eighth-grade parties aren't that amazing tbh. My cousin's taken me to a few high school parties. Those are way the fuck better. I can't wait till we're going to those together." She hugged Sophia and drove off down the street. "This is still gonna be hella fun."

"What time is it?" Sophia reached down at her boot to adjust how her foot fit inside.

"Like ten-twenty-ish," Clara replied. "Party started at like nine forty-five, so we gonna arrive at like the perfect time."

"Lit," Sophia said, coming out muffled from speaking downward.

Soon the two pulled up at a massive mansion. The three-story house seemed gigantic, even for Sophia. Thirteen cars, maybe more, were parked outside and in the driveway. Electronic music was blasting, and neon lights shining through the windows made Sophia anxious to get inside. Her mouth dropped into a smile, and she whipped her head back at Clara. Clara jerked back and forth with teeth smiling.

Sophia walked into the hotel-sized house and was immediately met with hugs from girlfriends and waddups from multiple guys. Sophia had always wanted to go to a massive house party like she'd heard about from all her friends. For the longest time, she thought they were overrated until she showed up at the one she was at.

Apparently the kid who was throwing it had gotten his older sister to buy alcohol and pot for the party.

She had a huge childish grin across her face as she followed her friends around the house. There was a girl doing a handstand with a funnel filled with beer leading into her mouth. Some kids were doing flips into the swimming pool, and others had their arms around each other, letting loose on the couches beneath them.

"Wanna beer?" a boy asked Sophia.

"Don't drink." Sophia smiled.

"You will tonight." He laughed, handing her the bottle.

She laughed with him and shrugged, pouring the beer down her throat. She exhaled hard after chugging the beer in under ten seconds. The boy stood in front of her, awestruck.

"Easy," she said, slamming the bottle down.

The boy smiled. "That's what I like to see! Another one?"

"Fuck it." Sophia nodded, grabbed one for each of them, and ripped the caps off.

"Hey, lemme time you on this one," the boy said, pulling out his phone. He scrolled through the apps and opened the stopwatch. "All right, ready … go!"

Sophia started chugging as her friends came around the corner to the bar. They cheered her on as she finished the last chug and slammed the beer bottle down on the countertop.

"Seven seconds!" the boy yelled. "No fuckin' way. Hey yo uh—"

"It's Sophia!" Sophia shouted over the music into his ear.

"Grant!" he shouted back. "Here, take it."

Sophia grabbed the phone and reset the stopwatch. "Go!" she yelled.

Grant turned the bottle upside down and leaned back. "How'd I do?" Grant smirked.

Sophia stared at the timer in disbelief. "How even? 4.68 seconds!"

"It's a secret!" Grant chattered. "Shots?"

"Let's do it." Sophia wanted to make the most of her night and jogged over to the liquor cabinet. "Vodka or whiskey?"

Grant pulled out two shot glasses from one of the shelves. "Vodka. Smirnoff!"

Sophia ran back with a bottle of Smirnoff already half empty. She poured both glasses to the brim. Grant looked at her and then at the glasses and laughed quietly.

"Full thing, huh?" he asked.

"Think a small girl can't handle it?" Sophia challenged.

"Naw, just like lightweights can't," Grant commented on Sophia's size.

Sophia wanted to prove him wrong and placed the glass on a table. She put her arms behind her back and smirked at Grant. She had seen people drink shots with only their mouths on Snapchat from other parties and figured it couldn't be that hard. She leaned down and cupped her mouth of the shot glass.

Sophia gripped it with her lips, leaned back, and swallowed the fiery liquid. She snapped in Grant's face proudly, "Satisfied?"

"Not bad," Grant noted and opened up his throat for the vodka. Sophia stood astonished at his skill.

"Wanna know the trick?" Grant asked and pulled her over.

She laughed hysterically and nodded. Her vision lagged slightly behind her nods, and she started feeling a buzz.

"Had surgery on my throat when I was in the womb because the cord thing wrapped around my neck. They kinda fucked up a bit, so the muscle that would be my gag reflex is cut short, and now I don't need to swallow if I don't want to," Grant explained.

Sophia gagged exaggeratedly in disgust. "That's nasty." Sophia laughed.

"It's not that hard to do even if you have the muscle at the normal length. Just gotta concentrate on something really hard. You can tell because that muscle won't tense up."

"How do you concentrate like that?" Sophia asked.

"Like this." Grant finished and leaned in and kissed her.

Sophia wasn't prepared for a kiss and initially pulled away. "What are you doing?"

Grant looked around the room scratching his neck. "Uhm, I was kissing you."

Sophia hadn't kissed someone since sixth grade, and she wasn't completely confident in her abilities. But she liked the feeling of Grant sucking on her lip, and she craved it now that they'd stopped. Grant started sauntering away from the painfully uncomfortable situation.

"Sorry." Grant put his hand up and turned around to go outside to the pool.

Sophia didn't want him to go and strutted up to him, stumbling once. She tapped his shoulder, and as he was turning back around, she pulled his head toward her and his lips onto hers. Grant clutched the back of her head and pulled her hair. Sophia put her arms around Grant and scratched his neck. She felt the muscles in the back of his throat relax. They stopped and pulled away from each other.

"Worked right?" Grant grinned after pulling away. "I concentrated hard enough on you."

"Yeah, you did." Sophia looked up at Grant.

"Maybe I can show you again somewhere else?" Grant said, darting his eyes between Sophia and the upstairs bedrooms.

"Mmm-hmm. But I want you to teach me better this time." Sophia gave a mischievous grin and gripped Grant's hand, and he led her into a bedroom upstairs.

Sophia missed a step on the stairs, and Grant turned back. She waved him off, but her vision lagged heavily as she stared down the hallway.

"Take a vid!" someone downstairs yelled as Sophia came stumbling out of the room Grant had pulled into.

Her bra was barely hanging onto her chest, and she wildly swung her leather jacket, now covered in vomit, over her shoulder. The button on Sophia's pants was undone, and she nearly fell down the stairs before Grant caught her. He had no shirt on, and his jeans had blotches of vomit smeared into them.

A bright light of a phone camera flashed through the crowd of kids watching Grant help the obviously plastered Sophia down the stairs. She came to a rest at the bottom of the stairs. Grant pulled her jacket off her shoulder and held it out in front of the two teens. The rest of the kids at the party, including Clara, were bent over laughing and pointing at Sophia.

Sophia leaned forward and squinted. It was indeed Clara cracking up over Sophia's drunkenness. Sophia wanted to yell at her but couldn't get the right words out, and Clara started moving through the crowd. Sophia lost sight of her.

"Yo please send that to me!" a random boy yelled at the multiple boys and girls filming the incident.

"Wheresh Claraaaaa," Sophia sputtered out with her head cocked to one side and her eyes moving rapidly.

Grant turned to her. "Shut the fuck up. Talking will make this worse for you."

"Nooooo, I wanja zee Claraaaaa," Sophia mumbled through saliva drooling out of her mouth.

Grant rubbed Sophia's shoulder and spun back toward the crowd. "Anyone named Clara here?"

Sophia saw a hand wave and then Grant point toward the hand. "You know Sophia?"

Sophia heard Clara's voice. Clara lied, "Not that well. Wish I did so I could've given her a better outfit to wear."

The crowd erupted in a series of laughs. Sophia couldn't believe her friend had abandoned her. Everyone knew Sophia hung out with Clara, but no one knew that they were practically best friends. Sophia made a mental note that Clara now was a former best friend.

"Good one." Grant rolled his eyes and continued to shield Sophia from the blinding lights of the cameras.

"Graaaaant. Grant. Grant!" Sophia shouted. She started

laughing. Too many thoughts were flooding her mind at once, and her mood switched from sadness to hilarity in milliseconds.

"I said *shut up*," Grant said, backing over to her. "What do you want?"

"Your penis is teeny weeny," she whispered, now laughing to herself. In her inebriated state, she thought she might be able to redeem herself by making a joke about Grant.

Grant couldn't make out her statement and leaned closer to her mouth.

"I saaaaid …" Sophia hiccupped and shouted, "Your peeenis is a teenzy one!"

Grant blushed, and the whole party roared. Grant dropped the leather jacket back onto Sophia and got up.

"Get out." Grant gritted his teeth, pulling Sophia up and walking her to the door.

Sophia's arms reached out, aimlessly looking for something to grab onto as the room whirled around her.

"Guyssss?" Sophia pleaded between sloshes of drool. "Grant, I was keeeeeding."

"Get the fuck out!" Grant bellowed.

Sophia looked back at the kids, and her mood switched back to sadness. Everyone had turned on her. She went from the cool girl who could chug beers faster than a guy to the drunk hoe.

"Just leave. Don't embarrass yourself anymore." Clara chuckled at Sophia walking out of the crowd.

"Fuck you, Clara," Grant said while ushering Sophia out.

"What?" Clara asked.

"Fuck you! You're a shitty friend," Grant yelled, opening the door.

Someone shut the music shut off, and the crowd went quiet. Sophia looked at Clara, and Clara carefully walked back into the crowd.

"You should go." Grant looked down at Sophia and looked away.

Sophia stumbled onto the pavement outside, and the door

slammed shut behind her. Sophia was staggering down the street toward her house, a mile away. She had thrown up six more times, and her jacket was soaked. Her fumbling hands had managed to pull her bra back on fully and were working to brush the vomit off her jacket.

The sound of sirens in the distant signaled to the slowly sobering up Sophia that it was time to hide under some low-hanging pine trees for a bit. Her jacket hung off some of the branches of the trees from her neighbor's house, and she crouched behind it. She peeked out into the darkness from underneath the trees as headlights of police cars came shooting down the street, presumably to Grant's house. Sophia choked back her tears and began blubbering. Soon she lay down on the damp ground underneath the tree and started to weep heavily.

The morning dew soaked into Sophia's hair, and she jerked herself awake. It was still dark out, and she was freezing. Sophia spat out the grass, which had made its way into her mouth as she dozed on the front lawn of someone's house and pulled out her phone: 6:30 a.m. She gasped and instantly stood up, forgetting where she decided to sleep. Branches scratched her head and ripped out some of her hair.

"Shit," Sophia said, holding her head.

She felt her head with her fingertips. Blood pulsed underneath, partially due to the scrapes caused by the branches, but also due to an immense hangover taking her head by storm. She moaned and crawled out from underneath the tree. The leather jacket hanging on the front of the tree was now dripping off the remnants of her vomit. She grabbed it and shook it off as she made her way down the street.

Sophia began to run, and once she reached her house, she caught her breath. Sophia collected herself and opened the door as quietly as possible. The door clicked.

"Thank God," Sophia said to herself and leaned against the door.

"Thank God for what?" her father said from across the room.

Sophia spun around and saw him lying on one of the couches in the living room. "Look, Dad," Sophia started.

"No, I get it," he said, standing up in his pajamas. "Think you're some jailed teen that *deserves* to get out for a night to go have fun. Think that you have it so rough living in this house with anything you could possibly want, but you gotta get out and live because that's what angsty teens do."

Sophia adjusted her vomit-covered jacket on her shoulders. She watched her father squint at the jacket and then widen his eyes. She could see his cheeks tense up.

"Come over here," he demanded. "Now."

Sophia shuffled over, too scared of her father's wrath to cry.

"Breathe," he said, crouching next to her.

She exhaled hard into his face. Mr. Milverton nodded and began to shake with anger.

"You know when I had my first drink … It was legal!" he shouted. "I waited for everything until it was legal."

"Dad, it's been a seriously long night, and I don't mean to be disrespectful, but right now none of what you're saying really matters to me."

"That so?" Mr. Milverton leaned into her face and back out again. He stuttered with rage, "So so so so what? You think what you did was justified because you had a long night." He used his hands to gesticulate air quotations.

"Dad, I …" Sophia paused, choking back the sob that instinctively rose in her throat. "Every single one of my friends at the party I went to laughed at me."

"That's tough, wow," Mr. Milverton said, unimpressed. "Yeah, what you went through tonight sounds really hard. You have any idea the kind of shit I went through as a kid. When I was short, they used to—"

Sophia continued to stare at the marble floor of the entryway to their house. She started to cry hard. She was ashamed of herself. All she wanted was to go out, have a good time, maybe get a little tipsy, and come back. Sophia hated the way she looked, hair disheveled, clothes falling off, her bra hanging on for dear life, and vomit on her clothes. She didn't want to look in a mirror for the rest of the week, let alone look at her father. She had always respected how restrained he was. The man rarely, if ever, swore around her, and this encounter was the first time he'd raised his voice over a yell at her in years.

"Grow up!" Mr. Milverton bellowed. "Oh, your friends laughed at you? That sounds *really* hard. So tell me: is there more? Hmm? Is there? Or is that it?"

Sophia couldn't take his yelling. She wasn't used to it, but at the same time, she understood. She had disappointed him in more ways than one. Her father always made a point of how he never snuck out, never touched alcohol until he was twenty-one, and never did anything sexual with someone past kissing until he was eighteen. And she did all of those in one night.

Regardless his carelessness got to her, and she couldn't take it. She didn't expect her father to this angry, and she snapped. "I had sex with a guy, Grant, and I threw up during the middle of it!" Sophia screamed. "Happy?"

Mr. Milverton closed his eyes and turned his back to her, rubbing his hands over his face.

"Yeah." Sophia wept. "I came downstairs, and everyone was recording. I was wasted, but I knew what was happening somehow. They kicked me out, even Clara. So yeah, it was fucking tough."

Mr. Milverton turned back around and let out a calming sigh. "Remember how we said you'd get your permit at the end of December? Make that the end of the December of freshman year. No phone either for the next three months. And, uh, if I ever see this Grant kid around the house, you're paying for your own college. Got it?"

"You even care about me? Your only daughter?" Sophia cried. "I tell you all this, and you punish me? I just lost all my friends, my dignity, and my reputation. Don't you care?" She thought this would make him see her plight, to help him see where she was coming from.

"Your life, your choice," Mr. Milverton said, walking back over to the couch.

Sophia watched, astonished, as he turned on reruns of Sunday night football on the flat-screen TV. She held back a scream and ran into her room.

Sophia had hit what she thought was rock bottom. Her friends left her, her first time having sex was ruined, the perfect night ended in shambles, and her asshole, verbally abusive, father didn't love her anymore. She wanted him to hit rock bottom, so she went into her closet and grabbed a belt. She couldn't see any other way for him to love her again, and she knew that he would be destroyed for the rest of his life if he found her hanging from the wall the next morning. She wanted that. There was nowhere else to go; her life had crumbled around her just because she wanted to have a good time.

Sophia wrapped the belt around her neck, tightening it to the maximum length she could. Sophia placed the open hole of the belt on the end of a coat rack nailed into the wall. Sophia struggled to stand up, wanting so desperately to kneel and leave. She pondered on the thought as her throat began to close. She knelt and hung momentarily. Sophia could hear the blood shooting through her face, and her throat began heating up. She began sweating as she struggled to breathe.

Would it be worth it? *Hitting rock bottom means there's nowhere to go but up, right?* She started choking on air, and she thought about graduating high school, turning twenty-one, graduating college, falling in love, finding a career, getting married on the beach, playing with her kids at a park, and watching the sunset with her family and grandkids. Her vision started going black, and she stood up again.

Sophia took the belt off and fell onto the ground of her bedroom trembling. She coughed so hard that she dry-heaved and shook with fear over what she had nearly done. Sophia lay on the floor quivering, and after catching her breath, she was finally able to cry for everything.

EMMA

A text from Shaun came in. "Hey, Em. Sophia and her family just came over for dinner, and they just left. I guess she wanted me to tell u that her dick-ness toward u ain't personal."

Emma read Shaun's text to herself. "Oh, aight cool. If you see her before I do at school, just tell her it's all good. Hey btw Ted's gonna be working late hrs this wk at his VERY successful bar lol. If you wanna maybe see a movie sometime tomorrow, I will be free from the kraken for two days, until he comes home at normal hrs."

Emma patiently awaited Shaun's response. Three dots appeared on Emma's screen. She tapped her foot waiting for his instant response. Eventually the three dots disappeared, and she sighed. Placing her phone down on the kitchen countertop, she went to grab a glass of water. As soon as she walked away, her phone buzzed, and she sprinted back over to it.

"Sure. New *Fast and Furious* movie?"

"Yeah, down. 6PM?" Emma texted back in a flurry.

"Ya. See u then. <3."

Emma smiled at it and hesitated to respond with a line of emojis but decided against it, deeming the thought immature and pointless. She put the phone in her pocket and went to grab a glass of water. She filled it up with tap water, the only option in her house. Up until the sixth grade, when her parents divorced, she was used to walking on hardwood floors with expensive furniture and a backyard twenty-five-yard-long swimming pool. Filling a glass of water with the faucet was virtually nonexistent at that time because her fridge had a dispenser on the outside of it for convenience.

Emma took a gulp of the glass of water and ahhed in satisfaction from the cold water. She nearly went upstairs to go to sleep when she looked through the kitchen window and noticed a black Bentley parked outside her apartment. The lights of the car cut through the foggy night air, and the windows were blacked out. Emma heard a door close and saw someone step out of the car.

"Hey, Mom!" Emma called through the apartment. "You expecting anyone besides Ted tonight?"

"No, why?" Mrs. Walsh shouted back from her bedroom.

"Uh, never mind," Emma replied.

Emma grabbed a knife, placed it through her belt, and sat on a bar stool near the kitchen counter. She couldn't be too careful. Since Ted wasn't there to scare off any robbers or tweakers and she couldn't imagine her mother being strong enough to protect her, Emma got prepared. Emma waited, glancing at the clock in the kitchen every five seconds or so.

Confused by the length of time it was taking for the person to reach her door, she went back to the kitchen window. The person had stopped at the edge of the pathway to her apartment. She squinted and could see it was an average-sized man with a low-hanging trench coat. *Who was it?* Maybe it was Ted, but this man was too stocky. She could see him pacing back and forth, and she put the knife back into the rack.

Eventually the man straightened out his shirt and began his walk to the house. Emma ducked down and made her way to bar stool she was sitting on. She waited and soon heard a slow, lackadaisical gait on the steps to the apartment. There was a knock on the door. Emma hesitated for a moment and then strode over to the door. She grabbed the handle and pulled.

Emma stared blankly at the man in front of her. He had a clean-shaven face. He was heavily built and wearing a business suit. The long trench coat was nearly hitting the ground as it swayed in the cool night breeze.

"Are you like a Mormon or something? Because my mom isn't that religious."

The man chuckled. "No, I am not a Mormon. I would look about thirty years younger and be riding a bike as my means of transportation. It's Dad."

"Excuse me," Emma asked. She didn't process what he'd said and just stared at him. "Dad?" Her father jutted his head out at her. "Nicholas?"

Emma didn't believe him and gazed at his attire: trench coat with a nice suit underneath. His muscularity was too high, but his voice was uncanny, deep and intimidating yet soft. It took her a moment to recognize him, but he was indeed her birth father.

"What are you saying? What!" Emma slammed the door in her father's face.

She never thought she'd see him again. He came back out of nowhere and just expected her to be happy to see him or something. Ted would be home soon and see him, and the heat between both men would be another thing Emma would have to worry about. Ted's territory would be encroached on by her father. He couldn't have come at a worse time, as Ted was getting more and more hostile. It had been five years already. He should've just made it permanent.

"Mom! Dad's at the door!" Emma fumed.

"Let him in then. Never heard you call Ted Dad, but glad you're making progress," Mrs. Walsh shouted back.

"No, like Dad Dad, Mom! Like Nicholas Legra is at the door!" Emma screamed.

"What?" Mrs. Walsh came shuffling out. She quickened her pace to the door and yanked it open.

Nicholas was walking down the stairs when the door opened. He whirled around to see his ex-wife. "Cynthia." He grinned slightly.

He glanced up and down at her as Emma came into the doorway. "You both … you both look great."

Mrs. Walsh clenched her jaws. "Nic, why'd you think today would be such a good time?"

Nicholas started back up the steps. "Now is as good a time as any, I suppose."

"Or as bad a time," Emma interjected.

If he thought he were going to just waltz back into her life, Nicholas was wrong. Emma didn't believe he thought he was coming back just because she thought that he wanted forgiveness for not being around when Christina died. Maybe he deserved it, but Emma wanted to see him beg for it. *If he hadn't left in the first place, Christina might not have … No, she wouldn't have died.* Emma knew it, and she was hoping her mom recognized it too.

"That's true as well." Nicholas nodded. "I know how hard it's been for you—"

"No, you don't." Emma raised her voice. "You don't know anything. You don't care. You just want us to say, 'Oh, it's all right. You weren't here when Christina …' It's not all right."

Nicholas exhaled hard. "Em, please."

"Don't fucking Em me." She had never sworn at her father face-to-face, and God, it felt good.

Emma stared at him, unblinking from her blinding rage. Her lip shook, not out of sadness but out of anger. She had more to say but was so filled with hate that she couldn't spit it out. Nicholas didn't deserve anything. He didn't deserve forgiveness. He didn't deserve a soldier's welcoming.

Yet when she realized who was standing on the porch, a part of Emma was relieved. A very small part, granted, but she thought that perhaps if her father were around, Ted would lighten up. He always hated Nicholas.

"Emma." Nicholas rubbed his scruffy face. "I know. I missed out on our daughter's whole high school career, and now she's not here for me to come back to."

"There ... was ... a ... funeral," Emma said with each word getting harder to push out of her mouth.

"I know," Nicholas said, his voice getting lighter.

If Emma even heard him whimper, she was booking it upstairs. She wouldn't hear his fake emotion.

Nicholas squeezed his mouth, dropped his hand, and raised his shoulders up, tensing them. "But after what I'd done to this family, I couldn't go with peace in mind. I didn't want it to be an event that I showed up. You had the right to celebrate her life in peace, and I didn't want to cause any more distress. I didn't want anyone to feel any more pain because of me."

Emma was gritting her teeth and then relaxed her jaw. As much as she hated to think it, Nicholas seemed sincere. She made the tiniest adjustment of her mouth so that one side moved up a single millimeter into a nearly microscopic smile. It would not have been noticeable to anyone if he or she had even blinked.

"I had to come back though, especially after Christina. I can't miss out on the life of my other daughter," Nicholas explained.

Cynthia had barely moved since Emma started talking. Her eyes were half-shut, and her arms were at her side. Emma could almost smell her carelessness.

Nicholas stood in the doorway and untensed his shoulders. "If you want to contact me, I'm staying ... I'm staying at the Barkley Lodges. Just ask for Nicholas."

"If I want—and that is a big if—if I ever want to see you, I'll know where to find you." Cynthia grunted.

"Great. Well, great." Nicholas nodded.

There was the sound of a truck coming down the street with no muffler. Nicholas turned to see Ted pulling up on the other side of the street in his pickup truck.

"Oh, I should be going."

"You should." Cynthia rolled her eyes.

Emma pressed her hands over her mouth, anticipating the storm about to erupt between Nicholas and Ted, mumbling to herself, "Ohhh my God."

Ted stepped out of his truck, heavy metal blasting. He walked around to the other side of Nicholas's black Bentley and saw Nicholas walking to the car. Ted smirked at him and released a puff of smoke from his mouth.

Ted held his cigarette down by his side. "Are you a friend of Cynthia's or something?" He sneered.

Emma saw that Ted didn't recognize Nicholas either. He really did bulk up during his time away. Emma started to breathe out, hoping they would just pass each other and Nicholas would leave.

"We've met before, Theodore." Nicholas sighed and stretched his hand out to Ted's. "Nicholas Legra?"

Ted took out the cigarette. Emma saw his smile of confusion and saw his mouth drop a tad and then close. She knew Ted had recognized him. Ted glanced down at Nicholas's hand and up at Nicholas.

"You." Ted grimaced.

"Me?" Nicholas stood still, holding his hand in the air between him and Ted.

There was a pause, and then a wad of spit shot from Ted's mouth into Nicholas's palm. Nicholas stared down at his palm and then at Ted, who looked about a quarter of the bulk of Nicholas. He winced and scrunched his mouth up at the saliva hanging from his hand. He shrugged and wiped his hand off on Ted's gray bomber jacket.

"Watch it." Nicholas snarled and tapped Ted's cheek lightly before stepping into the Bentley.

Ted was disarmed. He looked up and saw Emma and her mother standing in awe of the event that had just taken place. It was one of the first times Emma had seen Ted look weak in front of someone else. So in a quick effort to save face, Ted turned to the Bentley and crouched down next to the window. He tapped the glass, and Nicholas rolled it down for Ted to speak to him.

"You better leave right now. You have no right being here. I'm taking care of this family better than you ever could have. Get the hell outta here. I own this place."

"Sure." Nicholas started the car.

Emma saw Ted reach behind his back and lift his bomber jacket. She saw the butt of a knife poking up out of Ted's jeans. She hated Nicholas but despised Ted far more. She nodded up at Nicholas, and he looked at her. Emma shook her head at Ted's back. Emma wasn't a psychopath. She didn't want to see Nicholas hurt by Ted. She didn't want anyone to be hurt by Ted.

Nicholas shifted his gaze to Ted's arm. "I wouldn't." Nicholas rolled up the window.

Ted stepped back from the window, dropping his shirt down and stood watching the street as the Bentley drove away. He took a puff from his cigarette and blew it out into the now-stale night air.

"All right, ladies. Back inside!" Ted shouted without turning to face Mrs. Walsh and Emma.

Cynthia walked back inside, while Emma stayed outside for a moment watching Ted. Her nose ran in the cold air, and she wiped it. Ted exhaled the smoke through his nose and tossed the cigarette on the ground. He used his shoe to stamp out the last ember from the front of the cigarette.

He frowned. "Tells me to watch it."

She wanted badly to hate her father for coming back without warning, but after seeing him stand up to Ted fearlessly, she thought that having him back might not be so horrible. She hadn't had anyone to protect her from Ted in years, and Christina was the only barrier between the two. Nicholas could be the new barrier and maybe even overpower Ted.

The next night Emma and Shaun entered the movie theater to see the latest in action-porn, the new *Fast and Furious* movie. The theater was packed to the brim with large groups of teens and adults shuffling around through food and drink lines. Shaun grabbed two hot dogs for himself and a plate of nachos for Emma. Emma squeezed between mountains of whining kids and their delusional inattentive parents, who were glued to their cell phones, to find a bag of popcorn and drinks. After her near marathon-level trek, she caught up with Shaun and placed their combined items for the cashier to scan.

"And that will be $39.83, sir." The cashier looked down from the stand at Shaun.

"This is a movie theater. Forty bucks? For real, dude?" Shaun questioned the cashier.

The cashier glared at him and air-quoted Shaun. "Yes, I am *for real*. Kid, there's a line forming. You wanna just pay?"

Shaun squinted at the cashier and at his wallet. "Shit." He turned to Emma. "I don't wanna be a douche, but I literally don't have—"

Emma chuckled. "It's okay. I'll just cover the whole thing. I think I owe for the other seventy times you've paid for me."

"Really?" Shaun made a sigh of relief.

Emma nodded. She felt bad always being paid for and was happy she was finally given a chance to cover Shaun.

"Thanks, babe." He kissed Emma on the cheek. He grabbed all the food, piling it high between his arms and chest. "How much butter on the popcorn?"

"Enough so at the end of the movie I feel like someone entering *The Biggest Loser* competition!" Emma shouted to Shaun over the roar of customers.

He laughed and walked to the condiment station.

"Enjoy your movie," the cashier said to Emma, handing her the change.

She smiled politely. "Thanks."

Emma jogged over to Shaun and grabbed her drink from under his left arm. She waited patiently as he filled the bag of popcorn with butter. He turned around and smiled at her. She reciprocated. He handed Emma the bag of popcorn and went to add condiments to his hot dogs. The night was going so well, but Emma could not enjoy it fully as she was burdened with the thought of telling Shaun about the return of her father. She didn't want him to overworry about her.

Being his first girlfriend, Emma presumed all Shaun did was worry about her. She disliked putting unnecessary stress on people, especially Shaun. Emma saw how concerned he was with how he looked the night they hooked up. She saw himself checking his body in the mirror. Emma saw his interactions with his parents. She figured she would just wait for the right moment to tell him about Nicholas's return.

Emma danced around the subject on their Uber ride to the theater. She talked about how someone showed up unexpected the previous night and about how she wasn't sure what to think of it. Shaun had pressed into the identity of the person, but eventually let it go.

"All right, donzo. Shall we?" Shaun extended his hand with the corniness of the lead actor of a high school drama.

"We shall." Emma played along and curtsied.

They sat down at their assigned seats in the theater. Shaun slurped his Coca-Cola during the trailers before the movie began. A trailer for a home invasion thriller came on the screen reminding Shaun of the topic Emma discussed with him in the car ride. He nudged Emma's elbow.

"What?" she whispered. The trailer depicting an uninvited guest had reminded her of her father as well.

"Trailer reminds me that you never told me who came to your house last night. Who was it?"

"Not important. I'll tell you later," Emma lied.

"You're sure? Made a pretty big deal about it in front of our poor driver," Shaun joked.

Emma nervously laughed, "Nah, seriously. I'll tell you in ... how long is this movie?"

"Like *King Kong* length, I think," Shaun whispered as he got shushed by the person next to him. He turned to the random moviegoer. "Chill, movie's not even started yet."

"Just be quiet!" the stranger whisper-yelled.

Shaun rolled his eyes and turned back to Emma. "With this dude next to me, these three hours gonna feel like eight." Shaun shook his head.

Emma laughed. "I mean the Rock is really hot though. Makes up for the cheesy ass lines squeezed in through the movie."

"Not as hot as me though, right?" Shaun grinned.

Emma snickered. "You're hot, but let's be real. The Rock was Hercules. He's literally a god."

Shaun frowned through a smile. "Oh yeah. Yeah true."

Emma saw his insecurity when he turned away from her. She wasn't trying to insult him. "You know you're still the hottest guy I know. But you can't compete with a fifty-year-old ex-wrestler."

"Fair enough." Shaun chuckled a little too loudly.

"Kid, shut the hell up!" the moviegoer next to him whisper-yelled again.

Shaun whirled around. "It's just the trailers. Would you relax!"

The moviegoer let out a long sigh of contempt.

Shaun leaned in to Emma. "I swear the only place you meet ruder people is at the post office, the DMV, or the passport place."

Emma stifled her laugh with her hands over her mouth, as she was getting dirty looks from the people next to her as well. "Or the ride operators at theme parks."

"So true," Shaun said aloud, which was the final straw for the man next to him.

The man tapped Shaun on the shoulder. Shaun bowed his head annoyed and turned around. "What?" Shaun asked.

"I am going to report you for disrupting the silence inside this theater and—" The man was cut off by a rush of audio coming from the speakers.

"Hey, look at that. Movie's starting." Shaun smirked and turned to face the screen.

The moviegoer turned away from Shaun and conceded as the white text of the credits zoomed around the sides of the movie screen. Emma leaned back in her seat, the thought of her father's return still nagging at the back of her mind.

"I saw you crying when Paul Walker drove away, you know?" Emma laughed.

"It was sad, okay?" Shaun chuckled, shaking his head.

The two teens walked down the aisle out of the theater and threw their garbage out in the allotted bins. Emma wrapped her arm around Shaun's soft, warm side, and he held her shoulder as they walked. She could feel his ab muscles tense as he laughed. It was such a calming way to meander around.

"C'mon though. That got you?" Emma smirked. "*Titanic* was way sadder than that."

"But did Kate Winslet die in real life? No! This was technically Paul Walker's last movie. It's sad, fam."

"Fam?" asked Emma.

"Babe?" Shaun inquired.

"Better. Anyways I'll give you a point on your argument for Paul Walker's last movie." Emma defended herself. "But I bawled at *Titanic*."

"Fair, but the whole Jack-Rose-Jack-I-love-you-thing got old." Shaun yawned, and they walked outside of the butter-reeking theater into fresh air. "Uber?"

"We could walk fifteen miles if you want?" Emma joked.

"I'll call an Uber." Shaun smiled and looked for the nearest ride on the app. "Damn, there's a dude just in the parking lot."

Shaun and Emma ran to where the Uber driver was waiting and knocked on the glass. The car doors unlocked, and Shaun and Emma hopped into the back seat of the Mercedes. The Uber driver turned back to face the teens. He had a pair of glasses on and donned a plaid shirt covering a gray wife beater. His jeans were covered in dirt, and a construction belt lay next to him in the passenger seat.

"Where y'all headed?" he asked.

"Uh, your place, right? Ted won't be home till like three, right?" Shaun looked at Emma.

"Hmm? Oh yeah, sure. Yeah, my place. You just gotta be outta there soon," Emma answered, staring out the window.

Shaun nodded. "South side. The Deepcrest apartments in San Mateo?"

"I assumed San Mateo since we are in San Mateo right now. The Deepcrest though? That's my area." The Uber driver nodded and stepped on the gas pedal, propelling the car down the theater's exit. "Name's Paul."

"Seriously? Just saw a movie with a Paul in it," Shaun said.

"Oh yeah?" Paul asked. "*Furious Seven*?"

"Yup," Shaun replied.

Paul nodded in agreement. "Mad good flick. I give it eight out of ten. Last bit was so sad."

"Ha!" Shaun grinned at Emma. "Someone agrees."

"Fine," Emma said exasperated, her mind elsewhere. She was back to thinking how to tell Shaun about Nicholas.

Paul's smile contorted as he held in a snicker. "Looks like you're in the doghouse, kid."

"Em, you good?" Shaun asked.

She nodded, looking outside at the highway as the car merged into the long line of vehicles approaching a sharp curve. Shaun playfully fell into her. She didn't have the patience to be cute and funny while she was so stressed about Shaun worrying. Still she could see that the longer she held out from telling Shaun, the more concerned he became.

"What's up? The dude at your house?" Shaun implored.

Paul interjected, "Kid, quit while you're ahead."

"Paul, you mind?" Shaun said toward the driver's seat and then back at Emma. "Babe, what's good? What's on your mind?"

Emma slowly turned to face Shaun, her eyes darting across his face. *Stop asking.* She wanted to just speak without him constantly asking. She shook her head.

"Nicholas Legra, you know my real dad? He's back in town."

Shaun's mouth dropped to the depth of the Grand Canyon. Paul whipped his head around at Emma, his eyebrows raised into mountains, and his lips pursed. He cocked his head to the left and began to awkwardly watch the conversation through the rearview mirror.

"What do you mean he's back?" Shaun questioned.

"I mean he's back, like back for good." She guessed it was time to spill everything. "Well, I don't know about for good. He just wants to be a dad again. Like he doesn't want me growing up without a father anymore."

"Well, I mean that's good, right?" Shaun asked in an empathetic attempt.

Emma snorted and twiddled her thumbs. "Good's a strong word."

Shaun shut his mouth. He leaned back in his seat and looked up in the rearview mirror at Paul's eyes. Shaun shook his head quickly at Paul. Paul shrugged.

"What do I say?" Shaun whispered into the front seat.

Paul grinned, jokingly whispering, "Whatever's in your heart."

Emma could hear them but was amused by Shaun's trying to help. Despite his clearly being worried, as she predicted, she was glad to see how much he cared. He was even willing to ask an Uber driver for help. Shaun rolled his eyes and flipped Paul off. Paul chuckled. Shaun leaned back in the seat, staring at the roof of the SUV. A pause filled the car like a cloud of fog.

"Nic came back, huh? I mean like … How does that make you feel though?" Shaun looked to his right at Emma.

Emma considered how Shaun would react to her venting to him; she considered how much she should lay onto him. But she knew Shaun was there to support her. He was the only person she knew who could support her and listen to her. He *was* a good listener.

Emma opened her mouth and sighed. Shaun leaned forward for her reply.

She moved her mouth around a couple of times and finally spilled out her train of thought. "I guess I don't know. A small part of me is happy to see him, but like I guess I'm just so fuckin' angry. Like you know? Like where was he during these past five years? Like remember the father-daughter dance in seventh grade? No other girl had to serve drinks. Where was he when my mom chose Ted of all people to marry as a second ... no, as a replacement husband? He said why he wasn't here for Christina's funeral, and his excuse made sense, but still, who misses his own daughter's funeral? Like agh!" Emma finished her rant. "Other moments like my eighth-grade graduation. First day of high school."

"First boyfriend?" Shaun added, his forehead moving down as he smiled sympathetically.

Emma smiled down at the floor. "I'm glad you're here." She held Shaun's hand and rubbed his fingers. "And like I don't even know what my dad likes or what he's even like as a person now. If he hasn't changed too much, he'd probably like you."

Shaun laughed. "I hope so."

Emma went on. "When he came back last night, he and Ted had an—" Emma used her fingers to air quote. "Encounter. But it wasn't bad, you know? Like it wasn't like a yelling match. Ted even seemed scared of Nic. Well, maybe not scared, but like intimidated. Know what I mean?" Emma looked at Shaun, and he nodded hard. "And although my dad's speech about wanting to be there for me seemed like horseshit, I don't know. I like to think it wasn't. I wanna have a normal family again."

"I don't really remember much about how your dad was before he left, but I definitely remember he wasn't a big bullshitter or a fan of it. I remember he yelled at one of the teachers for being a pathetic, lazy, spendthrift."

Emma grinned. "He wasn't a liar. That is true. Even when he left us, he was like, 'I'm sorry. It's just too much. I have to go. It's unhealthy otherwise.' We were struggling after the recession and shit. Except he was the one who handled all the money stuff, and he couldn't take the pressure. Asshole had no idea what dump I'd be living in after he left."

"But that's my point, Em. Like what if—what if maybe—I'm just saying, like maybe his spiel wasn't bullshit. Like why else would he come back? There'd be no other reason for him to drive all the way out here, buy a place, and visit you. He has to care a bit, doesn't he?"

Emma let go of Shaun's hands and leaned against the window squinting and pouting her mouth. "What the fuck? Why would you take his side?"

Shaun rolled his eyes and sighed. "Because I thought I was helping."

"Why'd you roll your eyes then?" Emma asked.

Shaun sighed again and put his hand up. "Just ... never mind. My bad. Sorry, I just thought like assuming he cared was a good thing. Forget about it."

"No." Emma shook her head and moved back up to Shaun. She admitted to herself that her dad was most likely being sincere. "You're right. Like he'd have no reason to come back if he didn't kind of care."

"Exactly." Shaun slapped her thigh in emphasis. Emma looked up him, confused. "I don't know what that was. That was such a dad move."

"Daddy?" Emma joked with puppy eyes and rubbed his thigh.

"Okay!" Paul waved his hand frantically. "Don't need to hear anymore. Actually it's a perfect time to cut that off because your chariot has just arrived at the Deepcrest apartments."

Shaun and Emma both laughed.

"Have a wonderful night, my young scholars," Paul said in a British accent. "In my land, we give those who serve us flawlessly a lump sum of paper currency."

Shaun cracked up and added a 30 percent tip on the Uber ride.

"The kingdom thanks you, sire, and you, m'lady," Paul continued the act.

Emma got out of the car with Shaun and closed the door behind her.

"Hi, Shaun," Mrs. Walsh said to him when her daughter and Shaun entered the apartment. Her extra-large shirt draped over her small body, and she pulled her pants up while walking over to Emma. "Emma?"

"Yeah," she said, leading Shaun over to the couch near the entrance of the apartment.

Mrs. Walsh whispered, "I know Ted is coming home later, so it's fine that Shaun's over now, but please have him gone early so we avoid another argument between the three of us."

"Mom, you don't have to whisper. He's not even here yet." Emma couldn't understand how her mother was so worried about Ted's reaction that she whispered when he wasn't around but acted like she was in a teenage romance when he was. A strange case of Stockholm syndrome, but with someone who supposedly loves her.

Emma stared off into the kitchen and realized she must've looked insane to her mother, and she snapped out of it.

"Oh right, well." Mrs. Walsh bent over in a sort of bow at Shaun.

Shaun nodded while turning on the TV. "Totally get it. I'll be outta here by twelve."

"Thanks, hun." Mrs. Walsh smiled politely. "How was the movie?"

"Great. Vin Diesel is such a good actor. Dude is crazy ripped for forty-seven too or however old that dude is," Shaun answered.

Emma nodded toward her mother's bedroom.

"Yes, yes. Don't be pushy, Em," her mother commented, interpreting the nod as a yell to leave. "Good seeing you, Shaun."

"You too, Mrs. Walsh." Shaun beamed, and he walked inside.

He pulled Emma down onto the couch with him. She fell across his legs and had to lean up to rest her head on his lap. Shaun glanced down at Emma's body, and she watched him.

"Caaaalm down." Emma laughed. "I'll be ready for something later. For now, *Teen Wolf*?"

Shaun rolled his eyes and sighed. "My guilty pleasure."

Emma pulled herself upright and grabbed the remote to find the TV show. She scrolled through the guide and then through the thirty-three saved episodes of the teen drama. Emma watched the remote icon surf the episodes. She also saw Shaun in the reflection of the window next to the TV, looking down at her. She could see him looking at her legs, her hands, her torso, and her face. She looked back at him, and they locked eyes.

Emma snickered. "That was some Romeo and Juliet-level romantic-ness."

"'Twas," Shaun said. "You know, you look really good right now. And I'm gonna use that as a horrible segue into how good I think it was to talk about, like what happened last night."

Emma cleared her throat, blocking out a sniffle. "Yes, it was. And that, Shaun, is the end of the discussion of me and my dad."

"Sorry, just wanted to say like it was … like I think we … never mind. Find the episode yet?"

Emma turned on the episode she chose, coincidentally titled "Muted." Shaun and Emma sat in silence as the TV show rolled through the intro and then the opening credits. Shaun looked over at Emma, and she felt his eyes on him. Whenever they watched a TV show together, they always ended up on top of each other, and Emma wanted for once to just watch the show. Then again Ted was coming home soon. *Fuck it.* Emma turned to Shaun and began furiously making out with him. Within five minutes, he was shirtless, and her pants and shirt were on the floor.

"We have like fifteen minutes before you leave, Shaun," Emma joked through a gasp.

Shaun lifted his mouth off her neck and looked away. "Damn."

"What?" Emma caught her breath. "The hickey isn't obvious, right?"

"Huh? Oh … no, I was saying like 'Damn, you think I can last fifteen minutes.'" Shaun looked back at her. He tap-kissed her and went back to kissing her neck and shoulder.

She slapped him playfully. "We are so not doing it right now."

"Why?" Shaun questioned.

"We don't have time. And I want it to be comfortable and not like where me and my mom sit to watch movies." Emma kissed his chest. "And especially because we don't have a condom."

"I don't know. My pull-out game could be fire," Shaun joked.

"Let's not test that theory." Emma chuckled and continued making her way down his chest and stomach.

Shaun scooted down and took off Emma's pants. "Then we'll just do the other kind of sex."

Emma felt Shaun's warm fingers slide her pants off, and he moved up toward her. Fifteen short, but to Emma seemingly long, minutes later, they were asleep on the couch, lying against each other's chests. And another thirty minutes later, Emma was awoken by the sound of a car door closing outside. Her eyes blinked open, and she checked the time on her cell phone, 12:54 p.m. *Shit*. She knew she should've set an alarm. They were so screwed. She leaned up and began shaking Shaun vigorously.

"Mmmm?" Shaun groaned, his face pressed against a pillow on the couch. "Hmm?"

"Ted's here," Emma whispered aggressively.

Shaun's eyes opened wide, and he fell off the couch with a thud.

"What? Where?" Shaun said, rolling on the ground looking for the brute of a stepfather.

Emma snuck over to the kitchen window. "Outside. He's pulling his sports coat and jeans out of the back seat. Get your clothes on right now."

"Shit, shit, shit," Shaun swore to himself, struggling to put his feet through the pant legs.

"Hurry the hell up!" Emma raised her voice slightly. "He's locking the truck."

"I'm trying," Shaun whispered back. His foot finally became unstuck as Emma rushed over and threw him his shirt.

"Here's your shirt," Shaun said through her top to her.

She shoved her body into the shirt and jumped quite literally into her jeans, carefully landing on the ground to make as little sound as possible. The sound of a mild gait coming up the steps came into hearing range. Shaun grabbed his shirt, slid it on, and placed the pillows back on the couch.

The lock on the door started turning, and Shaun and Emma fixed their disheveled hairlines. Emma turned the TV on again and played *Teen Wolf* from where they had left off.

"What do I say? What do I say?" Shaun whispered just as Ted was entering the house.

"Just roll with it," Emma whispered and stood up. She was just praying that Ted wasn't in full-Ted anger mode. She hoped he would just yell at Shaun once and go away. "Hey, Dad, this is Shaun. He's in my history class at school, and he is helping me study."

Ted stretched and was focused on placing his clothes on the coat hanger. However, once he turned to his right and saw Shaun give a quick head nod to him, his focus changed. Ted pushed Emma aside and strode up to Shaun, grabbing the remote from his side and turning off the MTV show.

"Why the hell are you in my house?" Ted implored.

Shaun stood up and smiled as a formality, and Ted moved in, staring into Shaun's pupils.

"Emma invited me to—" Shaun was cut off as Ted fumed.

"You mean *your daughter*, right? Not Emma." Ted glared at Shaun.

Ted's possessiveness embarrassed Emma. The only person she belonged to was Shaun, at the least the only person she liked belonging to, and maybe her mom if she were nice.

"Right, right, *your daughter* invited me to help with the world history test coming up … uh." Shaun looked at Emma to complete the lie.

Emma spat out a continuation of Shaun's response. "Tomorrow. The test coming up tomorrow."

Ted continued to stare into Shaun's eyes without turning to Emma. "Yeah? What's it on?"

"Oh, it's on the rise of totalit—" Again Shaun was cut off.

Ted rubbed his face, annoyed. He closed his eyes and shouted, "I didn't ask you, prick."

"Dad, it's on …" Emma started.

"Yeah," Ted added, attempting to call her bluff.

Emma saw Shaun nod at the calendar in the kitchen. Emma looked back, and it was a picture of Italy. She smacked her lips while clearing her throat. "It's on the rise of totalitarianism and fascism in Italy under Mosahlini."

Ted's eyes moved around the outline of Shaun's figure, and he snorted. Ted slowly turned around to face Emma, who gave a purposely cute smile. Ted shook his head. "It's Mussolini. Can't even pronounce it right. No wonder you have a fuckin' eighty-four."

"Like I said, Dad, Shaun's helping me with my grade," Emma said.

Ted nodded skeptically and turned back to face Shaun. "That true, kid? You helping my daughter with her grade?"

"Yes, Mr. Walsh," Shaun lied.

Ted's scowl turned into a smile, and he laughed for a moment and then shoved his body within inches of Shaun's face. Shaun didn't flinch, but tensed his muscles, anticipating a punch.

"Yes, sir. It's sir to you. Know what respect means?" Ted shook his head. He backed off momentarily and then made his way back to Shaun, "You know, Shaun. I didn't get an email today from your fat bitch teacher. God, what's the whale's name?"

"Mrs. Morton?" Shaun suggested.

Ted nodded sharply and tapped the center of Shaun's chest. "That's it, Mrs. Morton. But, uh, she didn't send me no email about a test. Any idea why? You're a smart kid. Maybe you have an idea why the parents wouldn't get an email on a test on a topic as important and controversial as fascism?"

Shaun shrugged. "Sometimes Mrs. Morton forgets to put it online, which is why you wouldn't receive the email."

Ted studied Shaun's face and exhaled his alcohol and nicotine-reeking breath upon him. "Maybe." Ted was nodding, accepting the lie.

Shaun let out a breath of relief as Ted pulled back for the second time. Shaun cracked a joke for good measure, playing along with Ted's personality. "Yeah, probably all the cholesterol getting to her head."

Ted audibly made a slight chuckle. "Emma, this is why you gotta stop drinking all those smoothies and shit when you go out. Don't wanna end up like Mrs. Bypass. Ain't that right, Shaun?"

Emma looked down at her figure, which did look a little overweight. She had stopped caring whenever she was shirtless with Shaun, but now that Ted mentioned it, maybe she could stand to lose a few. She wished she were was skinny as Sophia. Emma knew Shaun said she was beautiful, but he could've been being nice. She tried not to focus on it.

"Yeah." Shaun squeezed a laugh out. He clenched his fist, and Emma shook his head at him. She knew he realistically wasn't going to attack Ted, but she used the head shake as an insurance policy. "Don't wanna look like the before pictures on weightwatchers.com."

Ted chuckled again and nodded in acceptance of Shaun's dig.

"It worked," Emma mouthed at Shaun.

"Well, since it seems like everything is simply peachy. I'm gonna go to—" Ted stopped talking.

Emma squinted at Shaun, confused by the pause in Ted's speech. She looked up at Ted and saw him begin to shake, and she followed his gaze to the sock. A drop of sweat leaked down her brow, and her eyes widened. She mouthed the word *sock* to Shaun. He looked down and realized only his left sock was on. Shaun muttered a line of expletives to himself, and Emma's whole body became soaked in sweat.

Ted crouched down next to the sock and pulled it out from under the couch. Emma knew it was probably sweaty from when Shaun was on the couch with her.

"Normally seeing a sock here wouldn't bother me, Emma. You know? Like maybe Shaun just took off his shoes to relax on the couch and forgot to put this sock back on. Maybe, Shaun, you stepped in a puddle earlier today, and this never dried out." Ted began walking back over to Shaun. "But you were on the couch when I came in, there was no rain for the past three weeks, and clearly this wasn't under the couch on accident. Unless you know of socks that can magically squeeze between couches and the floor beneath them. Still I will be as understanding as possible." Ted made a sinister smile and folded his hands on his stomach. "Were you fucking my daughter tonight?"

"What?" Shaun asked.

Emma could see that he was surprised. His eyebrows raised, eyes wider than a whirlpool. Technically they hadn't had sex *sex*. She knew if she chimed in, Ted would know she was trying to cover. She kept her mouth shut.

Ted cocked his head to the left, acting confused. "You don't know what that means, fucking?"

"No, I know what it means," Shaun answered, and his voice cracked.

"You nervous?" Ted insinuated. "I mean it's a simple question. Yes or no answer. Did you fuck my daughter tonight?"

Shaun gave a quick and resounding, "No!"

Ted stepped back, grinning. "Wow, packed some fire in that word. Sounded almost like you were defending yourself, kid."

Ted strutted up to Shaun and pushed his greasy hair back over his fade. Emma could smell the beer, leaking from Ted's pores, from across the room.

"Put your mouth near my ear. I just want to be sure about what that was." Ted smirked.

Shaun's voice shook. "No." There was a pause. "No, sir, I did not

555555

fuck Emma's puss tonight." Shaun asserted himself. "Good enough?" He pulled back from Ted's ear and glared back confidently.

Ted chuckled. "Wow, you are something else, Shaun. You might just be really confident or just a damn idiot. But respect to you, most kids would be shitting themselves by now." Ted turned around and walked to the bedroom.

Shaun exhaled a long breath, and Emma's mouth dropped.

"But Shaun." Ted looked at him before turning the corner.

"Yes, sir?" Shaun asked.

"You should leave right fuckin' now. And if you come here again, just don't okay? I won't be so nice." Ted left the room.

"I'm gonna go." Shaun smiled at Emma.

Emma's mouth was still hanging wide open, and she struggled to get out a sentence. "Uh, yeah. Uh, okay. See you."

Shaun chuckled. "That last line I said was a stupid move."

"It was really hot though." Emma closed her mouth and simply stared in disbelief at Shaun. The only other person to stick up for Emma was Christina. So that would make Shaun more like a brother? *Ugh, disgusting.* Emma pushed the thought from her mind.

Shaun grinned. He looked at his feet and then at the sock that Ted had left on the ground. He grabbed the sock and flashed a peace sign. The door shut, and Shaun left the apartment. Emma slowly shuffled over to the couch and flopped down across it. She could tell that things were slowly getting better. Not only had her father stood up to Ted, but the only boy out of eight that had met Ted, the only boy she cared about, and the only boy she loved, did not back down against him.

She knew that if some boy, as seemingly unimpressive and unintimidating as Shaun, could hold his ground, she knew she could give it a shot. He was far more muscular and could at least last a couple of minutes in a throwdown with Ted. Shaun wasn't even that assertive of a kid. Emma thought she could be strong after seeing Shaun do it nearly effortlessly.

JACKSON

Jackson lay awake in his bedroom at ten at night. He had just woken up sweating. Not the scared sweat. The anxiety-type sweat. He rolled off the edge and took off everything he wore except for his boxers. Jackson flexed briefly in the mirror. He leaned off the bed, placing his feet on the edge to do fifty-something decline push-ups. He stood up and wiped his body until it was free of sweat. Jackson pulled his phone off the charger on the lampstand and fell back on top of the dark comforter on his bed.

He swiped across the screen and found himself yet again opening kikmessenger. The app, originally intended for global communication, was instead being used by countless teens, men and women with middle-aged crises, and pedophiles to send nude pics and sexts to any person they desired. Now there was a small percentage of people who would use it as an alternative to their phone's regular messaging app, but Jackson was not part of that small group.

Jackson opened his most recent conversation with Chris Stellanar. "You there?"

He waited a moment and watched eagerly as a bold D appeared, indicating the delivery of his message. A bold R would signal the person had read it, so Jackson leaned up anxiously awaiting the response. The five seconds passing felt like five hours, and Jackson cracked his neck.

The R appeared. "Yeah, what's up?"

Jackson smiled. "Was asleep and woke up after finding myself dreaming of you."

Another R appeared, almost immediately. "Mmm. Wanna tell me what that dream was about?" Chris responded, followed by numerous winking emojis.

Jackson bit his lip and tried cracking his neck, but the air pockets in his joints hadn't reformed. "All you need to know is that we were alone. I'll let you figure out the rest ;)" He hated himself for texting Chris while he was with Sophia. He wished he'd never met Chris. He wished he had kept his thoughts to himself freshman year, but that was in the past.

Since then, Jackson had managed to text Chris for over a year without people knowing. Jackson knew he was being a horrible person to Sophia, and he wished he'd had the balls to just dump her. She was such a nice girl, and he used her as a way to keep up a good image.

"I like the sound of that, <3 <3 <3!" Chris responded.

Then there was a texting pause from both ends of the conversation.

"Sry I'm bringing this up again, but isn't it such bullshit that the only way we can communicate is on this shit? I mean we live in fuckin' Cali. You'd think people wouldn't care."

Jackson sighed. He agreed wholeheartedly, but he also wished people weren't so hypocritical. If they just accepted him, he could've left Sophia *and* be with Chris, and it wouldn't matter. It would be his own damn business.

Jackson typed away. "Tru. Funny thing is the liberal-ass kids at school think it's weirder than the hicks. Ironic af bruh."

"Yo for real, Jackson. Like the kids who are gay as hell at school, but have always been gay, like obv gay, are mad accepted all the time. We can't fall into that category cuz like I think they think we tryna fit in a group we don't belong. In all honesty, bruh, u and me been through more shit than the fags have."

Jackson was texting back as fast as possible. He was exploding with how much he agreed. Everyone was forced to accept the gay kids who were always gay, but God forbid an allegedly straight kid come out. Jackson couldn't think of the last time he'd heard a gay kid called a fag. And whenever he heard someone say how much hate he'd endured, Jackson couldn't stand it. He knew he'd gone through more hate than the kids who were always obviously gay. And Chris probably went through more than Jackson.

"Hahahah, yo Chris don't put that shit in text. Don't need someone seeing you say that. Get fuckin' expelled if they did."

"No one reading these anyway, dawg. Someone found me texting you, I'd rather get hit by a truck than get expelled."

"Hahahahha fr. Anyways I think the reason ppl give us more shit is cuz we broke the image of ourselves. Like I was the typical straight rich-ass jock on some Zac Efron *High School Musical* shit, dude. U were pretty much the same right?"

"Close enough."

"Yeah so when we told people we swayed both ways, even the PC kids flipped out cuz it's like we taking credit for something that didn't seem like ours. Idk, just tryna see both sides of it." Jackson was trying to be realistic, but he hated everyone for what all did to him.

"Those kids are still assholes though."

Jackson slapped his lips together, nodding. "Well, yeah obviously. The friends that left me and the ones that left you can suck my dick. But yo, Chris, didn't you have anyone that sided up with you?"

"Nope. Just figured out how to get thru it. Why? Did you?"

"Yeah, one kid. Isaiah Porter." Jackson had never really brought up something this personal with Chris.

"Y that name familiar?"

"Well, he died during our sophomore year. So there went my best friend and defense of my circumstance."

"Oh, shit. Yo, Jackson, I'm so sorry. Shit. What the hell? How hasn't that come up before?"

Jackson wiped his eyes. He rarely, if ever, talked about Isaiah, but he felt comfortable around Sophia and equally comfortable talking to Chris about it. "Yeah, well talking about how my friend died ain't my favorite topic. So that's that."

"I get it. Yo I gotta get off soon."

"Aw why?" Jackson asked.

"I'm tired as balls, and it's nearly 10:45 PM. I can hit u up after school tomorrow, dude."

"Ugh, fine. We needa find a better way to talk. Typing this much is hella annoying."

"FaceTime? I can do it later tomorrow night."

"Sounds g," Jackson said back.

"Aight. Ay, you wanna see a preview of the perks of video chatting?"

"Whatchu mean?"

"This."

Jackson read the text and waited. Soon a fully nude picture of Chris popped up onto Jackson's phone, and his mouth dropped. Better than the same pic of Sophia? He wasn't sure but leaned toward yes.

"Damn!" Jackson typed. "Chris Pine got competition hahaha."

"Thanks, dude. Maybe I can see a preview too ahahah," Chris replied with the winking face again.

Without hesitation, Jackson undressed himself and sent a nude to Chris as well. He trusted Chris well enough not to show anyone, given that their texts had never been shared.

"Damnnnn. Wish we could talk more, but I gotta go to sleep."

"For sure, Chris. See ya," Jackson replied and turned off his phone.

He had never seen another guy naked aside from a shitty porn. This was different. It was a personal connection, one that he hadn't felt with anyone for a while. Not even Sophia, sadly, could make him feel as normal and relaxed as Chris did. No one else but Chris Stellanar knew or even remembered what Jackson had admitted during the summer two years ago. The connection between Jackson and Sophia was strong, no doubt, but he could never tell her how much he liked guys too. He wished he had the courage to break up with her and just text Chris and be honest. Still he knew Sophia wouldn't be able to handle it because he lied to her so well about how much he cared.

Whenever he and Chris talked, he knew it was the one time and place where the hypocritical kids couldn't judge his life, where the activists, who fought for social justice but called him a switch hitter, couldn't insult him, where his parents, though well-meaning in their intent to guide his life choices, couldn't advise him, and where Sophia, the nicest, most genuine girl he had ever met, didn't have to know about his infidelity.

SOPHIA

"You think the chili and guac is better than the chicken?" Sophia asked Jackson as they entered the cafeteria's lunch line.

"Don't you mean the diarrhea or chicken?" Jackson replied sarcastically.

Sophia shook her head and smiled. Jackson laughed and held her hand against his thigh. She let go only to grab her food, the chicken rather than the diarrhea. The rest of the people in the lunch line jostled them apart, and she lost him for a moment. Sophia went to pay for her food and then walked around aimlessly after exiting the buffet line.

She was trying to find the baseball cap of Jackson before he came from behind, hugging her tightly. He laughed, and they kissed. Sophia went to sit down, and Jackson practically carried her to the lunch table. The cafeteria was packed to the brim with kids like a sardine can. Sophia could barely hear Jackson during their conversation due to the roar of people talking with the sound of a thousand jet engines. The cafeteria cooks made one last call for chicken, and a new influx of freshmen came sprinting into the line.

Sophia shook her head. "Amateur hour over there." She pointed behind Jackson, and they watched the freshmen shove through everyone to get to the food.

"It was a good year for me though." Jackson shrugged.

Sophia cocked her head. "Well yeah, you came here before all the PC shit."

Jackson laughed. "What are you talking about? You're like the most liberal PC person I know."

"Liberal doesn't mean PC. Liberal means—" Sophia was cut off. She wanted to say that liberalism means equality for everything and no constraints. She believed in freedom of expression, speech, thought, and religion. Her mother taught her as much.

"Okay, okay, okay whatever. You always make me feel dumb when you go on your long ass political rants." Jackson waved his hands at her, joking, "You'll def be a politician."

If she made it to graduate school, that was what she wanted, but she felt she wasn't smart enough. Sophia loaded pieces of chicken into her mouth with the cafeteria's plastic fork. She beamed through full cheeks. "That's the goal."

Jackson nodded. "Course you gotta get those grades up."

Sophia rolled her eyes and poked him with the fork playfully. "Cool it, Jackson."

He snorted a chuckle. Sophia watched him pull out his phone and begin texting away rapidly. Normally Sophia wasn't interested on what he was doing on his phone, but the randomness and urgency of his typing speed bothered her. *And why is he smiling?*

"Baseball coach?" She tested him.

"Hmm? Oh yeah. Dude just gave us a stupid afternoon practice schedule. Asking the team if they know, uh …" Jackson lost his train of thought.

"Yeah?" Sophia prodded.

Jackson leaned in at his phone. "Uh, sorry. Just asking if they know why he changed it up so fast." He smiled at Sophia insincerely.

"Ah." Sophia acknowledged his lie and began getting warm. She hadn't felt as paranoid as she did about what was *really* on the phone than about anything else in a while.

"Yo, Soph turns out the chicken was diarrhea too," Jackson joked. "Mind if I hit the restroom really quick?"

"That's so gross. Just go." Sophia chuckled phonily.

He laughed and leaned in to kiss her, and Sophia tapped his

lips with hers, slowly watching where he placed his phone. Jackson placed his phone down on the table and left to use the restroom. It was unlocked. They trusted each other enough at one point that they could leave their phones unlocked without going through them. But something went off in Sophia's head, and her trust of Jackson tore a bit.

She smiled at Jackson as he went out of view. When he did, she grabbed his phone and went into his Snapchat. Nothing. She went to his email and sure enough found no notices about a change in practice schedule. However, Jackson had the Kik app hid in a different folder, only accessible by looking up the app. She began to relax and talked herself into thinking it was just his mom messaging him.

Sophia placed his phone back on the table just as it vibrated. She opened the notification from Chris S. The notification took her to Jackson's Kik app.

"Skype call later tonight?" Chris's text read.

Confused, Sophia scrolled up through the conversation, and then she saw it. Sophia saw the nude picture Jackson had sent from the night earlier in the week along with countless sexts and nudes sent between the two boys. She nearly threw up in her mouth. She felt horrible betrayal. *That stupid, cheating, smooth, handsome, fucking liar. I should've broken it off when I felt he was off. Did he ever really care? How long? When? How? It wasn't because I'm ugly, right? He had to go for a guy over me?* No, Sophia knew damn well she was better looking than most of the other girls. So many questions mixed around in her mind.

Sophia dropped the phone on the table, and her face turned red with anger. She wanted to cry or yell, but in the crowded cafeteria, she knew she would she look insane. Sophia sat with her hands being crushed underneath her thighs, staring at Jackson's phone. A ringing in her ears set in like a grenade had gone off in her right next to her. She looked around, and the room whirled in slow motion. The laughing of cliques of teens rang out like ten thousand decibels. All the happiness on people's faces became distorted, and her eyes landed on the face of Jackson as he ran into the cafeteria. His hair was disheveled, and his jacket was soaked with sweat from his undershirt.

Sophia got up slowly like a lion ready to attack its prey. Sophia grabbed his phone off the table. She stormed over to Jackson, phone in hand. His eyes landed on her when she was fifteen feet away, and he covered his face and shook his head. *Did he think it would be that easy?* Some sophomores stopped talking and pulled out their phones in anticipation of a confrontation between the two kids.

"Sophia." That was the only word the helpless Jackson was able to get out of his mouth.

Sophia slammed her fist into Jackson's cheekbone. *That liar.* He stumbled back, holding his face with one hand. The other hand was gesticulating at Sophia rapidly, desperately trying to wave her off.

"I should have known. I should have fucking known!" Sophia's voice started out soft and grew into a contained yell. "First time we were alone in that park drinking, I thought something was a tiny bit off."

"Sophia, please. Yo, I'd be pissed too, but you've met my dad. Yo if he finds out—"

This time, Sophia cut Jackson off. "All you ever did was lie to me. The town slut going out with Jackson Decker. Everyone was telling me to watch out. And I defended you like the dumb bitch I am!" Sophia snapped.

As more people gathered around, she couldn't hold it in and started crying, feeling devastation. "You couldn't even find another girl to fuck? I'm so fuckin' low on the ladder there was no one else below me, huh? Couldn't even call a hooker. Had to go for a guy?"

"Soph, don't," Jackson begged.

It was too late. Sophia opened the pictures of Jackson and Chris Stellanar. Sophia held up the phone. "Apparently I'm too much of a whore to even do it for him."

Kids all around her gazed at the phone and pointed. Jackson's pictures flashed the audience, and Sophia moved her thumb up the page to Chris but stopped. Sophia realized how much she could do to Chris by showing his pictures around, and she turned off the phone. Jackson was the one at fault; Chris was just a bystander. Sophia didn't care to ruin him, but she wanted to humiliate Jackson.

Emma spoke up from behind Sophia. "Soph, you don't know what—"

"Shut the hell up, pier girl." Sophia scowled her. Sophia's anger was running out, and it showed as more and more tears fell. The wrath turned to depression and confusion.

"How? Why would you do this to me?" Sophia finally yelled. The noise in the room besides Sophia's and Jackson's voices was nil. A feather falling would be like a gunshot. "I trusted you! You're the only guy I've ever trusted enough for a relationship. And you leave me for another fucking guy! Fuck you!"

Jackson stood in silence, his face pale. His mouth was moving in circles, presumably trying to talk.

Sophia wasn't done. "Lied to my face today." Sophia stopped yelling. "Thought I could trust you. I gave you my trust, you idiot. I thought every guy just wanted me for a good fuck. I thought you wanted something else!"

Jackson looked away.

"Guess I was wrong. You didn't want either." Sophia finished her speech and threw his phone against the wall. She shuffled out of the circle that had formed, pushing people out of her way. She paused, and she saw Chris Stellanar watching her from the back of the cafeteria. He exited quietly. Sophia looked away.

The cafeteria cleared out as the bell rang. She turned back to see Clara and her friends glaring at Jackson. The baseball team laughed uncontrollably. Jackson stood in the cafeteria emotionless. She'd never seen him so careless, and she was already remorseful. She didn't want to feel that. She wanted to be angry, livid, and vengeful. But there was something in the way he slumped and slogged his way to class that Sophia felt horrible about.

Sophia kept walking, eventually running out of the room,

covering her face with both of her hands as she sniffled her running nose. She left the building and jumped into her car. Sophia reclined the chair of her car all the way back and lay still, unable to even find a reason to continue bawling. Emptiness consumed her.

For Sophia, the rest of the school day went by in a blur so when she got home and her father asked, "How was school?" even the normal grunt of "fine" wouldn't move from her brain to her mouth.

"Jackson and I had this thing," she said sullenly.

"Oh?" Mr. Milverton stood up from his desktop computer. "Like what?"

"I guess he's bi or gay or something," Sophia said vaguely.

Her father gave a look of utter confusion. "Not where I thought this was going at all."

Sophia nodded, void of emotion. She couldn't believe what she did. There wasn't enough anger left for her to justify ruining Jackson's life. *But he deserved it*, she thought. *Yeah, this was his fault. Well, no, he just cheated. I exposed him.* She didn't know what was going to happen with Jackson, but she didn't care too much about the future. Shock and awe were even absent from her mind. There was no going back now. Sophia needed to accept what she did.

"Well, did he like just tell you?" Mr. Milverton asked.

"He left his phone open at lunch while using the restroom. And like the whole convo before he left was interrupted because he kept texting someone. Turned out to be this dude. They were sexting and shit."

"What? How long?" Mr. Milverton moved closer.

"Months. Years?" Sophia stuttered.

Mr. Milverton embraced her out of instinct. It was a rare event, Mr. Milverton's hugging Sophia. Such a massive man had the emotional control of a drill instructor. All she needed, for as long as she could remember, was the embrace of her father. She had almost forgotten what it felt like, warm and protective.

"It's fine. At least it will be," Mr. Milverton whispered his deep voice into her ear. "It doesn't sound true, I know. And me saying 'It doesn't sound true' doesn't sound true. But it is. Trust me, growing up I had one success with a girl for every fifty errors, and when that success fell apart, it was crushing. Give it some time though."

"But like I should've seen it coming. Maybe not the gay thing, but just something. Everyone, I mean not like everyone, but a lotta people told me to be careful or like watch out for Decker or whatever. I don't know how I didn't see that he never cared."

"Maybe." Mr. Milverton pulled back, smiling. "I will say though it's the first time I've heard of a breakup where the guy left the girl for another guy."

Sophia laugh-cried. The joke was one of the first times her father cracked a joke to her in she didn't know how long.

"Therefore ..." Mr. Milverton caressed Sophia's neck gently before letting go entirely. "It sounds more of a Jackson problem than a you problem."

Sophia shook her head, looking around the house to avoid eye contact. "No, it's definitely a me problem."

"No, it's not. You can't blame yourself for everything, even though I do."

She looked up at her father as her tears finally subsided. "What?"

"I'm just gonna blow through this, all right? Emotional stuff for guys is just ... I'm gonna blow through it." Mr. Milverton sat down, rubbing his hands together and then stopping. "I apologize for the last, what, fifteen years? Growing up, I wasn't always ... Well, I was a little shorter and, uh, horizontally challenged."

Sophia made a small laugh.

"Yeah, all the yoked guys thought I was super rad too." Mr. Milverton rolled his eyes. "I figured out over the years that I fit pretty well into lockers, trash cans, and ice boxes."

Sophia couldn't imagine her father being thrown around. He

never acted submissive to anyone. Whenever she saw him, she saw a tough, fearless, intimidating man.

"My da—" Her father's voice cracked. He looked down. "My *father* didn't help either. War hero, bronze star, purple hearts, the whole nine *hundred* yards. My hero. Mouth off to that guy, and I was handled how he handled the Fritz in Europe. He helped me figure out the many uses, aside from holding your pants up, that belts provided."

She'd seen the scar on her dad's face before. He always said it was from falling off his bike when he was kid. It was probably from the belt.

"He was treated like shit as kid too, and I guess he thought that anyone who wasn't treated like shit or wouldn't stand up for himself needed to learn how. Unfortunately I must've inherited a version of his teachings. That night during your eighth grade when you came back from that party …" He chuckled awkwardly. "Reminded me of coming home from school every day. I wanted you to figure out how to deal with things on your own instead of complaining about it. The motto I inherited from my father was along the lines of 'Every kid needs to be bullied; otherwise they'll never appreciate an easy life.' Clearly not the right motto."

Sophia was astonished. It made sense. Sometimes her father would be a nice guy, but when he got angry, she knew she needed to get out of Dodge. Even after nearly ending her life and after everything he'd said to her throughout her teen life, Sophia wanted to forgive him. She even sort of understood her dad and grandpa's toughness policy. Her dad didn't have the best way of conveying it. After her dad had been so strict on her for so long, Sophia had learned to deal with her own problems.

Sophia nodded. "In a weird way, I get that."

"You shouldn't get that. That's not how you treat your kids. I was on the receiving end too. It's not right." Mr. Milverton nodded slowly and then faster and finally stopped. "Anyone can be a father; not everyone can be a dad. I'm gonna be a good dad, Soph."

"You already are, Dad." Sophia blinked out the last tear from her eyes and sniffled the rest away.

He smiled. "I'm not letting that kid Jackson around here again, not after what he did to you. You okay with that?"

Sophia laughed. "More than okay with that."

"How you feel 'bout some frozen yogurt?" Her dad stood up.

"I'm down," she said and grabbed her car keys.

Sophia may have felt like a four-year-old grabbing frozen yogurt with her dad, but it was refreshing. She rarely did anything alone with him. One good thing that came out of Sophia's finding out about Jackson's other life was how close it made her and her father again. Having him back on Sophia's side made her feel strong but safe again. It was like she had someone to protect her from people like Jackson.

Although Sophia's mother was puzzled by the sudden connection between her husband and daughter, she didn't question it. When Sophia's father didn't know how to advise her, Mrs. Milverton stepped in and talked about her own breakups from high school. While Mrs. Milverton gave life advice, Sophia's dad gave her the support she needed to get to the end of the week.

When it *was* the weekend, Sophia invited Emma to go out to lunch at the local burger joint. Shaun tagged along.

"He was like 'Imma be a good dad, Soph,'" Sophia said to Emma.

"There is no way in hell *your* dad said Imma." Shaun laughed.

"Something close to it." Sophia smirked.

Emma smiled. "It's good to see you like this. Like I don't know if I've seen you happy since January or something."

"Same," Shaun added. "When you came over for dinner the other night, I was like 'Damn, she keeps up this depressing shit it's gonna be a long ass night.'"

Sophia laughed. "Yeah, because you were *really* good at keeping the tone up."

"I'm a natural," Shaun retorted.

"Yeah, I would know." Emma jokingly rolled her eyes.

"Still, I'm not gonna lie. I kinda feel bad for—" Sophia was interrupted.

Emma cut her off, pointing the fork from her salad at Sophia. "No, you don't feel bad for him. That feeling is what got you into this shithole in the first place."

"True, but I did it to him. I mean, seriously, Decker's prolly gonna get bullied the rest of high school. It'll be my fault," Sophia said compassionately.

"Naw, he's a dick getting what he deserves." Shaun stuffed his face with a burger. "Yo ith wuv Awbeffwe shoh badash—"

"Finish the damn bite, Shaun. Sound like Stephen Hawking." Emma laughed.

Sophia nearly spat out her drink.

"I wath thaying." Shaun swallowed the burger meat and punched his chest. "Ahem, I was saying that it was honestly so badass when you waved his phone around at the school. I was like 'bout damn time.' The kid with his dick out in the pic prolly shit his pants."

Emma shook her head at Shaun very slightly. Sophia's eyes widened as Chris Stellanar had just walked in. Shaun put his hands up, confused. "What?"

Sophia nodded just to the left of Shaun's head. He turned around slowly. Chris Stellanar was in line, grabbing a burger. The trio watched him, and he turned around and locked eyes with Shaun.

"Get down," Shaun said, ducking.

Sophia shook her head and spoke through gritted teeth. "Shaun, you're the only one getting down. He already saw us. Coming over. Get up."

Chris stopped at their table and looked down at Shaun, squinting.

Shaun slowly raised his body off the booth seat. "Ah! Found it."

Shaun flashed a quarter as everyone stared at him. Sophia sighed as Emma face-palmed.

"Sophia, could they see my face?" Chris asked her.

"What?" Sophia responded with a question.

Chris got down next to the table. "My face. Could anyone see my head in the pic you flashed the whole fucking school?"

Shaun slurped his Coke loudly. "They saw one type of head."

Emma punched his shoulder. Shaun grinned with his hand over his mouth.

"Watch yourself, Shaun. I can just tell everyone it was you in the pic."

Shaun settled down.

"No, Chris," Sophia finally answered. She wasn't 100 percent sure that no one saw the face, but even if they did see the picture, she assumed they were too far away to actually tell who the face was. "No one saw it was you. I turned my phone off because … Look, no one saw."

"Oh," Chris replied. "Thanks." He nodded at Emma and Sophia and ignored Shaun before leaving the diner.

Sophia looked at Shaun and Emma. "Why didn't he ask about Jackson?"

Emma jumped in to answer first. "Prolly didn't care. Prolly still reeling from the whole ordeal. Didn't wanna make the convo more awk than it already was."

Shaun cut in. "No way. It's called survival of the fittest. Every man for himself. Capitalism."

Sophia pushed her hands over her face, slightly irked. "Where'd you find this kid?"

"Near the bottom of the barrel," Emma joked.

Shaun was left uncomfortably silent, and Emma and Sophia laughed. He chuckled slightly and moved on from the insult.

"Honestly, I hate to say it, but Shaun sounds right. He probably didn't care about Jackson, which makes me feel worse about what I did. I didn't like read the texts one by one, but from what I saw, there was a lotta dirty talk." Sophia half-smiled. "It's nice to know that he was getting used by Chris, but it still hurts."

"Don't even think about it. It's over. Push Jackson from your mind, babe," Emma said with her hand on Sophia's wrist.

"She's right," Shaun said. "Don't need any more negative vibes. Can't hope for a better past, right?"

"Yeah." Sophia pulled out her phone to check the time. "Damn, I gotta go. It's nearly three o'clock."

"Really? Oh, fuck yeah." Shaun jerked around in his seat. "God of War comes out in like six hours."

Sophia turned to Emma and rolled her eyes. "Okay then, I'm gonna go."

"Aight, see ya." Emma stood up to hug Sophia. "I'm serious though. Shaun's probably serious too, but like move on from Jackson quickly. You're strong enough to be without someone like that."

"Pffff, I better be." Sophia laughed. "Thanks anyways."

Emma nodded, and Sophia turned to Shaun to give him a brief hug. "Peace, dude. Go kill some people in your game."

Shaun bowed at Sophia, sensei-style, and Sophia laughed on her way out the diner.

SHAUN

Later that night Shaun asked if his parents would grab him breakfast for the next day. Unfortunately for him, his dad was stressed from a fight with his superior at work, and his mom was going to sleep. Annoyed, Shaun grabbed his skateboard and walked to the door.

"Honey, where are you going? It's almost nine." Mrs. Baxter scurried up to him in her light-blue nightgown.

"Uh, to the store?" Shaun said, reaching for the door handle.

"Oh. Well, if I knew you were going to go by yourself, I would have gotten dressed. Do you want me to drive you down?" she asked with a motherly smile.

"No, no, no, I can fit the stuff in my bag," Shaun said, inching to go outside.

Mrs. Baxter moved up to the door and held the frame. "Well, I just want you to be careful. It's dangerous this late."

"Mom, this is not Compton, not even close. You're acting like how you do even when we see a homeless guy on the streets. If he's in like a twenty-yard distance of the car, you lock the doors faster than the flash," Shaun commented on his mother's mannerisms.

"You can't be too careful." She crossed her arms.

Mr. Baxter looked up at the two from the phone screen he was staring at from the kitchen. "Just let him go, hon. He's sixteen. I was driving to San Francisco with my friends when I was sixteen."

"Thanks for the support, Derrick." Mrs. Baxter stared down Mr. Baxter.

He shrugged, turning his attention back to his phone

"Thank you, Dad. Good Lord." Shaun rolled his eyes and left.

"Well, be careful, Shaun! Don't talk to anyone you don't know!" Mrs. Baxter yelled out the door.

"Yeah, yeah, bye. Love you," Shaun shouted and skated down the street.

"Raisin Bran, Raisin Bran, Raisin Bran," Shaun mumbled to himself as he fingered the aisle of cereal boxes at the grocery store. He stopped looking for a moment and thought, *The fuck am I? Ninety? Raisin Bran, for real?"*

Shaun laughed to himself and continued searching for the box. He glided down the aisle on his skateboard and finally came to a rest on his desired cereal box. He held it in his left hand and used his right to grab the end of the aisle and propel himself out. Shaun looked left at the directions for milk and saw none, so he turned right, and his eyes fell upon Emma's father, Nicholas Legra. *Man, the guy really did bulk up.* Not that he was ever fat, but he walked around like Dwayne Johnson now.

Shaun whirled back around on his board and skated to the produce section without considering how he would escape. Although he knew he would have to leave the section sooner or later, as the temperature was freezing, Shaun began wondering how much the cereal and milk was worth and thought maybe he could just leave.

He decided upon it and placed the cereal down on some kumquats. Shaun got off his board and walked to the exit of the building near the produce section. There was a sign on the elevator, and as Shaun neared it, he was able to make out what it said.

"Out of order. Please use the stairs on the south side of th—"

Shaun read aloud. He shook his head and wiped his sweating hands over his face. "You can't be serious. My fuckin' luck."

Shaun slouched his shoulders and pulled his board over and hopped back on. He gave himself a quick pep talk. "Just be cool. It won't be awkward. Just say hi and leave. If he recognizes you, just say hi and leave. If not, per-fect. Yeah, he's older. You're older. He won't recognize you in a million years. You're chillin. Easy."

Shaun rode to the side of the produce section, picking up his cereal as he went. He pushed himself to out into the open and stopped. He faced the line of aisles leading to the cashiers and more importantly the stairs and alternate elevator. Shaun pushed himself down the aisles slowly, if he ran the chances of someone yelling "thief" skyrocketed.

Shaun was almost at the cashier and turned around on the board. No sign of Nicholas. Shaun turned back around and had to jump off his board as Nicholas moved out of the way.

Shaun scratched his head, avoiding Nicholas's gaze. "Sorry 'bout that. Should've been paying attention."

"Don't worry about it." Nicholas stretched his shirt out and walked away.

Shaun made a sigh of relief and started to push off down the aisle when Nicholas spoke again. "Hey, kid," he called to Shaun, who was desperately trying to inch away from the encounter. "Random thought, but, uh, do I know you? I feel like I know you. By any chance, did you go Brent-Ryan Middle School? BRMS?"

"Yeah I did. To be honest, you seemed familiar too. Are you Mr. Legra? Emma Leg … well, Emma Walsh's father?"

"I am." Nicholas nodded happily with a smile. He outstretched his palm. "Is it Seamus?"

"Shaun actually." Shaun smiled, shaking Nicholas's hand.

"Knew it was an S," Nicholas said. "You played flag football, right?"

"Mmm-hmm." Shaun smiled back.

"D-line?" Nicholas pointed at Shaun.

"Offensive mainly." Shaun corrected him.

Nicholas snapped his fingers. "Close enough. Yeah, I didn't recognize you for a moment. You definitely …" Nicholas flexed his arms at Shaun. "Definitely, uh." He motioned from the ground up to the ceiling at Shaun. "You definitely grew up? What do you guys call it? Glow up?"

Someone actually noticed? People could tell he was in shape. He'd never had anyone outside of Emma and his parents say how good he looked. Who knew Nicholas Legra would be the person to confirm what people had said about Shaun?

Shaun laughed. "Sure, glow up. Thanks."

"Yeah, you look good, man." Nicholas lightly punched Shaun's shoulder, laughing. "Bet it isn't hard finding a girl in high school, eh?"

Shaun nodded awkwardly. "Naw, it's not."

Nicholas smiled with his mouth open. "Ah, so, uh, you go to school with Emma now, huh?"

"Yeah, yeah, I do. Same history class." Shaun revealed slightly.

"Cool, you guys are still friends from middle school then?" Nicholas asked simply to keep the conversation going.

Shaun had to tell him that he was dating Emma. It would be weird not to, and he assumed Nicholas would find out sooner or later. Shaun was hoping he wouldn't have to worry about a Ted-esque reaction given how much of a liking Nic had taken to Shaun.

"Yeah, uh, actually I'm her boyfriend," Shaun said carefully.

"Really? No shit, huh? Good for you getting out there." Nicholas laughed. "Better treat her well; otherwise you won't be around to be with her much longer."

Shaun opened his mouth, trying to decide whether to laugh or not.

"I'm just messin' with you, kid. Relax." Nicholas chuckled, slapping Shaun's shoulder.

Nicholas's hands seemed to be trying to break free of the sleeves of his bulging leather jacket. Whatever exercise he'd been doing came out in the shoulder-breaking slap. And although not as tall as Shaun, Nicholas seemed to loom over him.

"Sorry, I'm just so used to … Ted." Shaun felt strange talking about the new husband in front of the old husband. "Didn't wanna bring him up. Sorry."

"Kid, stop apologizing. You're fine," Nicholas responded.

"Yeah well, I'm just so used to his personality." Shaun snickered slightly. "For lack of a better term, sir, you're a breath of fresh air. He probably would have actually killed me."

Nicholas laughed. "Him? You're a machine, and he's a twig. *He* should be afraid of *you*."

"He kinda is. Well, no. He's scared I'm gonna corrupt or do something with Emma, or I don't even know anymore with him."

"No, you know what. He should be afraid of you. Stop saying sorry all the time. I mean obviously if you get in an argument with your mother, say you're sorry, but other than that, no. That guy feeds off people being weak. If you act like he's the boss of you, that's exactly how he'll act."

Shaun nodded in acceptance, considering Nicholas's words.

"Jesus, I sound like a dad." Nicholas chuckled ironically.

"Well, like, you are." Shaun smirked. It was weird hearing that from the real father of Shaun's girlfriend. Yet the comment was reasonable. The guy probably hadn't been a dad in the conventional sense of the word since he left Emma's family.

Nicholas snorted. "Yeah, well, trying to be. Hey, does, does Emma ever talk about me? Anything? When I showed up, she and her mother were a little shocked. Rightfully so, but still, does she ever say anything?"

"I mean, in general?" Shaun asked.

Nicholas nodded, leaned on his back foot, and folded his arms. What was Shaun supposed to say? Emma had both appreciated and hated her dad in the thoughts she disclosed to Shaun. He could tell Nicholas only the good, but what would Emma want him to say?

He just stood, scrunching his shoulders and stuttering out nonsense syllables.

Shaun explained, "Well, there was some good, but I mean also some bad. I mean I'm not sure what she'd want me to say."

"Yeah, sorry. I realize that was very forward of me." Nicholas slumped a bit. "It's fine actually. You don't need to tell me. I wouldn't want to mess up you guys' trust for my benefit."

Nicholas sighed and nodded at Shaun. He readjusted his grip on his bag of groceries and started scuffing away. Shaun could see how badly Nicholas wanted to reconnect. He couldn't just let the guy leave without giving him *something*.

"She said she wants a normal family again," Shaun stuttered out. Nicholas stopped in his tracks and turned to face Shaun. "I'm not sure if she like exactly was referring to you. But she liked how you handled Ted."

"Really?" Nicholas lit up.

Shaun nodded and swallowed. "I mean, yeah. I feel like she's angry at you but wants to see you again too. I don't know. I might be wrong."

"No, that's good enough for me. Thanks, kid." Nicholas nodded with a grin. He walked back up to Shaun and shook his hand. "I like you, Shaun. Glad you and Emma are happy. Good kid."

Shaun chuckled. "She said you'd say that."

Nicholas scratched his eyebrow and nodded to the side. "Yeah, well she was right. Women are always right."

"I mean not alw—" Shaun started.

"No, trust me, kid. They're always right. Even if they're wrong, they're right. Your life with will be easy with women if you're always wrong." Nicholas laughed. He patted Shaun's shoulder and turned to go to the cashiers. "Good seeing you, man."

"You too, Mr. Legra," Shaun said and retracted his hand.

Nicholas patted his shoulder and turned to go to the cashiers. Shaun smiled and got back on his board. He grabbed his milk and eventually let the blatantly obvious happiness disappear. It was a completely different interaction than when Shaun met Ted, and it was refreshing. He now understood why Emma wanted an old family back, even though she probably meant she wanted her dad back.

Nicholas was completely different from Ted, like polar opposites. Nicholas was cool and warm; Ted was offensive and sleazy. Nicholas had a certain confidence while Ted's aura gave off arrogance. Shaun hoped Emma would be seeing Nicholas more. She deserved to be happy.

He bought the cereal and milk and made his way into the elevator. Then he skated out and rode home.

"Shaun Baxter!" Mrs. Baxter shouted upon her son entering the house with his groceries. "We agreed on a ten o'clock arrival time, young man."

Shaun sighed, and although he knew they had not agreed upon anything, he heeded Nicholas Legra's brief advice. "Yeah, you are *right*, Mom. It's nine after ten, and I'm late. Won't happen again." Shaun smiled acceptingly and hugged her.

She nearly cringed in expectance of a massive hour-long dispute, but embraced her son as well and then let go before the hug reached too long of a length.

"Love you. Goodnight." Shaun walked away.

His mother's mouth dropped, and she watched him go place the cereal in the cupboard and the milk in the fridge. Shaun walked into his room and shut the door. *Holy hell, it worked.* Shaun wished he had tried being a nice son earlier.

EMMA

Emma sat on her couch watching *Black Mirror* but wasn't paying attention. She hadn't been able to focus on much since she saw her father for the first time since sixth grade. She was reminiscing about his leaving. She struggled to remember the day it happened. She had repressed the sour memory

Nicholas left Emma's family when she was eleven *and* during the Great Recession. Emma knew he had lost his job but didn't know why he had to leave. Plenty of other families just downgraded their living styles, but her dad just left. Her mother said he was just going to look for different hospitals to work at, but Christina and Emma knew that was a lie. Well, Christina knew and told Emma.

Emma missed Christina more than ever now, as well as her guidance. She was the one who told Emma the truth about Nicholas's leaving. She wanted Emma to be strong and move on from it. Emma could see Christina was hurt too, but she never showed it. Emma always wanted to be as strong as Christina was and could only pull it off when Christina stood up to Ted every now and then.

But for fuck's sake, if her Dad hadn't left, Ted wouldn't even be in the picture. Her mom was just too weak to live alone. She was in denial. That had to have been it. She told Emma that Nicholas was just gone to get another job, but she must not have been able to handle it herself. Emma knew Nicholas was gone permanently, well, until now.

But that year he left was still the best year she had with him before he disappeared from her life. The second *Insidious* movie came out, and she forced Nicholas to take her to the movies even though she was still two years from turning thirteen. When the jump-scare in the hospital happened, her dad flew back into his seat. She remembered laughing so hard and teasing him for being so scared. That was the funniest thing.

The credits on the *Black Mirror* episode started rolling, and Emma saw herself smiling in the reflection of the TV. She stopped her unconscious smile. She liked the good memories of her dad. Maybe he could come back for a bit.

Out of the corner of her eye, Emma saw the screen on the home phone light up. *Incoming call.* The phone rang several times before Cynthia came out from her room to answer. Her hair was a mess, and she was brushing it out of her face.

"I swear I call the heater guy twice today, and *now* he calls back at ten o'clock," Cynthia said, irked. Emma chuckled. Cynthia grabbed the phone. "Hello?"

Emma rested her head on the edge of the couch, listening intently on the phone call.

Cynthia looked back at Emma, confused. "Sorry, who is this?" She pressed the phone into her shoulder and whispered to Emma, "Probably a crank." She drawled into the phone, "Hellooo."

A long sigh came from Cynthia's end. "What do you want?" she asked, annoyed.

Emma leaned up, surprised by her mom's tone. It was definitely not a crank call.

"Well, you are bothering me, but please continue." Cynthia cut him off. "Nic, no. Not right—" Nicholas interrupted Cynthia.

Emma stood up off the couch. *My dad is calling us? Why? What'd he need?*

"Speaker," Emma whispered.

Cynthia stared at Emma and slowly lowered the phone, clicking the speaker icon.

"Cynthia, please. I just want to talk with you and my daughter. I haven't been able to for too long." Nicholas sounded desperate.

"You just came by a couple weeks back. What are you talking about?" Cynthia replied snidely.

"Well yes, I came by. But to be fair, I was cut off by the all-powerful Theodore Walsh."

Emma nearly lost it. She guessed her father hadn't lost his sense of humor.

"That's your problem, not mine. You leave for five years and miss Emma now. That's your fault." Cynthia countered.

Emma shook her head at Cynthia. She mouthed "what" back at Emma.

"No, you're right. Absolutely right, but I'm doing well now, and I—" Nicholas said.

"Yes, I saw the Bentley. Very impressive," Cynthia droned sarcastically.

Nicholas begged, "Look, I just want a chance, even if it's this one time. I just want one time to talk with you guys, no matter how long."

Cynthia sighed again, almost loud enough that they could have been talking face-to-face. After her talk with Shaun, she knew her father deserved a chance. She nodded almost seizure-like at Cynthia. She looked at Emma and back at the phone, gritting her teeth.

She took in a breath. "Fine. Tomorrow afternoon. You get half an hour, three to three thirty."

"Thank you, Cynthia. Thank you—" Nicholas was cut off again.

"Bye." Cynthia hung up.

Emma walked back to the couch and plopped down. She guessed she was seeing her dad.

"So how's school going?" Nicholas smiled and sat down on the couch inside the Walsh's house. Emma sat away from him on the other end of the couch.

"Not that well. She has a few Bs and—"

Cynthia was interrupted midsentence. Emma spoke. "He asked me. You can tell because he looked at *me*."

Nicholas raised his eyebrows at Emma.

Emma avoided his gaze. She sighed. "Doing fine. Three As. Three Bs."

"Better than I did sophomore year. Then again I spent most of that time getting high." Nicholas attempted to lighten the mood.

Cynthia glared at him from behind the couch.

He got the hint, correcting his statement. "Of course smoking is bad. Don't smoke. No ma'am."

Emma nodded, avoiding speech.

"How's, uh, whatever you're into now?" Nicholas tried.

"Really?" Emma flattened her stare at him.

"Sorry?" Nicholas asked.

Emma replied, "Whatever I'm into now?"

"Yeah, what? I don't know," Nicholas explained.

Emma shook her head a bit. "I'm into drawing, like art. Not like Picasso, just like sketches of stuff."

"That's cool." Nicholas complimented her.

Emma smirked. "You don't think that. I mean it's not really that fire anyways. It's just sorta relaxing."

"Naw, I'm all about art. Salvador Dali knew what was up." Nicholas nodded uncomfortably at her and Cynthia. "I may be a surgeon, but I can appreciate some fine art."

Incidentally his random guess of a painter was who Emma idolized. The surrealism genre of art fascinated her, and she had to contain herself when Nicholas openly said anything about Dali. Ted wasn't even smart enough to know the name Dali outside of a Kanye West song. Emma couldn't ever imagine going to a museum with

Ted and could only see his using a sculpture as an ashtray. But going to one with Nicholas? The thought seemed clear as day.

"Oh yeah, he's like one of the best." Emma cracked a smile back at Nicholas.

"Yeah, him and Ernst. Fire, as you say," Nicholas joked.

"Yeah." Emma barely laughed at his dad joke. She wanted to like him again but kept thinking about why he left in the first place. *Why didn't he just make an effort?*

The small amount of fun stopped, and the awkwardness crept back into the room. Nicholas nodded while looking around the small duplex.

"Oh, I saw your dude, Shaun, yesterday at Safeway."

Emma perked up. "Really? What'd you guys like talk about?"

"Oh, I just reminisced about high school. Talked about how he's doing and how I'm doing. I like him. Glad it's working. Good pick." Nicholas grinned.

Cynthia shook her head and glared at Nicholas. "Yes, because the Walsh women always pick amazing partners, right?"

"Yeah, *Theodore* proves it." Nicholas winked at Emma.

Emma stifled a laugh. His slightly irking jokes at Cynthia made Emma see another difference between Ted and Nic. Nic actually knew how to joke around without crushing your feelings.

"Bad choices aren't genetic. If you're happy with Shaun, I'm happy with Shaun."

Emma smiled and bowed her head once. She turned to her mom. "At least someone likes him."

Cynthia rolled her eyes and looked at the clock, three nineteen. The time moved ever so slowly for her, but fast for Nicholas and Emma, whose time spent with each other was at least decent. The mood was about to fall though.

"I just have a question?" Emma asked, leaning forward from her end of the couch.

Nicholas cocked his head up.

"Why'd you leave?" Emma implored. She wanted to hear what his answer would really be like.

Nicholas looked up at Cynthia. "I lost my job. Recession hit us like a train." Nicholas gave the short answer.

"It hit other families like trains. Much bigger trains." Emma huffed.

Nicholas shrugged. "Well, sometimes you have to make decisions that affect you and other people. I didn't have much of a choice honestly."

Emma furrowed her brow. "Didn't have much of a choice? What about like staying home? You didn't even try."

Emma started getting angry. She had dealt with Ted all those years. She dealt with Christina's dying and her mother's not caring to help. She did everything on her own. What could Nicholas possibly have been dealing with that was worse than what she did?

"Yeah, I did."

"Leaving doesn't equal trying; it equals leaving." Emma raised her voice.

Cynthia looked at her surprised.

"Why don't we just go back to art? We were having such a good time," Nicholas said.

Emma shook her head. "I wanna know why you didn't try. I wasn't just gonna like you instantly for coming back for thirty minutes."

"I told you. I did try. Emma, I tried." Nicholas nodded at Cynthia. "You know I tried. I tried to keep us afloat."

"Didn't seem like it to me." Cynthia didn't defend him.

Nicholas looked back at Emma. "What do you want from me? What do you want me to say, Emma?"

"I want you to tell me why you had to abandon me!" Emma erupted. She stood up from the couch. She was fed up with Nicholas's avoidance of questions. She wanted an answer. "Why'd you h—"

"Because I couldn't see everything go!" Nicholas shouted. "I worked for everything we had. I did everything for you, for

Christina, for Cynthia. I know I should have stayed! We could've easily changed areas and gotten cheaper things. I was too proud to see everything fall apart."

Emma fell silent. It was not the admission she expected. She thought he was going to say that something went wrong, but the problem was only him.

"My pride." Nicholas raised his hands up, slapping the couch with them. "That's why everything went to shit. I lost my job, and the money stopped. Everything started collapsing. I didn't want to accept that everything I worked for was going away. I didn't want to see you go with it. So I left first. I know what I did. I put what I wanted over you."

Nicholas inhaled hard after nearly losing his breath from his explanation. Cynthia stood with her arms at her sides, stunned. "It was my fault you lost everything." Nicholas was shaking. He mouthed, "It's true. I couldn't handle the pressure, so I gave up like a bitch." Nicholas wiped the sweat off his forehead, which had accumulated during the spat.

"I appreciate the honesty," Cynthia said.

"Two years spent sleeping in a car gave me perspective on what really matters."

Cynthia nodded. "I'm sure."

Emma didn't know what to say. She wasn't sure if she appreciated the honesty like her mother said. Her dad left because he was basically materialistic. He cared more about a house and car than his kids? She did like that he told her the truth. She wanted to be less surprised at the admittance. Sometimes the truth just hurts.

"All right, well, it's almost time for you to go, Nic." Cynthia pointed at the clock.

Emma looked up—3:28 p.m. *Well, that went fast.* But at least Emma had the answer she wanted. She wasn't fully happy to have Nicholas back, but she was happy in the direction everything was headed.

"Right, well, if you ever wanna reach me. Here, I'll write my number," Nicholas said, pulling a pen out of his jacket. He took out his wallet and wrote on the back of a parking pass. "That's my number. And that's my address, 684 Barkley Lodges."

"Cool," Emma commented. *That was it, huh?* She was glad he was leaving so she could be in her thoughts for a bit, but at the same time knew everything would go back to normal with Ted once Nic left. "Well, bye." She waved at him as he opened the door of the apartment.

Cynthia held the door open for him.

"Good seeing you guys. Emma, Cynthia." Nicholas waved back at Emma and shook Cynthia's hand.

Ted was just pulling into the drive, and Emma saw his eyes go wild upon seeing Nicholas. He stepped out of his car and walked at a brisk pace toward Nicholas.

"No, sorry don't have time for this. Gotta get to church." Nicholas towered over Ted and held his arm against Ted's chest like a running back stiff-arming the defender.

Ted stopped and attempted an insult. "So you like saw the light recently while I was here for Cynthia and *my* daughter?"

"Nope, saw it a while back. Hit rock bottom so only other way to go is up," Nicholas shouted back as he strode into his Bentley. "You're halfway there, right? If you need some help, you should come with me."

Ted sneered at Nicholas, and a flea landed on his greased-up hair. Nicholas waved at Ted and drove down the street.

"What was he doing here?" Ted implored to Cynthia.

"What? Nothing, Ted. He just wanted to talk," Cynthia said, hugging Ted's arm, attempting to pull him into the bedroom.

"About what?" Ted continued his questioning.

"He just wanted to talk, Ted. He hasn't seen Emma in years so he just wanted to talk with her," Cynthia answered too defensive for Ted's liking.

Ted looked at her and studied her desperate facial expression. "You want him over me, don't you?"

"What? No. He won't come back here, Ted. It was a one-time thing," Cynthia pleaded.

Ted stared at her hard and then turned to Emma, who was sitting on the couch staying quiet at all costs. "What 'bout you? You want him back?" Ted cocked his head.

Emma shrugged slightly.

"No, I know you do. Lemme tell you something. He doesn't care about you like I do. Neither does that Shaun prick. Shaun just wants a good fuck, and so does Nic, Cynthia." Ted spoke the unintelligent thoughts running through his mind. "I'm your father, and while you're under this goddamn roof, you're not seeing that Shaun kid or Nicholas again. Understood?"

"You're not my dad," Emma swore at Ted.

"What'd you say?" Ted shook Cynthia off his arm and marched over to Emma. "Lemme hear it again."

Emma stood up proudly and leaned into Ted's ear whispering, "You're not my dad, so fuck off."

Ted reeled back. His eyes darted back and forth on Emma's eyes. She was testing out standing up to Ted. Since Christina left, all she did was submit. Emma couldn't stand staying in that state of mind.

Ted smirked. Then his smile turned sour. He stepped forward to her and pulled back a haymaker before slamming his fist into Emma's eye socket. Holy shit. It felt like a baseball just broke her skull. Her vision bounced around, lagging behind where she was focusing on. She turned and fell face-first onto the ground. She'd never been hit by Ted, and she never believed she would. All of his threats against her were only threats; this backed up her reasoning to step up to him. It might have been a mistake.

She wanted to cry, but every time her eye tensed up, it felt like she was getting punched again. Blood flowed around her head, and she could hear her veins pumping the blood around. There was a ringing in her ears, but she made out Ted's distinct voice going through it.

"Let's go," Ted grunted.

Emma moved her head slightly, her neck sore. She looked up to see Ted dragging Cynthia away.

"No, she needs ice. She can't sleep without ice," Cynthia begged, scratching Ted's neck.

Ted grabbed Cynthia by the wrist and shoved her forward. Emma could see he was losing it. Her mother's denial started dissolving into acceptance of how Ted was. Not that Cynthia was always weak, but Emma certainly had never seen her attack Ted before, even in the slightest.

Ted shook his head. "Well, she'll understand what it's like to take a hit. She'll survive."

Emma woke up with the taste of iron in her mouth, like a four-year-old who had gotten curious and licked a penny or dime. She leaned forward and felt as if an altitude drop had occurred only in her forehead. *Probably a concussion.* Her head was throbbing, and she made her way, stumbling, over to the sink. Blood spilled into her mouth. *Fucking Ted. Guy should disappear and pull a Nicholas.* She wondered if Ted had ever been punched. If he had, he hadn't been hit hard enough. Emma wanted to walk into Ted's room right then and beat his face in. She didn't care that she couldn't see. He needed to bleed.

She pulled out the check that Nicholas had written on hours earlier and blinked hard trying to read the address. The only person she wanted to see, despite everything he said, was Nicholas. He may have been a coward years ago, but she needed someone who could care about her and in a way that wasn't borderline pedophilic unlike Ted.

"86. No, 64. 684. Blake?" Emma read, confused. Her vision came into focus. "684 Barkley Lodges. Right, the rich place."

She opened the Uber app on her phone and looked for nearby drivers. The man who drove Shaun and her back from the theater, Paul, popped up two miles away. She selected him and grabbed her coat off the rack near the front door. She stepped outside into the brisk night air. She breathed out, and a thick mist formed as she exhaled.

"Middle of spring, and it's freezing in California." Emma snorted.

Soon Paul showed up outside her apartment. He stepped outside the car and opened the passenger side door for her.

"Ah, madame, your chariot awaits." Paul smiled at Emma. "Holy shit! What happened?"

"The king who rules my castle lost his temper." Emma smiled sullenly.

"Hey, no wait. You need to see a doctor or CPS or something." Paul furrowed his brows. "Seriously I got into plenty of fights as a kid and not going to the doctor left my vision at ... Well, I wear glasses for a reason."

Emma smiled. "Thank you, but no, Paul. I just need to get to the Barkley Lodges."

"No, no, no, no, no." Paul let go of the car door. "I'm calling 911. You need a doctor."

"I don't need that. I need to get to the Barkley Lodges now," Emma tried to shout, but her eye pulsed with every word. "My doctor lives at the Barkley Lodges."

Granted Nicholas was a surgeon, but it was close enough to the truth.

Paul squinted at Emma. "You're that close with him or her? It could be a her. I'm not saying all guys are doctors. Not that I thought—"

"Paul, please just drive," Emma said. Sure, he was a nice, funny guy, but God, he didn't know when to shut up.

"Okay, fine, but I really think you should consider calling CPS and doctor or vice versa."

"It's fine. Can we just go? I need to get there and back here before my stepdad leaves for his night shift," Emma explained. "I'll only be there for around twenty minutes, so could you wait in the parking lot?"

"In the parking lot? Outside the complex? Now hold on. I'd love to rack in the dough, but that's gonna cost quite a bit more if I wait and drive you back."

"Fine. Just drive please." Emma rocked in the car seat anxiously.

Paul shook his head and sighed as he ran around into the driver's seat. "Your chariot departs for the Barkley Lodges." Paul dipped his chin at Emma, and the car sped off.

Emma slowly moved her finger toward her eyelid and retracted it back as soon as it hit skin. A sharp throb ran through her eye and right nostril, and she opened her mouth, flexing her facial muscles from the pain.

"Here," Paul said, handing her a water bottle. "Need something cold on that."

Emma raised the bottle at Paul in appreciation and pressed it against her swollen eye. It slightly hurt, but it numbed the area.

"So is your doctor just your fine young prince?" Paul prodded.

Emma grinned. She enjoyed Paul's fake, cheerful role-playing demeanor. The man knew how to make the humor just dumb enough to lighten any darkness in the ambience.

"No, no. My first king lives there. He returned from afar many fortnights ago. He used to love my queen, but money troubles within the kingdom got in the way," Emma confessed, feeling comfortable with Paul.

Paul nodded. "Yes, I understand such troubles. A great trouble hit years back, and I lost my living quarters temporarily. Luckily my loving queen supported me in seeing we earn it back."

Emma understood. She wasn't about to tell Paul her whole life story, but it kept an awkward silence from creeping in. Besides, Paul was a pretty likeable guy—strange, but likeable.

"I can assume your new king is in dislike of your old one's return?" Paul asked.

Emma shook her head.

"Fa sho." Paul broke character. "Well, not gonna lie. I can see that. Try as I might, your manner is unchanged from my jesting. Imma just let you chill for the rest of the ride, gucci."

Emma laughed, "Gucci, Paul."

After driving on the empty night highway, strangely reminiscent of the night of Emma's sister's crash, Paul exited and pulled into the Barkley Lodges. Emma staggered out of the car but regained her balance before Paul could follow her.

"I'm fine. I'm fine, thanks. Twenty minutes max. Okay?" Emma asked.

"I'll be waiting." Paul gave her a thumbs-up.

"Sick." Emma gave one back and ventured for a jog, but the throbbing in her head held her back from doing so.

"696, 694, 92, 90." As Emma neared her father's apartment, she quickened her gait. "88, 86, 684."

Emma caught her breath and stopped. She stood outside on the front porch contemplating if she should even go inside. After waiting for a couple of minutes, she approached the door, and just as she was about to knock, the lock clicked, and the hinges swung the metal door out of the way.

Nicholas was staring at the welcome mat, aiming to fix its symmetry with his foot. "I was about to finish some paperwork when I saw a certain Walsh coming from the parking lot."

A painful tear leaked out of Emma's swollen eye. "Dad."

He smiled and looked up at her. "Did you just—" His smile faded. "What the heck? How in the hell did that—"

She rushed forward, and he pressed her head into his linebacker-sized shoulder. She cried against his sports jacket, one hand around his back and the other stuck covering her pulsating left eye. She inhaled the pleasant smell of his deodorant rather than the dank smell of Ted's cigarette smoke. Nicholas held his daughter still while she wept in the doorway.

He reached behind her and closed the door. Emma ran out of water to dispense from her tear ducts, and she slowed her breathing to longer dragged-out breaths. Nicholas let go of her, and she stepped back. He walked to the bar stools near his kitchen, which was nearly double the size of Emma's. Emma continued to wipe her tears as Nicholas sat down with a thud.

Nicholas pointed at her eye. "Did he?"

She bowed her head. Nicholas's face shook, and he gripped the edge of the stool so hard it looked as if it would break.

"Why?" Nicholas asked.

Emma coughed up the residue of her crying. "I told him he's not my dad and he could fuck right off." Emma looked around uncomfortably. It felt weird swearing so openly around Nic.

Nicholas rubbed his eyes. "That slimy ... Does he do this that often? Does he hit Cynthia? I swear if he hits you or Cynthia again.... I swear I'll—" He stopped and apologized. "Sorry, that's not right. Just that's not right."

Emma sighed. "I wouldn't have to worry about that if you hadn't left."

Nicholas took his hands off his face and slumped forward. He folded his hands. "I know, Emma. When I came back, I had no idea."

"You shouldn't have left in the first place. That's also not right." Emma didn't want to cry again. She snorted and swallowed to clear herself of mucus and crying drool.

"I know ... and ..." Nicholas exhaled with exasperation. "And I'm sorry. It's my fault. Where you are and who you live with. It's on me."

The apology was heavenly. Emma's mouth started dropping, but she caught herself and closed it. She nearly shouted. Not that it made up for everything, but Emma was a big fan of the word *sorry*.

It was a big step for Nicholas, she was sure, and definitely a big step for their reconnecting. She wasn't sure what her mom would think. She'd probably say he was lying, but Emma was right about Shaun, wasn't she? She was. Plus, Cynthia trusted Ted, and that got them in shit *ocean* without a paddle or boat.

"I appreciate the honesty." Emma repeated her mother's words with a smile.

Nicholas smiled again. "You want some coffee?"

"I actually need to go soon. Ted's gonna be leaving for his night shift, and I don't want him thinking I am where I am."

"No, you're not going back there." Nicholas shook his head violently.

"I have to." Emma averted her eyes. "Trust me. He'll call CPS and say you hit me. I'd still be here, and it would make sense. You know how Ted is."

"Fine, I'll just, I'll … goddamnit!" Nicholas groaned and walked over to Emma and hugged her again. "Fine. But I want you to know that if he does anything, I want you to know that it's okay to fight back. I know you're a strong girl. He wouldn't be expecting it. If you can't, call me as soon as you can. Okay? Call me, Shaun, 911, or something. Okay?"

"Okay, yeah, okay," Emma said into her dad's chest. She let go of the embrace. "I'm really glad you're back. I thought I … I'm glad."

"So am I, kid." Nicholas let Emma go and watched her leave.

Paul was standing near the car and looked up. "Madame?" Paul bowed at her and opened the passenger side door.

Emma hopped in, and he shut it. Paul fell into the driver's seat and reversed the car out of the parking lot.

"Sire," Emma rejoined. "Onward to my living quarters."

"As you wish," Paul stated.

Emma looked at him with a twinkle in her eye and reclined back in her car seat as they rode off to her apartment complex. Nicholas was back—really back. Not denial Nicholas. The real Nicholas Legra was being honest, and he wanted to help Emma. For the first time, Emma felt like everything would work out. If she could handle Ted, she could trust Nic to come to her aid.

She was determined to stand up to Ted on her own but was hoping it wouldn't come to that. Hopefully he would settle down. Maybe she could even see Nicholas on a regular basis. Ted was scared enough so it could work. No. She would have to wait, but she was okay with that.

JACKSON

M r. Decker paced around the kitchen, dragging his feet, making a sound akin to the scraping of sandpaper. Still dressed in a robe at one in the afternoon, he had a five o'clock shadow filling in. His hand was cupped over his mouth, and the caffeine from his third glass of coffee was still surging through him, causing a Parkinson's-like movement.

Jackson sat shirtless on a dining room chair on the other side of the kitchen island separating the two. Jackson anxiously tapped his foot, waiting for either of them to say something. Jackson had gotten used to any insult that came his way over the years and thus would be numb to any threat his father made when he finally decided to speak.

"How long was it going on?" Mr. Decker asked, flexing his facial muscles. "The messaging shit?"

Jackson raised his brow at Mr. Decker and then turned his attention back on the center of the dining room table, "Weeks? Months? Lost track of when I first messaged Chris."

"Why couldn't you have just stayed in the closet? Why not just let it all blow over two years ago and keep it that way?" Mr. Decker scolded.

Jackson bit the inside of his cheek. "Wasn't really my choosing to come out now."

"Your fault though," Mr. Decker added. "Wasn't my choice to have a fag son, but here we are."

Jackson looked up at the ceiling and back down at the table. "Here we are. You know that insult kinda got us back to square one."

"Well, what do you want me to say, Jackson?" Mr. Decker barked sharply, and then in a feminine sarcastic tone, he added, "Ooh, it's okay. You can be whoever you want. Everyone loves everyone. Hooray for us. I'm totally okay with you being a catalyst for everyone in this town reverting back to the old view of our family."

"Like I said, not my choice."

"Well, it is your *fault*!" Mr. Decker snapped. "If you like guys, at least take responsibility for the abnormality."

"Fair." Jackson didn't seriously agree with the abnormality line. He just wanted the torment to end.

Mr. Decker leaned over the kitchen island, both hands on the counter, "Goddamn right it's fair. Once your mother finishes wiping your phone, the only thing you'll be able to do on it is call or text us. No one else."

"Also fair." Jackson rested his chin on his arms folded on the table. There was no point in arguing because he understood too, from his parents' perspective, that he betrayed their trust. He hated them still, but he saw their perspective, another reason not to argue.

Mr. Decker narrowed his eyes. "Think you're being smart with me, son?"

"Well, yes in the sense that I think the punishment is smart," Jackson answered.

"Right," Mr. Decker said with a creased smile. "Well, to wrap this up, you even say the name Chris Stellanar again, you won't be spending the night under this roof. That's all I'll say."

No response came from Jackson, just a slight bounce of the head.

"Well, we are in agreement then." Mr. Decker pushed off from the island and left the kitchen.

Once Jackson heard the door to the master bedroom click and the shower water start running, he dropped his mask of nonchalance. He leaned back in his chair, with blood coursing through his capillaries so hard that the only thing he could hear was a short pulse in his eardrum every other second. His hands clenched in fists of rage and gripped the armrests of the chair.

Jackson stood up suddenly and slammed his fist against the wooden wall behind him. Pain shot through his arm, and he clutched his right hand trying to relax. He slammed it against the wall again and again and again. Soon a small dent formed in the wood, and his knuckles were bleeding.

Jackson stopped, and his blood ceased pumping so fast. "Fuck!" Jackson screamed and punched the wall so hard that his thumbnail cracked. He dragged his dripping knuckles across the yellow walls and fell down on his side, shaking with rage.

Jackson's friends had left him again too, leaving him in the state he felt most terrified in, isolation. Fear had taken over, and he was determined to prove to someone he wasn't thinking clearly when he messaged Chris. No matter his father, one of his friends, or the entire city, he wanted a chance to prove his innocence.

For all the high school kids knew, he had just sent some random guy a pic. They didn't know about the countless hours he spent confiding in Chris and the numerous rainy Sundays spent talking with someone he knew he could trust. With what seemed like the world against him and no Chris to be found, Jackson's fear of abandonment took over.

Something had to be done to gain his reputation back fast. He needed a get-popular-quick scheme. Drinking or hosting a rager wouldn't be enough mainly because everyone already knew he could chug like a Russian, and no one would come to a party he was hosting. Duh. Jackson barely had the will to wake up each day and go to school. Everything that happened was brought upon him by the stupid mistake of leaving his phone unlocked. Why didn't he lock it? Nothing would've happened if he'd just stuck around and held in his need to take a shit.

None of the kids on the baseball team thought he was normal. To Jackson, they were the ones who weren't normal. What kind of person turns on his friend when his friend is humiliated? The type of person who isn't really a friend. He probably wouldn't be able to get with another girl until college.

A lightbulb turned on. *Get with a girl. That was it.* If he could have sex with a girl and somehow get proof of it, maybe people would assume what happened was a misunderstanding. Yeah, he could just say he meant to text a girl and some gay kid responded, something like that. Jackson had to take a picture of himself, video, or something of him fucking a girl. Even just making out. Maybe he could set up a hidden camera and get someone over. No, that would look too weird to an outside viewer.

He didn't know what he'd do exactly, but hooking up with some girl was the only way Jackson could think to save his reputation. Whether it be some loner or a slut, he knew his friends would see it and respect him again. It would prove his straight-ness. Jackson hit himself in the head, trying to think of another solution to prove his worth among his old circle of friends. However, the limited space in his adrenal-testosterone-filled mind kept pointing at one vulnerable target. The most vulnerable girl he knew and knew was too much of a pushover to hate him forever. Sophia.

"C'mon, dawg. Pick up." Jackson spoke into a pay phone near a line of office buildings downtown.

Unless his father had suddenly become a federal detective, the call was untraceable. This meant his father would still think Jackson only used a phone to contact his father and mother.

The long dial tone sounded off at Jackson. He was trying to get a hold of one of his childhood friends, Hunter. Jackson's best friend, Isaiah, was the only person who stood up for Jackson and his coming out freshman summer. After Isaiah passed away during his sophomore year, Hunter was there to comfort him. Therefore, Jackson assumed he would have his best chance convincing Hunter that the incident at school with Sophia was a misunderstanding.

Hunter was definitely not in agreement with the idea of his friend's being part of the LGBT community but wasn't completely hostile over it anymore either. Another benefit of convincing Hunter first was to get a hold of his high school social status. Jackson had lost his smooth reputation and social level as well, so he needed all the help he could obtain with spreading the lie that his text was a mistake.

"Hunteeeeer." Jackson bit his tongue and gripped the tethered phone harder.

A click in the sound waves came into Hunter's ear and then the sound of someone's chewing gum and popping it. "Yeah? Who is it?"

"Yo, it's Jackson," he stated, exasperated.

Hunter sighed. "Whatchu got?"

"Yo I just wanted to say that—"

Jackson got interrupted. Hunter interjected, "That what happened in the cafeteria was staged."

"What?" Jackson asked, confused.

"Oh, sorry. Was Sophia a crisis actor?" Hunter snickered into the phone line. "The government told her to show a picture of you to everyone?"

"No, dude. C'mon. I was wasted when I texted that kid. It was just a stupid drunk text," Jackson started his story. It was not the best lie he'd ever told, but his actions would support it.

Hunter continued his skepticism. "Mmm, okay, sure."

"For real, that dude's not gay either. He's just some kid from my psychology class." Jackson threaded bits of truth into his lie for realism.

"What's his name then?" Hunter asked, believing he just caught Jackson.

Jackson had it all planned out in his mind ahead of time. He predicted every question Hunter would ask ahead of time and knew the answers to them. Jackson knew how to not answer. He knew what would cause further hurt for him or Chris, but also knew how to have a realistic lie.

"Chris Stellanar. He's that tall, skinny senior kid. Dude wears a Warriors cap all the time."

"Oh yeah." Hunter acknowledged his knowing of Chris.

After Chris smoothly covered up his own event with coming out, no one remembered it, and quite possibly the only person who knew about it anymore was Jackson.

Hunter poked Jackson mentally. "Yeah, I mean he could be gay though, bruh. How many black dudes you see wearing purple-red plaid and skinny jeans?"

"I didn't think a supposedly straight kid would notice," Jackson retorted.

Hunter laughed. "That was good. But I'm still not sure how you would, quote, drunk text a guy. Even if you were at a .38 blood-alcohol level, I'd still be surprised."

"The wonders of Jack Daniels are pretty insane." Jackson countered. *Fuck, I'm losing.* He was desperate though and couldn't give up the lie just yet. "In my mind, the word Chris came out like tsuchyich."

"So your natural thought was that tsuchickt or whatever was a broad who *needed* to see you naked?" Hunter howled. "It's a bit of a stretch, Decker."

Jackson fake-laughed with him. "Naw, dude, I was all kinds of fucked up. I was like, 'Screw it, man. Yeah, I'll send a pic.'"

"Jackson, Jackson, Jackson." Hunter laughed into a groan. "I'll give you an A for effort."

"Dude, what the hell? I'm serious, dawg. Matter fact, me and Sophia are still kinda tight."

Hunter huffed. "I'm sure."

Jackson kicked the brick wall the pay phone booth was hanging on. He didn't dare punch it in fear of breaking whatever was left of his knuckles. "Naw, like Sophia and I are mad tight. Feel me?"

"Whatchu talking about, dawg?" Hunter questioned him. "She was more pissed than a girl whose boyfriend left her for another guy. Oh wait."

"Hunter, like we boutta smash. I'm tellin' you, dude. Chicks get sooo vulnerable when they angry at you. Boutta get like some makeup pussy." Jackson cringed and smacked his forehead with the end of the phone. He was all in now. Somehow he was going to get back with Sophia.

Hunter paused and then whispered, "My mom just got home, so I gotta talk a lil quiet now. But mah homie, if you smashed Sophia fuckin' Milverton, damn. Hella people would prolly be back on your side. I obviously don't know for sure, but that would be insane. Chick's a fuckin' eleven outta ten."

"That's what I'm saying, dude. Me and Soph are smooth sailing with this shit under us. Her anger prolly gonna make it even more intense, dawg." Jackson added length to his already mile-long nose.

Hunter chuckled and whispered, "Damn, bruh. You better be sending me a pic of that sweet ass you taking."

"Hell yeah. Easy." Jackson was getting himself pumped up to regain his lost friendships and respect. "Imma hit her up on Monday. Parents gon' be out then."

"Yeee, dawg. Get it." Hunter backed Jackson's ego up. "But dude, I gotta be honest. That drunk text story is horseshit. Still as long as you smashin', I'm cool with it."

"You're a G, Hunter. Imma send you that booty pic aight?" Jackson spoke into the phone.

Hunter snickered. "Yeah, def send it. I gotta go, dude. My mom wants me to help with groceries."

"Chill, chill. Well, peace, dude." Jackson finished and hung up.

Jackson walked into the parking lot where his Jeep sat. He climbed into the front seat and leaned back laughing with a malevolent joy. He pumped his fist so hard that it nearly hit the sunroof. Jackson was imagining a utopian outcome from the encounter with him and Sophia. He would go to her house and apologize, but she would already be okay with it. She would have gotten over the whole ordeal, and they would hook up. It would be easy. They'd be doing it every day of the week after that. He'd be the most impressive guy at BRHS again. It could work. He could see it working. They'd be having sex on a regular basis with the occasional compliment about their relationship from a random classmate. He thought briefly about its going wrong, but no, it couldn't. It would absolutely go to plan.

SOPHIA

Sophia lay in bed, eyes glued to her computer screen and math notebook near her chest. With the relationship with her father finally coming back to that of a normal one rather than one filled with spite and anger, he had also started to support her more in the academic side of her life. Her father would occasionally defend her grades and work ethic in an argument with her mother and would aid in any way he could to tutor Sophia. Sophia's low Cs and Bs had gone up drastically with the newfound confidence she had gained from just a couple of weeks earlier. There were few to none what she called "shouting matches," loud arguments over her setbacks in her high school career. Sophia was motivated, and now that she had broken up with Jackson, she was relieved of many social stresses caused by the anxiety he would leave her.

However, less social stress meant more school stress and more time to improve. Countless days were spent staying up unreasonably late to get a high A on a paper, only to be met with an annoying 89 percent. Yet getting an 89 percent was still a shock for Sophia as she reminisced on the days when she would have killed for even a 75 percent. Sophia's whole weekend was spent studying for a unit test in a class, the bane of her existence, history.

At two in the morning on Monday, Sophia figured if she didn't know the material by that point, she wouldn't know it in a million years. The stress caused by her trying to maintain an 84 percent in that class combined with every single other class she was struggling with led Sophia to staying up another two hours. Come Monday afternoon, all Sophia had for homework was five problems of math, and it was a blessing for her serotonin levels.

"Hey, Dad?" Sophia shouted from her room. "Am I out of the Sominex pills yet?"

"Uh ..." Her father shuffled through Sophia's bathroom cabinet. "Got a couple left."

"Kay. I don't have that much work today, so I think I'm just gonna take a dose when I'm done with this math," Sophia replied.

There was a knock at her door, another new formality she and her father had been practicing to respect his and her privacy during work or family calls.

"Yeah? Come in," Sophia said without looking up from her math work.

"You really think you need these? They're not meant to be taken so often, Soph," her father advised, reading the label.

"I already read the directions, Dad. I got like no sleep this weekend and past week, and I finally have like no homework."

Mr. Milverton dipped his head at her and raised his brow.

Sophia looked up and stopped doing her math, sighing. "Look, I just really need the sleep today. Last time I'll take them until finals. How 'bout that?"

"How 'bout last time ever?" Mr. Milverton suggested.

She dropped her arms on her bed loudly.

"I just don't want you building up a dependency. That's all. So this time, and that's it. Like I say, once you hit eighteen, your life, your choices."

"I'll seriously be fine, but I get it." Sophia smiled and went back to her homework.

"Great." Mr. Milverton dropped her the pills. "I'm gonna go grocery shopping, get some gas, and finish some other errands I have to do before I forget. Want anything?"

"Nope, I'm all good. Just wanna sleep," Sophia said, getting irked that her father hadn't already left her room.

"Okay, I'll just go then. Love you." Mr. Milverton tapped her head and left. "Be back in an hour or so!"

"Kay!" Sophia shouted as her father left the house. She cracked down on her math homework and sped through the rest until her hand was sore from writing. Sophia sighed in awe. "Finally."

Sophia set down the pencil and went to grab a bottle from the pantry in the kitchen. She walked back into her room and downed the Sominex sleeping draught. Exhausted and dying for rest, she lay down, preparing for a much-needed deep sleep when the doorbell rang.

Sophia opened her eyes. She yawned, annoyed from being interrupted, and walked out of her room. "He forgot something, didn't he?" Sophia assumed her father to be standing outside the door. She assumed wrong.

Sophia wiped her eyes and opened the door. *Jackson. A normal Jackson? He isn't disheveled or overly dressed up. What is he doing here?*

"Oh God," Sophia said carelessly, her inhibitions lowered due to a longing for a doze. "Not now. Actually ever."

Especially that her father was gone, she didn't want to be alone with Jackson. Since she discovered what was on his phone and what he'd been hiding, she could only imagine what he was hiding from her then.

"Wait, Soph." Jackson pressed his hand against the door hand before Sophia could close it. His facial expression resembled a child lost in a department store.

Sophia, being the kind person she generally was, pitied Jackson. She knew the effects of the scene she made with Jackson in the cafeteria, and although 99.9 percent of her was telling her to shut the door and go back to sleep, that 0.1 percent snuck into her conscience.

She held the door open. "Look, I'm sorry for … the thing, okay? I didn't realize there was a past thing with that. My friend Clara— well, kinda my friend—told me all about it. So sorry."

"Thanks, I guess, but that's not why I'm here," Jackson said, angling to get a foot in the door literally. He continued his fake crusade to get into Sophia's bedroom. "I didn't wanna say sorry because I know how much you hate insincerity, but I did wanna say you don't have to feel bad about doing what you did. In all honesty, I would have poured acid over your phone if you did what I did to you to me."

Sophia questioned his intentions, and despite everything he put her through and everything her friends had told her, she opened the door fully, and Jackson waltzed in. Continuing her obliviousness, she invited him to sit on the steps of the fireplace. Sophia sat opposite of him, wrapping herself in a white blanket.

"I just lost it, you know." Sophia attempted to relate. She kept talking. "Like what you did was horrible, and I hope you know that there can never be anything again. I can't be with someone I don't trust and will never trust again."

"That's reasonable. I can't be with a girl for a while until I figure my own deal out, sexuality-wise," Jackson said.

"Yeah, I get that. I totally do. You need your time to readjust to the new attention, and I'm good with that. But I need time too. After this I honestly … I really just don't want to see you again until we both have our shit figured out. Sexuality for you and relationships for me." Sophia let loose with someone she swore she would never talk to again.

"Yeah." Jackson nodded. He looked like he'd just eaten a lemon. What did he expect though? Sophia wasn't going to budge on letting him back in.

Sophia was silent momentarily as well. "So who even like bullied you?"

Jackson breathed out strongly. "Like everyone. The class, parents, friends. Everyone, everyone."

"Why? Everyone's so like free and accepting around here." Sophia used air quotes. "I mean seriously. I'm accepting. I try."

"Yeah, you're a good person," Jackson said in the middle of cracking his neck.

"Maybe." Sophia acquiesced.

"Better than the people who gave me shit. All hypocrites. Won't put their money or I guess their beliefs where their mouth is when someone is being attacked," Jackson confessed. "Better than me too."

Sophia felt for Jackson and understood the pain he undertook, but she still believed she needed to cut him out. She didn't want him to do anything to hurt himself. Sophia just wanted him to be happy and to be in a position where he felt satisfied enough to move on. However, even Sophia knew Jackson couldn't be fixed with a snap of the fingers.

"Well, responsibility is a good step to me, Jackson Decker." Sophia smiled and stood up. "I'm honestly dead tired though and just took a sleeping draught. So I'm gonna have to ask you to leave, if that's good?"

"Oh yeah. I said my bit," Jackson said and stood up.

Together they walked to the door. Sophia smiled. "I hope you can change for the better. Good luck." She kissed him on the cheek, and she walked down the hall and shut the door to her bedroom.

Jackson opened the door, and a warm breeze rushed in. Jackson closed the door. Jackson remained as quiet as possible as the door shut and waited for any creaking of the floor near Sophia's room. Jackson stood at the welcome mat until his foot almost fell asleep. Jackson gritted his teeth, trying not to yell. The overwhelming kindness and genuineness Sophia displayed to him almost made him reconsider what he had told Hunter the previous week. He began to consider how much his reputation was really worth, but he somehow managed to kick the angel side of his conscience to fall back in line with the devil.

Jackson slowly removed his shoes and placed them to the side of the mat. He slid down the hallway, every step placed with just enough pressure on the hardwood floor to ensure no sound would be made. He kept his hand over his mouth and shortened his breathing.

Jackson stopped just outside of Sophia's door and pressed his ear against the wood. Jackson's sick ears heard snoring, and it was bliss to him.

He slowly turned the knob, and the door creaked open. The creak grew louder and louder until Jackson was so tense that he wanted to vomit. Jackson came to the side of Sophia's bed, and he paused, hesitating. His palms were sweating. His legs were shaking to the point he appeared slightly neurotic. Jackson stared down at Sophia's limp, unawake body and froze. As if falling to his death, his life flashed before his eyes, knowing that once he laid his hand on any part of her there was no going back.

"Hughk." Jackson gagged with terror and anxiety. He held his mouth with one hand and leaned over Sophia with the other. The bottle of Sominex pills sat on her nightstand. He realized she was out cold and carefully slipped down Sophia's jeans and panties.

Jackson was dripping sweat now as he pulled out his phone. He rubbed his hands over his face and through his soaked hair. Jackson pulled down his sweats and boxers in preparation. Blood pumped at astronomically high rates. Synapses fired, releasing dopamine throughout his body, and his muscles tensed as he pressed the button to take the photo.

As the button clicked, he noticed the flash and ringer were both left on by his mother's reset of his phone. It was the moment he went from a boy desperate to regain social status and to be accepted among society to a person who had embodied the worst of society's outcasts and criminals.

Sophia's room, completely blacked out from any afternoon lighting, lit up like a concert strobe light, and the camera clicked at full volume. Jackson dropped the phone and hit the hardwood floor with a loud thud, triggering the flash and click of the camera several times as it rattled to a stop.

Sophia awoke from her nap, wiped her eyes, and turned around to see a blurred image of Jackson. She felt a cool rush of air hit her naked back and realized it was a breath. She blinked and rubbed her eyes and saw Jackson standing above her half-naked. Sophia, still partially under the effects of the draught, turned to the ground and saw Jackson's phone lying still.

She realized her pants were off when she reached down for her pocket. Sophia connected what was going on and screamed at the top of her lungs. Jackson stood behind her frozen, watching Sophia as her weak, now adrenaline-filled arms tried to help her up. Sophia squirmed, and Jackson made his judgment call and pressed her back down on the bed.

"Jackson!" Sophia wailed.

Grabbing at anything at arm's length, Sophia blindly searched for a weapon. Jackson pressed her head into the pillow, and her legs went wild, kicking any part of his lower body she could.

Sophia shrieked and finally grabbed hold of her pencil lying on the side of the bed. She aimed the point at where she thought Jackson's torso was and began swinging as hard as she could. Sophia barely nicked his chest, drawing blood, but Jackson grabbed the pencil and threw it away. He fell on top of her and pressed her arms underneath his chest, behind her back. The pillows and sheets muffled her subsequent yells.

A lock clicked somewhere in the house. Sophia turned toward the sound, but Jackson missed it. Jackson aimed his torso at Sophia's vagina and closed his eyes in desperation to find an excuse to not continue. He found none. Sophia continued screaming into the sheets and swung her fist back over her head, crushing Jackson's eyelid into his skull. Jackson head-butted her neck and exhaled. He reached under her shirt and grabbed her breasts. Sophia cried when Jackson pressed himself inside her.

Mr. Milverton, who had just gotten home, looked up from the door and slammed it shut. He could've sworn he heard someone yell. Sophia looked up at her desk and reached for her lamp. Jackson thrusted, and Sophia had grabbed her lamp. She hit it against both of their backs.

Mr. Milverton dropped the groceries and nearly tripped over

Jackson's shoes. He looked down and realized they were men's basketball shoes. Mr. Milverton took off his tie and loosened the shirt around his neck.

He ran up to the door to Sophia's room and banged on it. "Sophia!" Milverton roared.

"Dad!" Sophia cried for him.

Jackson covered Sophia's mouth and held her jaws shut. Mr. Milverton heard the bed shaking, and he pulled on the doorknob so hard that it broke. Mr. Milverton pressed his back against the wall for support and slammed his foot against the door. Four kicks later, the door caved and swung off its top hinge.

Mr. Milverton stormed inside. "Get off her!"

Jackson was groping Sophia under the shirt when Mr. Milverton tackled him from the side, both of them falling into a standup mirror. Sophia crawled up into a ball in the corner and wailed as Mr. Milverton grabbed the lamp and smashed the bulb part over Jackson's head. Jackson tried to pull himself off the ground, but Mr. Milverton grabbed him by the shirt and dragged him out of the room.

Sophia sat shaking in the corner, her eyes frantically searching for anything familiar, anything to relax her nerves. She was terrified and could barely catch her breath.

Mr. Milverton dragged Jackson's back against the ground outside and threw him against Jackson's parked Jeep. Blood dripped out of Mr. Milverton's shoulders from the shards of glass the mirror had embedded in him. Jackson panted heavily, his eyes bruised and forehead bleeding profusely.

"You should be dead right now. You know that!" Mr. Milverton shouted at the still half-naked Jackson. Mr. Milverton's whole body shook, and he slammed Jackson against the Jeep. Jackson opened his mouth to say something. Mr. Milverton leaned into his face, ready to attack again. "Mouth shut."

Jackson's eyes watered, and he nodded. Mr. Milverton pulled out his phone and dialed.

"911, what's your emergency?" the dispatch asked Mr. Milverton.

"Yes, I have the boy who just raped my daughter standing in front of me. My address is 7221 Parkland Avenue, Freneau County." Mr. Milverton stared at Jackson. "Yes, yes, she's inside. I'm bleeding from my shoulders. The rapist is bleeding from the head and chest. Glass fell on me and him and … Yes, inside the house."

Jackson sputtered out reddened drool.

"He's now bleeding from the mouth." Mr. Milverton kept a straight, unchanging facial expression. "No, not life threatening. I'm fine. He'll survive. My daughter needs help though. I need to help her right now, so can you send some … on their way? Great. How … five minutes? Okay. Thank you."

Mr. Milverton looked up to see one of the neighbors pushing his recycling bins outside. "Hey, can you watch this kid for five minutes until the police come, Jeremy?" Mr. Milverton asked nonchalantly. "Just help me out."

The man, laden with terror at the sight of both males bleeding profusely, reluctantly agreed and walked over to Jackson as Mr. Milverton went back inside.

"Sophia?" Mr. Milverton called as he entered her room. "Sophia."

His eyes fell upon his frozen daughter. Sophia's eyes were transfixed upon her bloodied mirror and lamp. Her body shook in anxiety, and chills ran down her back and legs. She looked up at her father, and he crouched down beside her. Her eyes were red, but she was void of emotion.

Sophia struggled to breathe between coughs and phases of nausea. She could barely comprehend her surroundings. But she understood one thing: her father was there. She held his hand and squeezed it. Her father held hers tightly, and they sat staring at each other on the floor of her bedroom. She forced a tiny smile, and her shaking subsided. Mr. Milverton wrapped his arms around his daughter, and he and Sophia remained like that while Sophia's heart worked to slow its beats.

Jackson, so desperate to regain his reputation, had raped the only girl who trusted him. The only serious relationship he had ever had in high school had ended because of him, and now it would be sending Jackson to prison because of himself. He thought of Chris and all the inadvertent fear he had sent him into, of his friends who now would be more separated from him than ever. The society that rejected him and he so badly wanted to rejoin would now permanently exile him.

"I'm sorry. I'm so sorry. This is so fucking. I'm so sorry," Jackson said out loud.

Jackson knew while assaulting her what he was doing. He knew before he did it. Jackson's insisting attempts at atonement went nowhere, as there was nothing to say. It was already too late.

Jackson yelled, "I'm sorry, Sophia!"

The shout echoed through the door of the Milverton's house, which was still open. Sophia heard it, and her heart began to race again. Mr. Milverton could feel it beat against his chest. He pressed Sophia's ears shut. Sophia looked up slightly from the ground at her father, and although muffled, she made out what he said next, "It's done now. You're safe."

No smile came onto her face. Nor a frown. She accepted his words and let her eyes rest on the hardwood floor again.

EMMA

Emma held an ice pack to her eye as she texted Shaun with one hand, a skill yet to be mastered by any adult alive. Living up to the nickname Sophia had given her, pier girl, Emma suggested that Shaun go with her to the San Francisco piers that night.

"We can get Paul from Uber and take us up there for dinner or somethin. The ride might be more expensive than normal cuz it's like a forty-minute drive. But Paul's a chiller, so I think we'd be good."

"Aight," Shaun responded. "Come by in a bit then?"

"Yeah. Ted's gonna be around for a bit though, and after he hit me, he's not a really a fan of seeing u around."

"All right. Should I just hang out across the street or down the block?" Shaun asked.

Emma sped up the typing, occasionally missing letters with her thumb. "Sure, jus mak suree he can't see u."

"Aight. If I were there, I woulda killed him. I don't know if I *actually* would, but it'd b close. Even for Ted, wtf? Like shit. I swear I might've killed him if I were there. Why didn't u call CPS?"

Emma shook her head at his response. "Because I know Ted. He's a scumbag. He could cover his tracks if he were blind. My mom is close to seeing how he is, but she's still like … what's the girl version of being whipped?"

"It's still whipped lol."

"Oh. Well, yeah, she's still whipped. So I gotta just do me for now."

"Yeah, well if I were there, I'd fuck Ted up. Fr fr. Just like how does he think he can do whateva he wants w u? Like how tf u just think sum like that? Gets me so pissed."

Emma grinned. "Ur so protective <3."

"Of course. I love you, and Ted's actually psychotic." Shaun wrote back.

Emma laughed to herself, texting. "Not wrong there. Aight. Well, I'll see u when I see u, kk?"

"K yeah." Shaun finished his text.

Emma tossed her phone on the ground and crawled to the window. She stared out, slightly anticipating Shaun to already be coming down the road on his skateboard. Not surprisingly he wasn't, yet Emma continued to stare. She looked through her window at the entrance to the apartment next to hers. A small toddler stagger-stepped outside of the door followed by an ecstatic father and mother elated by their child's walking. The father picked the kid up by the arms and swung her over the steps, laughing with the little girl.

Not once had Emma ever seen her stepfather that excited by anything aside from his bartending. She watched the white-picket-fence family rush into their Toyota, the mom twirling the laughing baby in the air. Emma sat down smiling at the cluelessness and innocence of the child. She had been exposed to the depression of her father's leaving at such a young age that she barely remembered a time like that of the family outdoors.

Emma grabbed her phone and went to wait downstairs for a text from Shaun on his whereabouts. She made her way down the stairs, expecting to see the shoeless feet of Ted in the kitchen. There was no such sight, and Emma was relieved to be free of him for a brief period at her home. She sat down in front of the TV and stretched her whole body out on the couch. Emma pulled out her phone just as noises started coming from her mother's bedroom.

As the moaning grew louder and Emma had to cover her ears,

the thought of such a weasel of a man's having sex with her mom was unbearable and disgusting. Soon the moaning hit a peak and stopped. Emma slowly uncovered her ears, disturbed by the thought. The door behind the stairs to Emma's bedroom creaked open, and Ted walked into the kitchen sweating. He was just wearing boxers and a plaid shirt covering his white cutoff.

"Whoowee," Ted breathed out. "Damn, that woman knows how to suck a dick."

Emma said nothing but placed a heavy frown on her face without looking at Ted. Her mom was carrying on like nothing happened, like Emma hadn't gotten knocked out by Ted. Even with Cynthia's strange filter of delusion and denial, Emma wanted to believe she could be turned around. Sometimes Cynthia would see Ted for the maniac he was.

Ted grabbed a glass from the dingy metal cabinets over the sink. Ted filled it with tap water and smacked it down on the countertop.

"All right." Emma scowled at him, trying to ignore him.

Ted sighed and chugged the glass of water. His loud swallowing and dripping hair made Emma gag. "Emma, Emma, Emma. You always look so mad. Always so mad at me, but you never do anything about it. I'm starting to think you might actually enjoy having me around. Can't blame you since the other option is Nico the spic."

Emma was fuming. She swung her legs off the couch and placed her phone in her pocket. She'd had it with Ted. How dare he talk about her family like that? Ted didn't have anyone seriously related to him that still cared about him. And if he did, Emma had never seen them around. Sure, she didn't have the perfect relationship with Nicholas, and she didn't even fully like him. Still whatever she had with him right now was far better than any connection she'd had with Ted. Ted wanted her to do something about her anger. She was getting ready to. Her black eye struggled to open, and she looked up at Ted, her nose and lip shaking with rage.

"Oh shit." Ted grinned, and his mouth dropped. "Your eye is seriously fucked."

Emma grabbed the edge of the couch trying to remain still.

"You know, I think we need to go back to hitting kids. First time my dad hit me I was pissed too, but it taught me discipline, made me tougher. And look at you, like Ronda Rousey." Ted wiped his lips of the residue of the water. "The disrespect you show me just proves you haven't been taught well enough, but once the belt comes out, you'll understand. Every kid needs it once in a while. Bring society back to the good old days."

"The good old days when it was cool to hit kids?" Emma questioned Ted's brutal ethics.

Ted went on nonchalantly, "Well, not just with kids, with wives too. Sometimes y'all just need a good smack, understand who's in charge. Your mom likes it like that when I'm on top."

Emma liked her mom just as much as anyone in her situation would, but Cynthia was her mom. Before Ted, she loved Emma. To Emma, only she was allowed to insult Cynthia, no one else.

"Talk about my mom like that again, and I'll shove that glass up your ass." Emma defended herself like Nicholas advised, like Shaun had demonstrated.

Ted shook his head, sighing. "You never learn. Like I said, just need a good smack."

He walked over to Emma and easily backhanded her across her injured eye. It wasn't quite like salt in a wound, more like a twenty-pound salt-covered dumbbell in the wound. Emma turned around, stumbling. She regained her balance as black pixel-like specs flooded her injured eye.

"That hurt?" Ted asked.

Emma's ears were ringing, but she turned back to face Ted. "I think you missed."

Ted's jaw clenched, and he backhanded her again. Emma's temple spasmed, and a warm sensation came over her face. Blood rushed to clot the now-bleeding cheek Ted had hit.

"Suddenly you think you're tough? You're not." Ted turned to go back to Cynthia's room. "Just like every other woman in California, too stubborn to admit they crave dick just to get through the day. You all *need* our help because a boyfriend is the only thing keeping you from slitting your wrists."

Ted's warped point of view must have come from his father. From what she'd heard, Mr. Walsh wasn't particularly nice to Ted's mother either. Emma always assumed their relationship was reminiscent of Cynthia and Ted's. Mr. Walsh probably beat Ted into thinking the same way he did about women.

"Ironic, you can barely get through the day without alcohol." Emma was determined to stay strong besides the fact that her still-concussed head was foggier than San Francisco in the middle of June.

Ted's fist clenched, and he walked back over to Emma. "You really want another one?"

Emma stood still, waiting for the punch.

"What is it with y'all liking it rough?" Ted cracked up in Emma's face, with bits of saliva covering her cheeks.

The recurring insult against herself and her mom had finally tweaked her enough. Before Ted raised his fist to strike her again, Emma punched Ted Walsh in the nose. It was a weak punch, albeit, but a completely unexpected occurrence for Ted. He stumbled back, checking his nose for blood. Although confident, Emma hadn't fully understood what would come from the minor infliction on Ted's ego.

"Stupid bitch," Ted stuttered with anger. He grabbed Emma by the throat and shoved her into the TV, which fell over with a loud bang.

The sound of Cynthia's opening the door and scurrying into the room reached Emma's ears. "Emma!" Cynthia shouted and tried to run to her daughter.

When Cynthia attempted to protect Emma, Ted slapped her in the face. "Back off! She asked for it. She deserves it. It'll teach her some fuckin' respect," Ted barked at Cynthia and shoved Emma onto her back.

"Ted, stop it!" Cynthia roared.

Emma strained to focus on Cynthia. She could see her mother was breaking out of her view of Ted. Emma never saw Cynthia clench her fists.

Ted turned around, looming over Cynthia like a giant. "You have a better way to teach her? I'm the one constantly taking her shit and being disrespected. This is it. She needs to learn!"

Emma and Cynthia locked eyes for a moment. Cynthia swallowed and stared in disbelief at Ted. Her eyebrows wrinkled into an M.

"Ted, you need to leave my house right now," Cynthia said. "Get out."

Ted, who was about to hit Emma again, turned around and squinted at Cynthia. "Get out?" He stood up and stalked over to Cynthia insidiously. "Get out? I bought this whole fuckin' place for us. You don't like it? Fine, you leave. Take this bitch with you."

"I'm calling the police." Cynthia pulled her phone out and dialed 911. She waited as the phone rang.

Ted reached out for the phone, and Cynthia moved her arm away. He reached again and grabbed the phone. He ended the call and threw the phone away. Ted jerked his body at Cynthia, and she flinched back into the wall.

Ted chuckled. "Shouldn't have done that." Ted lowered his voice.

Emma saw Ted coming over and tried to pull herself away. Her minimal strength only allowed her to move so far as Ted raised his foot and slammed it on her calf. A thousand bullets could not have made up the pain that surged into her thigh as her shin broke. She tried to pull her leg up to clutch it, but the nerves must've torn around the broken bone. It was excruciating.

Ted moved away from Emma and walked up to Cynthia. Emma gritted her teeth, drooling through the cracks, and pulled herself up to the couch. She saw Ted smack Cynthia's head against the wall and throw her onto the staircase. She was probably out cold. It was now down to Emma. Emma was not letting Ted get away with this.

"My God." Ted sneered at both women. "You're pathetic, both of you are. It doesn't hurt that bad. C'mon, get up! Grow up!"

Emma turned onto her stomach and sputtered out blood that had drained from her noise to her throat. Her eye felt as if a train had rested on top of it, making it impossible to open. She tried to contract her eye muscles, but they wouldn't move. Her right leg and arms, however, still functioned. Emma mustered all the strength she had and pushed herself off the ground to stand on one leg and face Ted.

Ted fidgeted with his hands. He looked around the room and back at Emma. He moved forward and then back two steps. Ted snorted, and his eyes looked her up and down, widening slowly.

"You don't know how to raise anyone. Christina raised me." Emma maintained. Pointing at her mother, she continued, "You made my mom your bitch. She didn't do anything to deserve that, and you walked all over her ... and me ... and Christina. And you killed my sister. Christina drove so fast to get away from you that she crashed. You killed her."

"You don't know what you're talking about." Ted glowered. "Your sister, *my* daughter, died because of *her* choices. I didn't do shit. Just like you, she had no respect or appreciation for what I do to keep a straightened family."

"You?" Emma raised her hand at him. "Haven't done anything! Barely make enough at the bar to keep us above the poverty line. Look at my mom! Look at her!"

Ted rolled his eyes and swung his body around to look at Cynthia's unconscious body. He raised his brow at Emma. "Yes, that is Cynthia, and that's a couch, and that's a chair. What? You think you both don't deserve it? Telling me, your father, to fuck off the other night? Think you don't deserve anything? How am I the unfair one?"

"You're not my father," Emma growled. "You never have been. You never will be."

Ted cracked his knuckles and strode over to her when the

doorbell rang. Ted stopped in his stride and sighed. He walked over to the door and opened it partly. Emma could see Shaun through the crack. He was rubbing gum off the bottom of his shoe when Ted opened the door.

"Hey, Emma, I was waiting for a bit and didn't see Ted's car, so I thought I'd jus ... Oh hey, Mr. Walsh." Shaun looked up, shocked.

"Hey, Shaun." Ted sneered.

Shaun lied pathetically, "I know you don't wanna see me, but I just wanted to see if Emma were around. I had to, uh, give her my notes on world history."

"Shaun!" Emma shouted, elated at the sound of his voice. "Call Nicholas!"

"Bitch, shut up!" Ted bellowed.

Emma saw Ted had broken character, and Shaun was going to know something was up. Ted looked back at Shaun, and there was a pause. Shaun slammed his bodyweight against door just as Ted pushed it shut and locked it. Shaun continued banging on the door.

Emma yelled, "650-582-9988."

"What?" Shaun yelled and stopped hitting the wooden door.

"Nicholas's number." Emma repeated. "It's 650-582-9988!"

Shaun shouted back, "He's at Safeway ... leaving now ... on his way!"

Ted turned back to Emma. "You think Nicholas is gonna stop me? He's barely man enough to—"

Ted was interrupted when Emma kicked him in the balls. He fell to the ground and dry-heaved. Emma stepped over him. She pressed down on the hand Ted was using to stabilize himself, above the ground, and kicked him onto his back. Emma knelt next to him on her good leg and punched him repeatedly in the face. Her right arm tired soon, and she switched to her left. His face poured blood, and he reached up aimlessly, finally able to block her fists on the seventeenth jab.

"For Christina." Emma stood up and let Ted writhe in embarrassment and pain.

Ted glared at her and struggled to get himself to his feet.

"Nicholas is here, and he just called the police, Em!" Shaun shouted through the door.

She looked at Ted and smirked. "It's done."

A car door closed outside, and Ted looked up. Ted lunged once more at Emma and fell on top of her. Emma's broken leg was crushed under Ted, and she yelped with pain. Her leg was throbbing, and she pressed against Ted as he pressed against her throat. Emma smacked around at Ted, and her vision really started to fade to black. Her throat closed, and footsteps outside indicated Nicholas was about to attempt to break in.

Ted waited for a banging on the door but didn't expect the whole door to break open. He let go of Emma's neck as Nicholas and Shaun entered the room. Nicholas threw his jacket on the ground and wound up a punch. The amount of force that hit Ted nearly sent him through the apartment wall.

Nicholas grabbed Ted and pressed him up against the wall near the broken TV. "What did you do!" Nicholas roared. He shook Ted and smacked the back of his head against the wall. Nicholas had Ted quivering in terror and begging to be let go. Nicholas almost punched him again but refrained. "Why!" Nicholas yelled into Ted's ear. "Look what you did to them! To my family!"

Ted looked at Nicholas and twisted his face into a frown. Ted made no remark and settled down. Cynthia finally came to and rolled off the staircase. Emma pushed herself off the wall and fell to the ground, taking in deep breaths. She felt her throat for any cuts. It was only swelling, and she watched Nicholas and Ted.

"The family you've been so good to," Ted commented and wiped his gushing lips.

Nicholas fumed. "I left them. I didn't nearly kill them. Police are on their way."

Almost on cue, a police siren sounded in the distance. Emma exhaled sharply with a short laugh. Ted was going away. Nicholas let go of Ted and stepped back in a huff. Nicholas walked over to his ex-wife and helped her lean up.

"I'm so sorry I wasn't here sooner, Cynthia." Nicholas held her hand.

She smirked and nodded at Ted. "Just get *him* out."

"Oh, I will." Nicholas reassured her.

Shaun walked past Ted with a grimace. He looked down at Ted's white boxers. "Jail should be a fun time."

The sirens drew closer, and the sound of screeching tires echoed outside. Nicholas cracked his wrists and stood up, grabbing Ted by the collar and leading him outside. Ted maintained an upright stance, but Nicholas forced him to sit down on the steps leading into the apartment. Emma watched Ted sit, staring out at the road. She looked back at the floor and nearly fell onto her face.

Shaun ran over, caught her in time, and picked her up in his arms. "My God, the fuck he do to you?"

"A lot, but you see his face?" Emma winced as she staggered through the house.

Shaun nodded. "I bet your sister is proud."

"I hope so," Emma said through a surge of pain around her shin.

"No, she is." Shaun smiled and let Emma down as they made their way to the destroyed doorway of the apartment.

The police walked up the entrance to the house and came to a stop in front of the two men, Nicholas and Ted. It was finally happening. Emma could barely contain herself and struggled not to cry. The salt in the tears hurt her eye and cheek too much. She watched the officer's eyes switch between the sight of Ted's deformed, bleeding, swollen face and Nicholas's reddened hands.

The officer grabbed his cuffs off his belt. "Which one of you is Nicholas Legra?" the officer questioned. "There was a report of domestic violence."

Ted dipped his head at Nicholas sullenly. The officer questioned Nicholas on the matter, and Ted sat silent with the occasional grunt of agreement.

"Can't believe it." Emma choked up. "He's going away."

"And I'm gonna be around a lot more," Shaun said and kissed her forehead.

"Don't make me fucking cry," Emma joked. Blood spilled from her lips. "The salt in the tears hurts so bad."

"Sorry," Shaun said.

They watched as the officer ordered the defeated Ted to stand up and place his hands behind his back. His goatee dripped with a combination of mucus, saliva, and blood. Ted let the officer place the cuffs on him and dragged his feet as he was led to the cruiser.

"Goodbye, Ted," Emma muttered loud enough for only Shaun and her to hear.

The door to the cop car slammed shut, and the officer walked around to the driver's side. Ted looked up at Nicholas and then at Shaun and Emma. He nodded at the scene with an annoyed smirk admitting defeat. The cruiser drove off down the road with Ted in the back seat.

EMMA

A week had passed since Ted had been taken to be tried in court. He was inevitably found guilty of domestic violence, child neglect, child abuse, attempted murder, and, just barely, involuntary manslaughter relating to the death of Christina Legra. He was sentenced justly to a time long enough to think over his actions, twenty-seven years. Emma was taken to the hospital to treat her leg and bloated face. Shaun stayed overnight the first night with Nicholas and Cynthia.

Emma woke up to see Mr. and Mrs. Baxter standing in the hospital room, presumably to pick up Shaun in the morning and take him to school. Her throat was sore from Ted's choking attempt, and she didn't want to bother talking to Shaun or his parents. She watched Mrs. Baxter come over to Shaun. She could only see a fraction of what was normal. Her eyes were too tired and sore to move.

"Shaun," Mrs. Baxter whispered on Friday morning. "Shaun."

Shaun's arms were folded on the side of Emma's hospital bed, his head nestled in between them. Cynthia and Nicholas were on the other side passed out.

Shaun's mother tapped him on the head, and he sprung awake. "Yes, what do you want for dinner?"

She smiled warmly. "Honey, it's seven thirty-eight. Gotta go to school."

"No, I need to stay with Emmaph," Shaun slurred his speech,

attempting to rest his head on his forearms again and go back to sleep.

"No, we gotta go, kid," Mr. Baxter whispered from the entrance. "She'll be fine. Her parents are here. If she really *needs* anything related to her health, she's in good hands. She'll be fine without you for a day, Shaun."

"Mmmm," Shaun groaned, trying not to admit his being awake. "Fine, but I'm coming back once school ends.

"Fine," Mrs. Baxter said. "Let's go."

Mr. and Mrs. Baxter walked out of the hospital room and waited for Shaun in the hallway. Shaun stood up and shook the remnants of his tiredness from himself. He wiped the morning grime from his eyes and walked past Emma's bed. He dragged his hand across Emma's arm and unwillingly left the room to meet his mom in the white hospital hallway. Emma fell back to sleep.

Three hours later, Emma awoke again, still just as sore as before. Emma tried to move her leg but could barely feel her skin move. She panicked and pulled off the bedsheet. Thankfully, she saw it was just wrapped in a tight cast.

"Cool it," Nicholas said from the bedside chair. "We didn't need to amputate yet."

Emma leaned back, relieved. She looked at Nicholas and then at her mom, who had been watching her panic as well. Emma smiled at her mom, attempting to convey the happiness she felt with the absence of Ted. Cynthia smiled back momentarily, and then the smile turned into a frown.

"I'm so sorry, Emma. I should've kicked Ted out years ago." Cynthia leaned forward and held Emma's hand. She let out a few tears but no more. "I was trying to be a good mom. I just, I just didn't want you to have to have another person leave your life."

"Temporarily." Nicholas jeered.

"Mmm." Cynthia gave a minor smile back. Emma could tell she was beginning to accept Nicholas's return.

"In a very strange way, I understand that. I just wanted to have Christina's death mean something you know? Now it does." Emma accepted her mother's exasperated apology. "You should've handled Ted better these past couple years, but I also don't know how I would've acted if I were you. Regardless, I know you're a good mom. Which is why I think you should give Nic a chance. He was the only person, aside from Shaun, who protected us."

"Thank you, Emma," Cynthia said, wiping her eyes. "And thank you, Nic."

"It's why I came back. I wasn't expecting yesterday to happen, but the big dude upstairs has a plan I guess," Nicholas commented.

"I don't need to hear about you seeing the light, Dad." Emma's sarcasm filled the room like a chemical fume.

"Fine," Nicholas said.

Emma smiled and leaned back in bed. Cynthia released her grip on her daughter's hand and relaxed back in the bedside chair next to Nicholas. Emma had been protesting her mouth's desire to ask a question for the whole time she and her parents had been talking.

Finally she relieved the straining muscles of her own face trying to contain the question. "So could Dad come around more? Or can we go to see him more?" Emma asked her mother, impatient for an answer.

"Uh, wait, Emma." Cynthia paused.

"Yes." Nicholas nodded violently. "I'll get space cleared for you both, available for whenever you want. Just let me know."

"Really?" Emma beamed.

"No, wait." Cynthia shook her head slightly. "I'm still married to Ted, and although I am very thankful for what you did, I need to be divorced from him before I consider anything relating to you."

Nicholas conceded. "Oh. Of course. Stupid of me."

"But I'm not saying I'm not considering what Emma said." Cynthia curled her mouth into a smile at Nicholas.

Emma looked up, surprised at her mother's comment. She wanted to be able to have her family back together probably just as much as Nicholas did.

"I'm not sure how long it'll be before I'm ready for any major changes. But being here for us gets you a foot in the door at least." She winked at Nic. "Of course, for the time being we'll still need some money to cover our costs for things at the apartment."

"Anything, Cynthia, to be with the both of you," Nicholas begged.

Cynthia smiled cheekily. "Well to start, I could use some breakfast. What about you, Emma?"

Emma faked a groan jokingly. "Oh yes, please, a nice stack of pancakes."

"I get it." Nicholas sighed and stood up. He mouthed at Cynthia, "Thank you."

Nicholas walked over to Emma and stroked her head before leaving to grab breakfast for his family. She had hit a new level of happiness and nearly screamed when Cynthia nodded to Nicholas's "thank you."

Nicholas left the room, and Cynthia exhaled. She relaxed and folded her hands on her lap in a quaint, mom-like fashion. Emma stared into oblivion, unfolding all the possibilities that remained on the horizon for her now that Cynthia had at least opened the door to Nicholas. Emma had finally gotten what she had needed desperately for so long, a family.

SOPHIA

Calming wouldn't be the right word to discuss how Sophia's mom felt when the family discussed what happened between Jackson and Sophia. Although after she stopped wanting to kill Jackson Decker and her phase of fury passed, she was calmer than previously. She laid off asking Sophia how she felt unless Sophia openly brought it up. After having grown more sensitive to Sophia's wants, she obliged when Sophia requested that she not be taken to a sexual abuse treatment facility.

Sophia had no desire to have to go to a place so sterile, as she described the buildings. Sophia knew that sooner or later the news would get out that Jackson had assaulted her, and she knew it would bring controversy to her reputation as the town slut. But at that point, she couldn't have cared less. The event would bring possible unwanted attention to her family, but as long as she knew Jackson was in a cell with only a metal frame to sleep on, she was carefree.

The moments following her father's leaving the room to talk to the police, who had come to pick up Jackson, were, in a word, cathartic. Sophia reminisced on the night when she had her first full conversation with Jackson on the bottom of the slides. She had felt so safe, so cared for. Same as Jackson, it was her first relationship where the trust or love wasn't one-sided. Sophia knew Jackson wasn't some desperate freshman asking her out or a senior looking to have his go with his first freshman. Jackson was a junior needing someone to trust with his secrets just as much as she was. It just happened that those secrets were that he loved someone else during their time together. Sophia remembered Emma's telling her to be careful, Clara's advising her on her choice of Jackson as a partner, and the moment she actually sided with him when he briefly bullied Emma.

"Was it my fault?" Sophia questioned herself. She knew the answer was a resounding no, but what if it weren't? She tried to rationalize a yes out of the question, "So many times ... told he was bad. Didn't care. Why didn't I care? Why didn't I fucking care?"

The questioning made the ordeal worse, and anxiety filled her lungs with each accelerating breath. She leaned up against the bed, pulling her pants back up all the way. Sophia looked down at the broken glass on the ground and wondered, "This wouldn't be here. None of this would be if ... should have listened to Emma. Desperate like him ... No, I'm desperate ... Jackson's ... evil ... pathetic ... gone."

Her dad came back into the room. "Hey."

Sophia's eyes refused to look up from the broken glass.

"He's on his way out. You're gonna be okay," Mr. Milverton said. The words shook from his lips.

"My fault," Sophia said, half-aware it was audible. "It is."

"No, it's mine. Shouldn't have given you those damn pills." Mr. Milverton crouched next to her. "Sophia, it's me. It's all on me. The party in eighth grade, being with Jacks—him, this."

Sophia ignored his continuing to stare, her void of emotion growing.

Mr. Milverton sighed and dipped his head in front of her to get her attention. "Me and your mother, we should've been paying attention."

"I almost killed myself that night after the party." Sophia sniveled.

Mr. Milverton cocked his head to the side. "What?"

"I did. At least I felt like I did. I tied a belt around my neck and stood on my tiptoes contemplating whether if it were worth living here until I was eighteen. Only reason I didn't was because I thought it couldn't get any worse." She wiped her eyes.

"Why didn't you tell me?" Mr. Milverton asked, his eyes tight and worried. He sat down on the floor of Sophia's bedroom.

"Because I didn't care!" she snapped finally. "It didn't matter, but now everything's breaking down. I thought it couldn't get worse then, but now I know the only thing worse than right now is death, and even that sounds like a step up. I feel paralyzed."

"Sophia, you came back from where you were in eighth grade. You can come back from this too." Mr. Milverton reasoned with her. "I'll help. I swear. I'll make sure no one ever puts a fucking fingernail on you again."

"What if you can't though? I mean what's gonna stop me from doing it this time? The moment I saw you come into the room, I knew Jackson was going away, but it was too late. It might be too late again for me to fix myself." Sophia gripped her legs close to her chest. She was trapped, and the room seemed darker than normal. Sophia didn't want it to lighten up. It would be easier if her dad just left and she fell into the darkness.

She wept. "What if this really is the worst it can be and there's no coming back from it? I mean, anything could happen now, and I would still remember this. I don't wanna live knowing that the only way to be sure it can't happen again is leaving everyone."

Sophia's dad folded his lips over one another and exhaled through his nose. "You don't know that it will or won't happen again."

"Exactly," Sophia said, semiconfused.

"But you also won't know what it's like to finally leave this shithole and go to college. You won't know what it's like to meet your husband. There won't be any kids if you die." Mr. Milverton went on. "You won't see an anniversary or grow old with someone. But you'll also never understand what it's like to be truly carefree, to not give a shit about what other people think. Doesn't any of that sound good?"

Sophia broke from her state of near catatonia and nodded. Her void of emotion suddenly filled up and overflowed. She wept and released the firm grasp of her legs, and a strong wave of warmth overwhelmed her as tears gushed from her eyes. Her father leaned against the bed and put his arm around her back.

Three days later Sophia sat up on her parents' bed after justifiably refusing to go back to her mattress until it was replaced. She sluggishly surfed the TV, and her eyes finally came to a rest on *Supernatural*. The episode played out in front of her eyes, which were now free from staring into limbo. Her mother came into the room toward the climax, and Sophia had to pause the suspense show.

"Hey, Mom," Sophia said.

"Brought you some lunch," she replied, holding up a quesadilla. "Homemade."

"Thanks." Sophia smiled politely at her mom who was attempting to reconnect. "I'll have it in a sec. It smells amazing though. We should talk."

Within milliseconds, Mrs. Milverton was on the edge of the white mattress with her hand outstretched to her daughter. "You're sure?"

"Yeah. Just say what you want you to say first, and I'll just answer anything because I assume Dad filled you in on everything."

"Of course, of course." Her mom nodded vigorously.

"I just don't really feel like repeating what happened in my mind." Sophia confided to her mom.

"Without a doubt." Mrs. Milverton leaned down. "I only want to make sure you are okay. And tell me if you want anything, anything at all. Just ask. I don't want you to feel like this is something we can't talk about."

"It is. I'm not sure where this conversation is gonna go since Dad told you everything already. I just know that sooner or later something's gonna happen again," Sophia explained. "Maybe not as bad, but I'll need you, you and Dad."

"I'm not going anywhere." Her mom rubbed Sophia's thigh softly.

Sophia flinched at the movement. "Can you not do that right now?"

Mrs. Milverton pulled back her hand. "Sorry, I wasn't thinking about it."

"S'fine, just need to get used to anyone doing that stuff again." Sophia made an apologetic smile.

Mrs. Milverton folded her hands on the bedside. "Can I tell you something?"

"Sure," Sophia said, anticipating a confession, the typical thing her parents did to make her feel more accommodated.

"I was at a party. I was your age. And someone had some cocaine, well, a *lot* of cocaine. I snorted so many lines that I nearly died. When I woke up, I was in the hospital, and I saw my parents there. I started crying and stressing out about what they thought of me. I told them it was all my fault and that I was so sorry, but all they cared about was if I were feeling okay or if I were hurt. The point being, no matter what happens, I'm here for you. Whether I'm actually here or not, just know that someone somewhere cares."

Sophia cracked a smile. "That was so cliché, Mom."

Although she was prepared for some sort of parable from her mother, Sophia was not prepared for that story and appreciated her mother's vulnerability.

Her mom sighed with a grin. "I know, but it's real. And I hope you know that you'll always be the stronger one between you and ... him. I'm sorry. I can't even speak the prick's name."

"It's fine. Neither can I."

"Good. He doesn't deserve any more attention than he gets in prison." Mrs. Milverton went on. "Well, even if you remember this for the rest of your life, just keep in mind that you survived. It seems like there's always a story of a teen killing herself over sexual assault or bullying. You will be known as one of the strongest people among your friends."

"What if I tell people and they don't believe me?" Sophia asked, unconvinced.

"*What if they don't believe you?*" Mrs. Milverton repeated the question.

Sophia shook her head, confused.

"I mean, who cares? You'll know the truth. That'll be enough anyways. All the people who lie about getting assaulted and get publicity will have to live with being part of a group of people they don't deserve to be with. You'll know what actually happened, and people will have to live without knowing the truth," Mrs. Milverton explained. "And if you decide to tell your story, you'll know you'll be helping someone else get through her own experience."

Sophia accepted what her mom said. "Thank you." Sophia nearly started crying again but held it in. "I needed to hear some of that from someone."

"Always, anytime." Mrs. Milverton almost patted her thigh but outstretched her hand instead.

Sophia held it firmly before her mom left the room, and she let the soft skin go once her mom walked away. Sophia fell onto her back on the bed. She stared at the ceiling, slowly letting her mind forget everything she once thought about Jackson. She remembered the good times with him, and it was hard. It was hard to accept that there *were* good times. Sophia wanted to forget them, but they were already fading.

She remembered the night in the park, seeing movies with him, and grabbing coffees, but she could barely recall what they said or did on those dates. She couldn't remember their conversations, and she knew it was better that way. The memories would drift back sooner or later, but for now they were leaving her, and for Sophia Milverton, it was a feeling of a sort of magnificence.

SHAUN—EMMA—SOPHIA

"All right, I'm leaving now," Sophia said to her parents and zipped up the side of her leather boots.

"Okay, honey," her mom said, her arm on Mr. Milverton's back. "Got your wallet. Got your phone. Is it charged?"

Sophia rolled her eyes and pulled out her phone. "Yeah, seventy-three percent."

"Oh, are you sure that's enough? We want to be able to reach you," her mom said, worried.

Mr. Milverton added, "Or so we can endlessly annoy you with texts while you're with your friends."

Sophia pointed her elbow at her Mr. Milverton. "Dad gets it."

"I stay with the crowd dawg, yo." Mr. Milverton cracked.

"Aaaand you lost it." Sophia laughed.

"It was a good five seconds being in touch with youth." Mr. Milverton nodded.

Sophia buckled her belt, fluffed her hair, and let it cascade over her shoulders. She finished putting on eyeliner and makeup. Sophia grabbed her lipstick out of her mini-purse and pressed it over her lips, turning the normal pink to a darker velvet. She smacked her lips and turned her head both ways, looking in the mirror in the foyer of her home. Sophia grinned, liking her appearance, and noticed her mom was frowning in the reflection.

Sophia turned around to look at her mom. "Mom, sooner or later, you need to let me go back out in the real world. What happens happens." Sophia rationalized. "I'll be fine, okay?"

"Okay, honey, we trust you. Just want to make sure you are careful," Mrs. Milverton said with an uneven smile.

Sophia hugged her mom and then her dad. "Guys, keep in mind that I'll be with one of the arguably, strongest, most intimidating guys from BRHS."

"He doesn't really know how to fight though, does he?" Mr. Milverton chuckled.

Sophia punched his arm playfully. "Soooo? Shaun looks tough, and he protects Emma like you don't understand. Trust me. I will be fine."

"Okay, okay, okay," Mrs. Milverton said, shooing her daughter over to the door. "Have fun!"

"I will!" Sophia beamed and left the house.

Sophia jumped in her Cadillac and drove down the road. She pulled over when she got to the driveway of Shaun's house on Maple Street, San Mateo. She pulled out her phone and texted Emma. "Nearly ready? I'll be there soon."

"Yeah, I'll be outside when u get here," Emma responded and slid the phone back into her short shorts back pocket.

Emma sat on the edge of the kitchen countertop looking at an old picture. She was at the top of the Empire State Building, smiling, with both of her arms around Christina. Cynthia was holding onto Nicholas's arm, and he was laughing, tongue out, like an ecstatic little kid. Emma took a picture of the photo and put the framed one back down next to a vase of roses given to Cynthia by Nicholas.

"Hope you're proud of me, Christina." Emma looked out the window at the twilight sky.

The sun shimmered on the horizon and prepared itself to

set. Emma hopped off the counter and landed carefully on her pressurized air cast on her lower leg. The door to the apartment was taken off and replaced with a newer one that didn't have its paint wearing off. Emma hobbled over to the door and opened it. It swung smoothly, and she stepped onto the porch. She sat down, and a tear came to her eye, remembering the last time she saw her sister.

Emma chuckled to herself. "Summer's almost here. I remember you wanted to go to Hawaii for the first time. I'm planning on going with Dad if Mom lets us."

Emma pulled out her cell phone and looked at the picture of her family at the Empire State Building. "If I do go, I'll bring you."

Emma smiled and placed the phone back in her pocket. She put her arms on her knees and rested her head on her fists. She looked around the porch and saw the dried drops of blood that had fallen from her body during the night Ted was taken away. The paint curled around them, as if trying to hide the evidence.

Emma stood up, took a picture of the blood, and made a note. "Emma 1, Ted 0."

Feeling satisfied, she sent the picture and caption to Shaun. She sat back down on the edge of the porch and waited.

Shaun laughed when the picture came through and responded, "All day."

"Hey, Dad?" Shaun called through the house.

His dad slogged over to the door and opened it. "I was just about to go to the dinner with your mother. What do you need?"

Shaun turned around from the desk chair he was sitting at and almost made his request when he noticed the suit his father was wearing. "Look good, dawg."

"You think so?" his father said cheerfully. "Got these cufflinks last weekend." He showed the golden bits to his son.

"Yeah, not bad. Navy blue makes you look like Skyfall Bond," Shaun joked.

"They make me look ten years younger? Should wear them more."

Shaun snickered. "Anyways, I was wondering when you wanted me back by?"

Mr. Baxter shrugged. "I'll text you. Just not past twelve, okay?"

Shaun was elated, and his eyes widened. "You'll let me go out till twelve?"

"Yeah, why not? You're old enough," Mr. Baxter answered.

Mrs. Baxter called from outside the house, and Mr. Baxter said his goodbyes to Shaun and left. Shaun had finally gotten freedom from his parents, and his happiness nearly hit the point of hilarity. When his dad left, he jumped up and down and shouted at the top of his lungs like a kid who had just gotten his first video game.

Shaun went into the bathroom and started his routine. Although he and Emma were together and his insecurity over being single had disappeared, certain aspects of his character would never change. He took off his shirt and flexed in the mirror to see any possible progress, and in fact, there was. Shaun questioned whether he was telling himself his abdominal muscles were showing or whether he had finally hit his goal of 10 percent body fat. Either way, Shaun's confidence shot up, and he continued riding the high that started with his parents' permission to stay out late.

Shaun sprayed four puffs of deodorant into the air and shook his head through it. He grabbed a stick of deodorant from his cabinet, rubbed it over his upper-upper body, and threw it to the side. Shaun squirted out some gel and coursed it between his strands of hair.

Shaun straightened his jaw, examining his face for any acne, just in case, and then he went about getting ready to leave the house. Shaun grabbed his wallet and phone and picked up the money his parents had left for him on the dining room table. He was patting his jeans to make sure there were no creases when a honk came from outside. Shaun went around the house and grabbed his keys before turning off all the lights. He left the house and walked outside.

As Shaun stuck the keys into the lock, another honk came from a Cadillac parked in Shaun's driveway. He turned around and flipped off Sophia.

"Hurry your ass up, then!" Sophia shouted from her opened window.

Shaun locked the door and jogged over to her car. "Sorry, princess," Shaun said upon entering the car.

Sophia turned around, grinning. "You can always walk to East Side."

Shaun put his hands up, surrendering jokingly.

"Good." Sophia laughed and put on "Shape of You" by Ed Sheeran.

Shaun closed his eyes and exhaled loudly. Sophia looked back at him in the rearview mirror. Shaun shook his head at the choice of music and looked up at her in the mirror. They looked at each other, and he smiled, mouth open, glancing at the aux cord.

"If you put on some weird heavy metal shit, you're walking." Sophia grinned cheekily and handed Shaun the aux cord.

He connected his iPhone to it and turned on "Psychosocial" by Slipknot. When the bass drum kicked in and the lead singer screamed the first line of the song, Sophia unlocked all the doors.

"You're walking."

"Kidding, kidding," Shaun laughed. "How 'bout this?"

Shaun scrolled through his library to "All Down the Line" by the Rolling Stones. Shaun braced himself for Sophia to yell at him to pass her the cord back, but none came. Instead she started bobbing her head to it. Shaun watched as she got into the beat, and when the chorus came, she belted out the lyrics. Well, that was a bit of a shock.

"I like it. My dad used to play this all the time," Sophia said and cranked up the music. "Haven't heard this in a while."

Shaun smiled. "Time to check off turning a cheerleader's music taste to rock from my bucket list."

Sophia laughed, and soon they were both jamming to the song. Shaun watched people go about their lives as Sophia drove down El Camino Real. Homeless people shuffled around their encampments, begging for food and money. Businessmen dined with their female coworkers at fancy restaurants. College students drank the night away, watching sports games at all the local bars.

The nightlife was vibrant in San Mateo that day. Shaun zoned out while sitting in Sophia's car and watched the blur of cars, in the other lanes, racing by. The sun, getting ever so close to hitting the horizon and disappearing until the following day, glimmered like a golden pearl in the sky. Shaun snapped out of it when the song automatically changed to, unfortunately for him, some weird heavy metal shit.

"Nope, hand it back." Sophia waved her hand for the aux cord.

"Wait, wait, wait. I have the perfect song." Shaun pushed her hand away.

Sophia turned and looked at him for a moment. "Shauuuun."

"One sec." Shaun fumbled with the phone and paused the extremely dark Anthrax song that aired for ten seconds. Shaun sighed. "Whew."

The car slowed to a stop outside a certain line of Deepcrest apartments.

"We're here." Sophia tapped Shaun's thigh and pulled up at Emma's apartment.

Shaun looked up from his phone, and his mouth changed from neutral to a smile as he saw Emma stand up from the porch. Emma walked to the car, and Shaun reached over to her side and opened up the door for her. She climbed into the convertible and grabbed Shaun's hand as he pulled her in. Emma shut the door behind her, and Sophia made a U-turn in the middle of the street.

"I'm pretty sure that's a double-yellow," Shaun said. "Like, you can't do that. So turn around again and go left at the end of the street instead."

"Killer boyfriend you have, pier girl," Sophia joked at Emma.

Emma laughed. "He is. *Most* of the time."

"*All.*" Shaun corrected her and kissed her cheek.

Emma beamed and held Shaun's hand.

"That's very cute." Sophia rolled her eyes.

"Yeah, honestly, Em. Your hands are already sweaty." Shaun laughed and let go of Emma.

Emma looked up at him, grinning mischievously. "Never minded me getting a little wet befo—"

"Okay! Okay!" Sophia shouted over Emma. "Don't needa hear that before dinner!"

Shaun blushed, and Emma lost it over his embarrassment.

"So where we going before the concert?" Shaun asked.

"Uh, nowhere, but there is a Round Table right outside the venue," Sophia said.

"Down," Emma said, searching through her bag. "I'll pay."

"No, I'm driving you. I bought the tickets to see A$AP Rocky. I'm buying you dinner," Sophia countered.

"I'm the guy here. I pay for all of us. I'm not letting a girl pay for me. It's rude, bruh."

"Well, I'm breaking through societal norms then, babe," Emma joked.

Shaun said, "Cut your hair like Rachel Maddow, then."

"No way. I'm not that into the women thing." Emma hit Shaun in the shoulder.

Sophia said, "Bill O'Reilly, Rachel. Chill out. I got it covered. I got the money."

"No, my dad unnecessarily gave me a hundred dollars. I gotta do something with it," Shaun begged.

"Fine." Sophia gave up.

"Fine." Emma stopped as well. "Dude, Soph, we sound like a bunch of senile grandparents arguing over who's got the check."

"That's sad." Sophia laughed and turned onto the highway. Sophia looked up at the rearview mirror and at Shaun, who had gone silent. "Hey, rock kid?"

"Rock kid? Is that like the dude version of pier girl?" Shaun asked.

"No, it's because you made me listen to Slipknot and Anthrax for ten hours," Sophia jeered.

Shaun chuckled. "It was like thirty seconds."

"Whatever, you said you had the perfect song." Sophia motioned at the aux cord.

"Oh yeah, Emma actually showed it to me one time. It's by the Foo Fighters. That too extreme for you?" Shaun jested.

Sophia rolled her eyes. "Play the fuckin' song already."

Shaun showed Emma the title, "Walk," and Emma nodded so hard it appeared she might have gotten whiplash. Shaun played the song and reached into the front seat of the car. He turned the knob on the dashboard up so high the electric guitar vibrated the car floor.

Sophia instantly felt the music and caught on to the chorus easily. She looked back at Shaun and Emma, who were dancing in the back seat, and they sang the lyrics all down the highway. This was what they all needed. Sophia had found a group of friends who cared—seriously cared—about her. Her failed relationship was no longer part of her mind, and her parents were more attentive but no longer overbearing. Shaun had moved on from arguing with his mom and was granted the freedom to have a normal teenage life by his parents. And Emma, a girl who'd started the year in a pit of depression, was taken to the Everest of happiness with a family together again and friends she could relate to and joke with and would never forget.

Sophia motioned for Shaun to pause the music briefly. He did.

Sophia confessed, "Kinda random, but you guys know when you're having a really shit day and like you're not sure if it can get better and you don't know if it's worth it to keep going?"

"I feel that more than you know, Soph." Emma looked at Shaun.

"Especially if it's because of your parents, for real for real," Shaun said.

"I just feel like this here, right now. This shows it was worth it. Right now makes everything we've gone through worth it." Sophia beamed and nodded at Shaun. "You can play the damn song now."

Shaun put the music back on just as Emma managed to yell something that came out inaudible and fragmented.

"What!" Shaun and Sophia yelled almost in unison.

Emma shouted again, and Shaun looked at Sophia in the mirror, shaking his head. "What!"

Emma grabbed Shaun's phone and turned the volume of the music down. She looked at both of them with a happiness only comparable to Shaun's and Sophia's.

The elatedness overflowed, and Emma shouted, "It's going to be a great summer!"

Emma unbuckled her seat belt and climbed into the passenger's side seat. Shaun moved to the middle seat in the back of the car and leaned forward to be between both girls.

"I love you, Shaun. There aren't words to describe it. And, Sophia, Christina's not here, but I think she'd be good with who I chose to fill what she left," Emma said. "No one else I'd rather be with right now."

"Same," Shaun said. "I won't forget this moment."

Sophia gripped Emma's arm. Shaun locked hands with Emma and placed his other arm around Sophia's shoulders. Sophia cried with joy and banged her head to the Foo Fighters' passionate drumming and Dave Grohl's voice. Not everything was perfect, and the year could have gone smoother, but Sophia was thankful for what she had. Singing with Emma and air-guitaring with Shaun made her hopeful for the rest of high school. In that moment, Sophia felt carefree. She was living without worry. In that moment, they were all having the time of their lives.

In that moment, they lived.

Printed in the United States
By Bookmasters